MISSING:

ONE BRIDE

Name: Randi Howell

Age: 24

Last seen: Squaw Creek Lodge,
            June 6.
            Wearing white wedding
            dress.

If spotted, please contact
Grand Springs Police Department
immediately.

REWARD $$$

Dear Reader,

Sometimes your life can change in a heartbeat. For the residents of Grand Springs, Colorado, a blackout has set off a string of events that will alter people's lives forever....

Welcome to Silhouette's exciting new series, 36 HOURS, where each month heroic characters face personal challenges—and find love against all odds. This month a would-be bride flees her own wedding and witnesses a murderous scheme. She takes refuge at the ranch of sexy, down-to-earth Brady Jones. The charismatic cowboy is lured by Randi Howell's air of mystery—but her secrets could cost them both their lives....

In coming months you'll meet a loving nurse who marries a co-worker to gain custody of the baby she helped deliver; a rough-edged cop who could mean the difference between life and death for a woman unjustly accused; and a secretary who discovers she is carrying her boss's child. Join us each month as we bring you 36 hours that will change *your* life!

Sincerely,

The editors at Silhouette

THE RANCHER
AND THE
RUNAWAY BRIDE
SUSAN MALLERY

Silhouette Books

Published by Silhouette Books
America's Publisher of Contemporary Romance

Special thanks and acknowledgment are given to
Susan Mallery for her contribution to the
36 HOURS series.

SILHOUETTE BOOKS

THE RANCHER AND THE RUNAWAY BRIDE

Susan Mallery

lives in sunny Southern California, where the
eccentricities of a writer are considered fairly
normal. Her books are both reader favorites and
bestsellers, with recent titles appearing on the
Waldenbooks bestseller list and the *USA Today*
bestseller list. Her 1995 Special Edition title,
Marriage on Demand, was awarded "Best
Special Edition" by *Romantic Times* magazine.

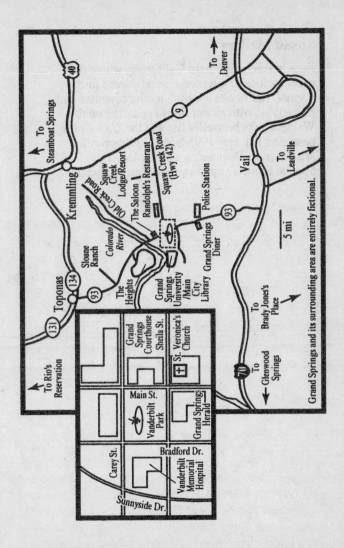

To Steamboat Springs

To Denver

40

9

To Leadville

To Vail

Vail

Kremmling

Squaw Creek Lodge/Resort

The Saloon

Randolph's Restaurant

Squaw Creek Road (Hwy 142)

Police Station

93

Old Creek Road

Colorado River

Sloane Ranch

134

Toponas

131

To Rio's Reservation

93

The Heights

Grand Springs University/Main City Library

Grand Springs Diner

To Brady Jones's Place

To Glenwood Springs

70

5 mi

Grand Springs and its surrounding area are entirely fictional.

Grand Springs Courthouse

Sheila St.

St. Veronica's Church

Main St.

Vanderbilt Park

Grand Springs Herald

Carey St.

Bradford Dr.

Vanderbilt Memorial Hospital

Sunnyside Dr.

Prologue

Brides were supposed to be beautiful and happy, Randi Howell told herself as she smoothed the front of her white satin wedding gown. Or at least reasonably attractive and content. Panic was not on the list of acceptable emotions. She didn't want to think about what she must look like, but she had a bad feeling her eyes were wide and filled with a hunted expression. Gee, at least a "deer in the headlights" look would make the wedding photos interesting.

"It's not so bad," she said aloud, wishing her voice sounded more confident. "After all, I'm marrying Hal. He won't be a horrible husband."

Despite the nerves banging around in her stomach and the alternating urge to throw up or break out in a rash, she had to smile at that one. Hal would be annoyed if he knew she thought of him as "not so horrible." Hardly praise every groom dreamed about.

Randi paced the length of the room. It was all of eight steps. The small meeting room, one of many at the far end of the Squaw Creek Lodge, had been converted into a temporary "bride's room" for the wedding. Although the ballroom had been festooned with flowers, candles and beautifully set tables for the reception, the decorations didn't extend this far back. The tiny room contained only an oval mirror in the corner, a florist's box with her bouquet, a folding chair piled high with her street clothes and nothing else. At least the room was carpeted. The hallways weren't. The only bright spot in an otherwise dismal situation was that she was alone.

Her mother had wanted to spend these last few minutes giving Randi instructions and reminding her how socially important the wedding would be, launching Randi into Grand Springs society. Randi grimaced at the thought, pleased she'd insisted on spending this time by herself. The only place she wanted to be launched was to another continent.

"Stop it!" she told herself firmly. "You're getting married. Hundreds of women do this every day. Love is a difficult concept at best. How do you know you don't love Hal?"

She stopped in midpace and slowly faced the mirror. The medieval-style gown clung to her from shoulders to hips, then flared out to the floor. The heavy satin swayed in counterpoint to her movements, creating grace from her tomboyish walk.

She raised her gaze higher, past the pearls her mother had given her to wear, to her face. Despite perfect makeup, she was pale, her skin nearly the color of ash.

The realization began slowly, a small kernel of knowledge that sprouted, then grew quickly, like one of those time-lapse images on television. It wasn't that she didn't *love* Hal, she wasn't sure she even liked him.

She'd fallen into the engagement, as she'd fallen into everything else in her life. Because it was easy. Easier than making her own way.

"I don't want this," she whispered, suddenly sure she couldn't marry Hal. But what was the alternative? How could she get out of this situation? One thing was certain. This time her daddy or her big brother Noah weren't going to come to her rescue. This time she would have to take care of it herself.

"Mom is gonna kill me," she muttered as she glanced around the room, trying to figure out what she was going to say to the older woman.

What if her mother tried to talk her into getting married, anyway? After all, everything was paid for, the guests were waiting. She had about three minutes of freedom left.

"I need more time," Randi said. "I have to think and figure out what I want. Dear Lord, this would be a really great time for a miracle."

She waited about two heartbeats, then figured God was busy. She was going to have to make her own miracle.

She grabbed her purse and considered writing a note. No time, she thought, hearing the organ music start another song. She'd been over the music list so many times, she had it memorized. The wedding march would begin next.

After slipping off her shoes so she could walk quietly down the linoleum floors, she left the bride's room and headed for the rear entrance of the ski lodge. At least it was June and she wouldn't have to worry about freezing. In the winter, she couldn't have gone outside in just a wedding gown.

The back door of the lodge was in sight when she heard voices heading her way.

"Drat." She glanced around, looking for a place to hide. There were meeting rooms on both sides of the hall. The first door she tried was locked, but the second gave way. She stepped inside and waited.

Barely breathing, she pressed her ear to the door. The voices got louder as two people walked by. From a snippet she caught of their conversation, she realized they were kitchen employees taking a break.

Randi breathed a sigh of relief. Now to escape.

But before she could open the door, the tiny hairs on the back of her neck prickled. She heard voices again, but these weren't coming from outside. They came from directly behind her. She wasn't alone.

Maybe it was the stress from the wedding, or her concentration on the people in the corridor, but when she'd first entered the windowless conference room she hadn't noticed the lights were on. A quick glance over her shoulder showed a couple of jackets tossed on a long conference table. There was an alcove to the left. She could hear the clink of glass, then noticed the smell of coffee.

Great. There was a meeting going on. She had to get out of here before someone saw her. Bad enough to be running away from her own wedding. Worse to be caught in the act.

"Jo will take care of the old broad," a strange male voice said. "That's her specialty."

Randi paused for a second. The statement didn't make sense. Then she realized the man must be talking about a nurse. For a while she'd thought about that as a career. After all, her brother was a doctor. Then she bit back a moan. The men having a meeting might be doctors, too. Oh, Lord, she probably knew them.

Get out! she ordered herself.

She swung the door open wide and took a step toward the now-empty hallway and freedom. As she shifted her weight forward, her stocking-clad foot came down on a carpet tack.

Life was not fair, she thought as she yelped involuntarily.

"What the hell?" another man said.

He rounded the corner as Randi hopped in place, trying

to balance on one leg while holding her purse and shoes and rubbing the injured foot.

She froze. The man approaching her was not a doctor. She'd never seen him before. But what really got her attention was the deadly looking gun he held in his right hand. The barrel was pointed directly at her.

She raised her gaze to his face. Above a close-clipped beard, dark eyes told an ugly story. This guy was going to kill her.

She waited for her life to pass before her eyes. Or did that only happen while drowning? She couldn't remember. She couldn't do anything but stand there, braced for the explosion that would end her life.

Instead, the lights went out.

The darkness was so complete, Randi thought she'd died. Then she realized the men were cursing and there hadn't been a gunshot.

God had provided a miracle, after all.

"Thank you," she said aloud as she bolted for the hallway.

Muffled curses followed her. There was a crash, and she assumed one of the men had run into the table.

Randi hit the wall a couple of times herself. In the distance, she saw an eerie red glow. The battery-powered emergency exit sign. She raced forward, slammed down on the bar to open the door and stepped out into the wet, storm-darkened evening.

Not bothering to look back, she headed for the highway. The ground was wet and rough beneath her bare feet; the rain drenched her in minutes. Without lights to guide her, she stumbled on the wet, muddy ground but kept on going. Fear provided an extra burst of speed.

When she reached the highway, she didn't see any headlights and nearly stamped her foot in frustration.

Then a low rumble filled the night and an eighteen-wheeler rounded the curve in the road.

Randi stepped directly in the truck's path and waved her arms. The driver slowed.

Two minutes later she sat high in the seat, wet and mud-spattered, explaining that she was running away and needed a ride out of town. She didn't mention the mysterious men with their guns, not sure what to say about them. Why on earth would anyone want to kill her simply for interrupting a meeting?

She tried to get her breathing under control. Terror and the damp made her shiver. What had just happened?

"Where you headin'?" the trucker asked, distracting her.

He was a burly man in his fifties. His kindly smile was comforting. And if not for the tight wad of tobacco between his lip and gum, she would think him perfect grandfather material. "Just about anywhere."

"I'm going to Phoenix."

"I've never been there. I think I might like it."

The trucker stared at her oddly. Randi figured she deserved it. After all, she *was* a runaway bride complete with a wedding gown, flowers in her hair and lacy but torn stockings.

She sighed. Just last week she'd given herself a stern talking-to about facing her problems instead of bolting. Of course, in this case, her problems were bigger than she'd first imagined. Better to run than be shot.

Why *had* those men pulled guns on her? What was Hal going to say when he found out she was gone? What was her mother going to say?

She stared out the window while the driver tried to make conversation. The rain was stronger now. It felt as if it had been raining for weeks. As they circled around

Grand Springs, she noticed there was a lot of mud on the highway and she didn't see any lights. Looked like there was still a power outage. Maybe it would be enough to distract everyone so they wouldn't notice she was gone.

If only that were true, she thought as the eighteen-wheeler drove southwest...toward safety.

One

Brady Jones leaned back in his chair, ignoring the loud creak as worn springs protested his weight. They'd been doing it since his dad had retired five years ago. Like everything on the West Texas ranch, the chair wasn't new or fancy, but it worked and he figured it would outlast them all.

He glanced from the application he held to the woman perched uneasily on the straight-back wooden chair in front of his scarred desk. When she caught him looking, she gave him a big smile that didn't make a dent in the worry lurking in her dark blue eyes.

Another hard-luck case, he thought as he dropped the application onto the computerized ledgers he'd been going through when she arrived. He'd always been good at spotting them. For one thing, the duffel bag at her feet was too small to contain more than a couple changes of clothing. She'd hitched a ride to the ranch instead of driving. Then there was the matter of her application. Too many lines left blank, too many vague references he wouldn't be able to check out. No home address. No relatives.

He should kick her out on her shapely butt, because he didn't need her kind of trouble, or temptation. That particular lesson had been hard won and never forgotten. These days he avoided women with mysterious pasts.

He *should* get rid of her, but as Tex would be happy to tell him, he was a bleeding-heart sucker for anything or anybody in need. So instead of saying the position had already been filled, he leaned back further, placed his booted feet on the desk and gave the woman an encouraging nod. "Why don't you tell me about yourself, Ms.—" he glanced at the application "—Ms. Rita Howard."

"I'm good with horses," the woman said quickly. "I didn't grow up on a ranch, but I've had lots of experience. I've been riding since I was about seven. I started with English and dressage, but one day I used a western saddle and I was hooked."

This time her smile reached her eyes, brightening them until they gleamed like sun-soaked lake water on a perfect summer day. Brady nearly groaned out loud. He didn't want to notice that, nor did he want to admit that he was itching to reach across the desk and touch one of the black curls springing free from her braid. She'd obviously combed her hair recently and braided it tightly in an effort to keep the curls in order, but it was a hopeless task. He would bet that by the end of the day, her hair was in complete disarray. Unfortunately, the image enchanted him.

"I worked in a stable all through high school," she said. "I know my way around horses, Mr. Jones—"

"Brady," he said, interrupting.

"Okay. Brady. I work cheap, I'm dependable, I don't make trouble." She shrugged. "I understand your reservations. You don't know me from a rock, so you're going to have to take my word about my good qualities." She bit her lower lip. "I guess that's it."

She had a heart-shaped face and a cupid's bow mouth. Stupid details to notice, he told himself. He would hire her or not hire her based on her abilities and his gut. His daddy had always taught him to listen to his gut, and so far, it had only let him down once. Of course, that other time had involved a woman, too, but he wasn't going to think about that now.

Logically he shouldn't give her a try. There was no reason to trust anything she'd said. Especially the part about not making trouble.

"There's one thing you left out," he said, lowering his feet to the floor. "You've got nowhere else to go."

He met her gaze squarely, watching pride wrestle with reality. If only she knew how hard he wished she would claim some other job opportunity or a friend willing to take her in. He didn't want this to be the end of her line.

She blinked twice, but didn't speak. He swore silently. She didn't have to speak; the quiver at the corner of her mouth said it all.

"I've gotten by before," she said, and rose to her feet. "I'll manage. Thanks for the interview, Mr. Jones." She picked up her duffel bag and an expensive-looking purse.

Brady waited for the feeling from his gut. There wasn't one. Only the voice in his head telling him to be damn careful because he'd been down this particular road before and it had a way of flattening a man.

"How about a week's trial?" he said. "If things work out, you can stay on."

She'd made it to the office door, where she paused, then turned back. "You're saying if I don't like the working conditions or job description, I'm free to move on to something more upwardly mobile?"

He grinned. "Sure thing. A place with a corner office, maybe."

Another black curl worked its way free and dangled by her cheek. She shifted her purse to her shoulder and brushed the strand away impatiently. "I'd like that. The job, not the corner office."

"Great," he said, even as his gut belatedly kicked in. The feeling warned him that the decision he'd just made was going to change his life forever. He could only hope this time it would be for the better.

He rose to his feet and named a salary. "That's weekly and includes room and board," he added. "The stables are your responsibility. You'll be up early. I want the horses fed by five so they'll have at least an hour to digest their food before the cowboys get them some time around six. After you muck out the stalls, you'll be responsible for exercising any horses not being used that day."

Rita nodded. "I'm familiar with the work involved. I know I don't look very strong, but I'm tough and I'm good. You'll have to wait and let me prove that."

Because he was ten different kinds of a fool, Brady actually wanted her to show him she was terrific. He wanted to be dazzled, and not just by her smile. Obviously he needed to get out more.

"You have a week," he said. "There are a couple of high school boys who work in the afternoon. They take care of the horses when the cowboys are done, so you won't be responsible for that. Any extra time you have, you tell Tex and he'll give you chores. You have Saturday and Sunday afternoons off."

"Sounds great. Is there something you want me to do now?"

"You can start in the morning." He studied her face, trying to discover her secrets. A pointless exercise. She would tell him or not, in her own time. Maybe it was better if he didn't know. For both of them.

He crossed the worn wooden floor and stopped next to her. Her left hand hung at her side. He picked it up and turned it over so he could see her palm.

At the base of her middle finger sat a large circle of

raw skin. Other blisters—some healed, some still filled with clear fluid—formed an angry pattern across her flesh. He rubbed a couple of thick patches, feeling the calluses formed by hard work.

Rita Howard might know her way around a stable, but she hadn't been doing the hard work until just recently. What was her story? Had she lied about everything?

He was so deep in thought he barely noticed the burning. When he registered it, he nearly flung her hand away as if it had bit him. Maybe it had.

Heat flared, starting in the center of his palm, going bone deep before boiling up his arm to his chest, then moving lower. Hot, mind-numbing, sexual heat—the kind that made a man behave like an ass, then not have the good sense to regret it in the morning.

He bit back a curse. He didn't need this woman on his property, and he sure as hell didn't need to want her in his bed.

His mind obligingly took that image and shifted it until he was lost in a mental tangle of bare arms and legs, burying his need inside her and his hands in her curly dark hair. According to his brain, a bed was not required.

Moving slowly, so she wouldn't know what he was thinking, he released her hand, then shifted and leaned against the wall. The action did two things. First, it put some distance between them so he could work on developing a little self-control. Second, it allowed him to casually adjust his position, folding his arms over his chest and crossing his ankles in an effort to draw her attention away from that part of him that had instantly and violently reacted to the unwelcome fantasy.

"Judging from your hands, you haven't been working with horses," he said, pleased his voice sounded completely in control. "What have you been doing?"

She shrugged, apparently unaware of the battle he fought for control. "A little of everything. I waitressed in Phoenix and found out I'm not much of a people person. I like them one at a time just fine, but the pressures of a lunch crowd are too much for me." She clutched her duffel bag close to her midsection. "In Albuquerque I worked as a maid in a big hotel. Now I'm here."

"Are you moving east?"

Her gaze darted away. "I don't have any specific plans."

But she *was* on the run. Had he really been hoping she was just some kid on a summer adventure? Life wasn't that simple. This particular woman was in trouble, and despite his wayward hormones, Brady was going to do his best to stay clear of her.

There was, however, one thing he had to know. "Rita," he said, his voice stern. He waited until she looked at him before continuing. "Are you on the run from the law?"

Her blue eyes widened and shock parted her mouth. Even before she spoke, he read his answer. Whatever her troubles, she hadn't done anything illegal.

"Of course not," she said. "I swear."

Conversations like this were not part of her life plan, Randi thought glumly, wishing there was a way to convince the man in front of her she wasn't a recently paroled felon. She wanted this job. More important, she needed it. Despite her proud words that she would get by, the truth was she was down to her last five dollars and getting pretty desperate.

"Okay," Brady said. "I had to ask. I hope you understand."

"No problem."

"Come on. I'll show you around."

He led the way from the office at the back of the barn

and through the stables. Randi followed behind. The familiar smell of horses and hay relaxed her. At least she would enjoy working here. She'd hated both waitressing and being a maid, although she'd kept the jobs until she'd felt the need to move on. After all, when one was on the run, one didn't get a whole lot of choices, employment-wise.

"Report any problems with the horses to me immediately," Brady was saying. "Even if it's four in the morning and you don't think I'm up. We've got a vet on call. I'd rather pay for an unnecessary visit than lose one of the animals."

"I can do that."

She glanced around at the large, clean barn. Judging from the little she'd seen, the ranch was successful. Maybe it was her imagination, but she had the sense that people had been happy here. At one time she would have laughed at herself and claimed she was being fanciful. In the past few weeks, she'd learned to listen to her senses. Being on her own had taught her to pay attention and trust herself. There was no one else she could depend on.

At the entrance to the barn, Brady paused. "The bunkhouse is over there," he said, pointing to a long, low one-story building on his right.

Big windows looked out on the lawn and the large shade trees beyond.

Randi settled her duffel bag strap over her right shoulder. "It looks very nice."

"Yeah." Brady was lost in thought. "I have a cook. Tex. He prepares three meals a day. The dining room is in front. He rings a bell when the food's ready. Don't be late."

She tried to ignore her growling stomach and the fact that she hadn't eaten yet that day. "No problem."

"Actually, there is." Brady shook his head and turned to his left. Away from the bunkhouse.

She followed his gaze and saw a white two-story house. A wide porch wrapped around the first floor. Late summer roses bloomed by the back porch.

"Well, Rita, we have ourselves a situation."

She smiled politely as she wondered if she would ever get used to her new name. At least she didn't stare blankly when someone called her that. When she'd first run away from the wedding and those men with guns, her only thought had been to stay alive. Changing her name had made her feel safer. It was probably unnecessary, but it was too late now. Brady thought of her as Rita Howard and that's who she was going to continue to be.

"There are over a dozen cowboys on the ranch," he said.

"Okay."

"Counting Tex and myself that's nearly twenty men. Except for my dog, Princess, a few of the cats and some breeding stock, you're the only female around."

"Oh." His words sank in. "Oh," she repeated as heat climbed her cheeks.

"Yeah. Oh. So I'm going to give you a room up at the main house. I'm the only one who sleeps there, and I'm about as safe as they come."

That wasn't true, she thought, eyeing his broad shoulders and muscular thighs. She would bet he could be pretty dangerous when he chose to be. What he really meant was he wasn't interested in her so she wouldn't have to worry. It was no more than she expected. While children didn't run in horror when they saw her walking down the street, no man had ever lost control because of her beauty, either.

"I appreciate the concern," she said. "It won't be a problem."

"It better not be. I don't want you making trouble with the men."

Rita grinned. "Brady, don't let that thought keep you up nights. I swear, if you catch me having my way with one of your cowboys, you won't have to fire me. I'll quit. As tempting as all that testosterone sounds, I'm going to do my best to resist."

His answering smile caught her unaware. His eyes got all scrunchy, and there was a dimple in his left cheek. Until this moment she hadn't noticed he was handsome, in a rugged cowboy kind of way.

Don't be stupid, Randi told herself. The last thing she needed was to start thinking of Brady as anything but her employer. Hadn't she learned anything in the past few weeks? She'd nearly married a man she didn't love, and running out on the wedding had almost cost her her life.

"Fair enough," he said, and led the way to the house.

Once inside, he quickly showed her around. She had brief impressions of worn but well-made furniture, lots of light and more room than a single man could possibly need.

"Is there a Mrs. Jones?" she asked as Brady headed for the stairs.

He glanced back at her. "My mom?"

"No. Are you married? Will your wife mind me being here?"

He turned away. "I told you that you were the only female here. My parents are away traveling."

"Then, I won't bother introducing myself to them."

As he walked down the hallway, he pointed to partially open doors and identified which belonged to whom. His room was at the top of the stairs, a guest room stood across the hall. His parents' bedroom was next to that and hers was down at the end.

The twelve-by-fourteen room had big windows that overlooked the barn and the bunkhouse beyond. She could see the leafy trees, the backyard and out into the open pastures. A tall dresser stood opposite the window. A desk sat in the corner. Like the rest of the furniture, the four-poster bed was light oak. The comforter and throw pillows were a neutral beige and light blue, and someone had draped a hand-crocheted throw on the foot of the bed.

"There's a bathroom in there," Brady said, pointing to the door on the right. "Closet's on the other side. There's towels, soap, I'm not sure what else. Let me know if you need anything."

She moved past him, into the room. Sunlight spilled onto the hardwood floor. Oval rugs sat next to the bed and in front of the dresser.

"It's great," she said. "Thanks."

"It's not fancy, but it's clean. A couple of ladies come in from town every couple of weeks and go over the place. They were here last week."

She touched the smooth surface of the dresser. "They seem to do a great job."

Brady stepped into the hallway. "Make yourself at home. You can use the television in the living room if you want. There's a stereo in the study. I know it's tough being in a strange place, so feel free to look around. Dinner's at five. We eat early so we can go to bed early."

At the mention of food, her stomach growled. No doubt the cook served simple food in large portions. She couldn't wait.

Brady hovered for a couple of seconds, then nodded. "I'll see you at dinner."

"I'll be there."

He left. She stayed by the dresser until his footsteps

had faded. A minute later she caught sight of him leaving the house and heading back to the barn. She crossed the floor and watched him.

If this were a movie from the fifties, Randi had a feeling John Wayne would be playing the role of Brady Jones. The rancher appeared to be honest, hardworking and trustworthy. There was something solid about him. Maybe it wasn't a romantic description, but it was one that made her feel safe. In the past few weeks, being safe had become a priority.

She folded her arms over her chest and curled her fingers into her palms. The action reminded her of Brady's touch when he'd taken her hand in his. His strong fingers could have crushed her easily, yet she hadn't been afraid. There'd been nothing threatening about his gesture, nothing sexual. He'd checked on her the way he would check on one of his horses—impersonally.

Except for a couple of pats on her butt when she'd worked in the truck stop, his was the first physical contact she'd had with a man in weeks. If things were different...

But they weren't, she reminded herself briskly. She was a runaway bride with no plan. A man had tried to kill her and she didn't know why. For now, all she wanted to do was survive and think. Eventually she was going to have to figure out what to do.

"Eventually," she said softly. "But not today."

She unpacked. As all she had were a spare pair of jeans, three T-shirts, one long-sleeved shirt and some underwear, it didn't take long. The bathroom vanity had double sinks and lots of drawers and cupboards. Her brush, toothbrush and toothpaste barely filled two shelves in the medicine cabinet. A quick glance showed her the shower was clean and there was bar soap as well as shampoo. She opened the bottle and sniffed the expensive liquid. It was a far cry from the cheap stuff she'd been using. Amazing what she'd gotten used to in such a short period of time.

As she crossed the bedroom and headed for the hallway, she realized that except for feeling safe and talking to a few friends, there was little she missed of her old life. She didn't even mind not belonging, maybe because she'd never belonged.

Briefly she allowed herself to wonder what her mother must be thinking. Assuming the older woman was over her fury. Randi shuddered at the thought of what her mother was going to say to her. So far, she'd avoided having that conversation.

"You're a chicken," she told herself. "A smart chicken, but a chicken all the same."

She'd wanted to tell everyone she was all right so they wouldn't worry, but she hadn't wanted to talk to her mother. Instead, she'd phoned her brother Noah.

She didn't want to think about that phone call she'd made the morning after she ran off, about the worry in his voice as he'd tried to talk to her through the static on the line. Eventually, they'd been cut off—by the stormy weather, she supposed. But in all these weeks, she'd never gotten the nerve up to call again. She liked to think she would have already gone back to face everyone—if it hadn't been for those men with guns.

But she hadn't mentioned them in her too brief conversation with Noah. Instinctively she'd guessed that he wouldn't believe her. Why would he? It was such an insane story, she barely believed it herself. In the light of day it was easy to laugh off what had happened as some bizarre misunderstanding. But at night, when she was alone, the fear returned, and she knew that those few seconds when she'd faced death had been very, very real.

At least she'd recognized her brother had been right with his assessment of her character before the wedding.

It *was* time for her to grow up. And that was what she was going to do while she was on the road. Grow up. Take responsibility for her actions and stop expecting other people to rescue her.

Maybe she should call again. It had been too many weeks since they'd tried to talk. But she didn't really have anything to tell Noah, or anyone.

She reached the bottom of the stairs and looked around at the large main room. Long sofas and overstuffed chairs filled the floor space. The homey prints, brass floor lamps and magazine-covered tables were so different from the cool elegance of her mother's house. There wasn't a non-functional antique in sight. Randi figured she should have been appalled or at least contemptuous. But she wasn't. If anything, the room drew her in, invited her to stay awhile, to be comfortable. To be safe.

This room felt like home.

She crossed to the fireplace and stared at the pictures on the mantel. They showed an attractive couple, first as newlyweds, then in different stages of their lives. Randi picked up one that featured the parents and an eight- or nine-year-old Brady standing next to a horse. He proudly showed off a blue first-place ribbon.

The couple stood close, their arms brushing in a way that was intimate yet comfortable. The man beamed with pride as he rested his right hand on his son's shoulder. Brady had his father's size and strength, and his mother's winning smile.

Randi touched the glass covering the picture and ignored the stab of longing. Someday she would find a place to belong and someone to love. Someday she would figure out what she wanted and be grown up enough to make it work.

Brady Jones was a lucky man. She hoped he was smart enough to appreciate all he had.

TWO

Brady stood in the entrance to the dining room and watched his men talk about their day. They were an interesting group, these cowboys he'd hired. Some had spent years on the rodeo circuit, some had grown up on nearby ranches, some hired on to escape a present or a past they couldn't handle. He was used to strays, but telling himself Rita was no different from anyone else wasn't going to cut it. She was a woman and that made her different.

Had he made a mistake? Maybe he should have turned her away, despite the fact she had nowhere else to go. There were cities with shelters. Not around here, but in the bigger towns.

He didn't want to be responsible. He didn't want to have to care about a stranger's fate. Yet he could no more escape that than he could change the color of his eyes or his height. He was his father's son, and he'd learned early to look out for people.

He heard footsteps on the concrete path and grimaced. He didn't even have to look over his shoulder to know it was her. Her step was lighter and quicker, her stride shorter. He'd hired a woman—what on earth had he been thinking?

As he turned to greet her, he reminded himself it was too late for second thoughts. He'd offered her a week's trial, and he wasn't about to go back on his word. He would make it clear to the men that she wasn't to be given special treatment, nor was she to be considered available.

She smiled when she saw him. Her hair was damp and pulled back in a tight braid. So far no curls had escaped to tease at her face and neck. Although she'd showered, she'd put on the same inexpensive, worn clothing. Times had been hard. For a moment, he allowed himself to speculate about her past, then he pushed the thoughts aside. As long as she did her job, her past wasn't his business.

"Hungry?" he asked.

She laughed and touched her flat stomach. "Starving. I could smell whatever is cooking the moment I stepped out of the house. I felt like one of those characters in a cartoon who floats along, inhaling the scent."

Her bright smile made him respond in kind. Then his expression froze as he realized she was hungry because she hadn't eaten that day. He wasn't sure how he knew, but he sensed it as surely as he believed the sun would rise in the morning. Dammit, why hadn't he thought to offer her something earlier? There was food up at the house.

He opened his mouth to apologize, then clamped his lips tightly together. Rita might not have a lot of money, but she had pride. Tomorrow he would casually mention there was food available for her whenever she wanted.

"You ready to meet the gang?" he asked.

She nodded. "I can hear their voices. There sure are a lot of them."

A faint ribbon of nervousness wove through her words, but she squared her shoulders and stepped into the dining room as if she wasn't worried at all.

He followed her and waited for the men to notice. It didn't take long. Within five seconds, the room was silent.

Brady glanced at Rita, who stared at the men. They

stared back. He wondered what she thought of his ragtag group of cowboys. Like good-working cow ponies, they weren't much to look at, but they got the job done.

In turn, he wondered what the men thought of Rita. She might not be conventionally pretty, but her big eyes and smile were lovely, she had great hair and the kind of shape that was pure temptation.

"This is Rita Howard," he said. "She's our new groom."

Several of the men reached up and pulled off their hats.

Rita smiled and said, "Hi." There were mumbled "hellos" in return.

Brady motioned to the table. "There's no assigned seating, so plant your butt wherever's comfortable. Tex serves plenty to eat."

"If it d-doesn't k-kill you on the way down," Ziggy said, smiling at Rita.

"I'm hungry enough that nothing's going to kill me," Rita said. "Who are you?"

"Ziggy."

"Nice to meet you."

One by one the men introduced themselves. They were cautious and polite. Brady figured that would last a couple of days, and then Rita would become one of the boys. At least that was his hope. Except maybe for Ziggy, who was staring at Rita with a wide-eyed puppy dog gaze. Ziggy and Rita were about the same age, although he'd always thought of Ziggy as a kid.

The sharp clang of a bell cut through the conversation. The men quickly moved to the table and took seats. Ziggy held out a chair. "M-Miss R-Rita," he said, his stutter more pronounced than usual.

Brady frowned. He didn't want her treated that differ-

ently. But before he could say something, Rita moved to
the offered chair and sat down.

"Thanks, Ziggy. Do you do this for a different cowboy
every night?"

There was a moment of stunned silence, followed by
an explosion of laughter. Ziggy's face turned nearly as
red as his hair. "No, ma'am. I ain't never held a chair
out for a man in my l-life."

"I see." She took a sip of iced tea. "Tell you what.
Tomorrow night I'll hold out your chair, then we'll be
even."

"Yes, Miss Rita."

She wrinkled her nose. "Just Rita, please. At six in the
morning when you come to collect your horse, I'm going
to be knee-deep in hay and horse manure. I won't feel
much like being called 'Miss Anything' then, okay?"

Brady saw that Ziggy had placed Rita to the right of
the head of the table. As if he, Brady, were responsible
for her. He was about to protest, then he realized it was
probably for the best. Thinking he had a personal interest
in Rita would keep the men from making any moves on
her.

"Grub's on," Tex said, walking in the room carrying
a large tray. He set it on a side table, then started placing
bowls and platters in front of the men. On his second trip,
he leaned close to Rita, caught sight of her and froze. His
gaze narrowed.

"Tex, this is Rita," Brady said. "She's the new
groom."

"Uh-huh." Tex straightened. "You much of a cook?"

Rita stared at him. "I'm terrible in the kitchen."

"Uh-huh. We don't do much in the way of fancy food
here. No decorated cookies or sushi."

"I've never had sushi," Rita said. "I always thought raw fish was something you fed to cats."

"Uh-huh." He returned to the kitchen.

Brady took his seat. "Tex takes a little getting used to."

"He's jealous because you smell better than the food," Quinn called from halfway down the table.

"Next time I won't bother showering," Rita mumbled under her breath. "Then that won't be a problem."

The dining room door opened and Ty stepped inside. A couple of men greeted him, but the majority didn't acknowledge his presence. The tall, dark-haired loner didn't encourage idle chitchat.

"Evening, Ty," Brady said.

"Boss." Ty walked toward the empty chair at the far end of the table, then paused when he saw Rita. "Ma'am."

"This is Rita," Brady told him. "She's the new groom."

Eyes so dark they were black didn't show a flicker of emotion. Ty nodded briefly to Rita, then took his seat. Brady resisted the urge to slide his chair closer to hers, as if it was necessary to claim her. The point was to treat her like one of the guys. If that was possible. He'd already done a lot more thinking about her than was safe.

"You planning on eating or do you want to just look at the food?" Tex growled when he returned with another tray.

Brady realized they'd all just been sitting there, waiting for Rita to start. He nudged her arm and nodded toward a bowl overflowing with mashed potatoes. She grabbed the serving spoon and dropped a mound of fluffy potatoes onto her plate. As she passed the bowl to her left, Tex set a huge platter of fried chicken in front of her, then glared defiantly.

Rita glared right back. "Looks great," she said, and speared the largest piece.

"You mean to tell me you ain't got one of those prissy little girl appetites?"

"That's exactly what I mean to tell you," she said, and took a bite of chicken.

"Uh-huh." Tex returned to the kitchen, but Brady would have sworn he was smiling.

Randi stepped out into the evening. The air had cooled some and the night creatures were warming up for their regular performance.

"Get enough to eat?" Brady asked, coming out of the dining room after her.

She laughed. "I can barely move. If these jeans weren't loose to begin with I would have had to unbutton them." She patted her stomach. "Three pieces of chicken, two servings of potatoes and vegetables, three rolls and dessert. Are you sure you want to include room and board in my salary?"

"The men eat twice what you do. It's all the physical activity. These guys aren't sitting behind a desk in some office. They're outside working hard."

At least they had an excuse, Randi thought. She'd been hungry from not eating much over the past couple of days. She shook her head, determined not to dwell on that. For now she was here and things were looking up.

She paused in front of the bunkhouse, not sure if she should say good-night or if Brady was walking back to the main house, as well. She took a tentative step in that direction and he moved with her.

"You made progress with Tex," he said.

"Uh-huh," she replied, trying to imitate the cook's low, disbelieving tone.

Brady chuckled. "He's proud of his culinary skills and enjoys people eating what he prepares. I'm sure he thought you were going to complain."

"About someone else's cooking? Never. Maybe tomorrow I'll take that second piece of pie and he'll actually smile at me."

"Oh, that's a tough one. It takes about a month of solid eating to earn one of Tex's smiles." Brady shoved his hands in his pockets. "The men aren't usually like that."

"I know." At his quizzical glance she shrugged. "They're showing off because I'm female and I'm new. They'll get bored soon and I'll be one of the guys."

"You sound experienced."

"I'm no expert, but I have a brother. He's a lot like that. In fact—"

Randi crossed her arms over her chest and bit back a groan. What was she thinking, spilling personal information like that? She had been so careful since she'd run out on her wedding. She'd never let anything slip. It must be all the food making her sleepy, or maybe it was the ranch itself. Maybe here she could feel safe for a while.

If Brady noticed her faux pas, he didn't let on. "I did warn you about being the only female around. But I think you're right. They'll get over it in a few days."

"I can handle meaningless flattery until then."

They'd reached the main house. Brady rested one foot on the stairs, but made no effort to climb up to the porch. "What makes you think it's meaningless?"

She glanced down at herself, then at him. "Let's just say I have no illusions."

"Then you have some misconceptions."

Randi wasn't sure how to take that. Brady didn't give

her a chance to respond. He jerked his thumb toward the house. "We've got a satellite dish on the ranch so you can get a couple hundred channels, if you want to watch TV. There's books in the library. I've got some work to do in my office, so you'll have the place to yourself. 'Night.''

With that he turned and walked away.

Rita stared after him. He moved easily through the darkness, walking a path he'd traveled thousands of times before. She waited until he disappeared into the barn before climbing to the porch and entering the house.

She touched the switch by the back door and lights sprang on in the kitchen. Having him come inside with her would have been awkward. Had Brady really wanted to return to his office to work, or was he giving her time alone so she could settle in? She suspected it was the latter. The guy was definitely a gentleman.

She left the light on for him and started up the stairs. Hal was socially correct and always knew which fork to use, but she wouldn't have described him as a gentleman.

Hal. The longer she was away from him the more she wondered why she'd been willing to go out with him or get engaged. Worse, she'd nearly married the man. What had been wrong with her?

Once in her room, she crossed to the window and stared out at the clear West Texas night sky. Stars twinkled. During the day the heat was oppressive, but at night it cooled off some. She inhaled the scents of horses and grasses, flowers and hay.

What quirk of fate had brought her to this particular ranch, to this place of misfits and strays? She thought about the cowboys she'd met at dinner. Ziggy with his stutter; Quinn, whose left arm and hand were nearly useless; Ty, the mysterious loner. There were others, a col-

lection that defied description. Oddly enough, she fit right
in. A woman on the run from a man she didn't want to
marry and two strangers who wanted her dead.

She leaned against the windowsill. Her gaze settled on
the barn, specifically on the light shining from an office
in the back. "Who are you, Brady Jones? Why do you
bother with the likes of us?"

She didn't have an answer and she didn't need one.
Around Brady, she felt safe. After nearly two months on
the run, there was nothing she wanted more, except maybe
to find a place to belong.

Her body ached with exhaustion, yet she made no move
to get into bed. Sleep was hard to come by these days.
Of course, tonight she wasn't on her own anymore. She
was on a ranch, surrounded by cowboys. Soon Brady
would return to the room down the hall. She wouldn't be
able to hear him, but she would know he was there.
Maybe that would be enough to allow her to relax. Maybe
tonight she would finally be able to sleep without dreaming or waking up at every unfamiliar sound.

Three

It was still dark when Brady made his way to the barn the next morning. There were lights on in the bunkhouse, and the smell of coffee wafted through the still air. He'd heard Rita walk past his bedroom door at ten minutes after four, so he knew she'd gotten up on time. At least one of his concerns had been addressed. Which left all the others. She'd claimed to have worked in a stable for several years, but without being able to check references, he had no way of verifying that information. Did she know her way around a horse? What kind of job was she doing?

He rounded the corner of the barn and found the wide double door propped open. The portable radio kept in the tack room had been placed on a bale of hay. Soft, classical music played quietly.

Rita stood next to a black gelding, her dark hair the same color as the horse's mane. The large animal dwarfed her, yet it was obvious who was in charge. She spoke in a low voice, keeping the animal's attention and helping it place her as she moved around its body, brushing its legs with a dandy brush. The gelding's ears moved back and forth as if absorbing all that she was saying, processing the information, then responding with a flick of its tail or a brief snort.

Brady walked past her without saying anything. Bent over the horse as she was, she didn't see him. He grabbed the feed clipboard and started down the center aisle.

According to Rita's notes, each of the horses had been fed the proper amount. They were all up and alert, with no obvious signs of illness. Brady randomly checked a couple of stalls. He found clean straw, empty feed bowls and plenty of hay and water. Behind the barn, damp straw had been spread out to dry in the morning sun. He scanned the clipboard again. She'd put a star by Casper's name and added a comment that she'd read the previous note about his injury and that this morning he seemed to be moving around without any discomfort. There was no swelling. In her opinion, he'd recovered from the sprain and was ready to start light exercise.

"Not bad," he said, making his way to Casper's stall. The gray gelding greeted him by making a snuffling noise and nudging him in the center of his chest.

"Too early for apples," Brady said as he rubbed the horse between the ears, then scratched behind the left one. Casper curled his lips back as if to say the attention was nice but he would have preferred an apple.

"Let's see if Rita's right about your leg, old boy." Brady stepped into the stall and ran his hands down Casper's left rear leg. An unexpected gopher hole had injured the animal. They were lucky it had just been a sprain. "Feels good to me. How'd you like a pretty lady to exercise you today?"

Casper snorted.

"We'll wait a couple of days before she rides you, though."

Brady patted the horse and walked to the front of the stable. "How's it going?" he asked as he hung the clipboard back on its hook.

Rita jumped, startling the gelding. She quickly placed her hand on the animal's neck and spoke soothingly before turning to Brady. She touched her chest and smiled. "You scared me."

"Sorry. I knew you didn't see me come in, but I thought you heard me rattling around in back."

She shook her head. "I guess I was involved with my work."

"Good." He stepped close to the gelding and ran his hands over the animal's back. "Nice job."

"Thanks."

She wore a T-shirt and jeans. Her braid had dissolved into a riot of curls. Green-and-brown stains dotted her thighs and her midsection; sweat made a damp patch on her back. There wasn't a speck of makeup on her face, no jewelry, nothing even remotely feminine. Yet her eyes flashed with intelligence and humor, and when she smiled he found himself smiling back. There was something about Rita Howard, something that made him wish he believed in taking those kinds of risks.

"I heard you go downstairs about four this morning," he said.

She bit her lower lip. "Did I wake you? Sorry."

"I was already up."

"Oh, I get it. You were wondering if I was going to show up on time."

"Don't take it personally. It happens every time I hire someone."

She laughed. "You didn't have to worry. I was so nervous about sleeping through the alarm that I must have checked the clock fourteen times. After the horses are exercised, I just might take a nap." Her laughter faded. "If you don't mind."

"Rita, you're only expected to put in eight or ten hours a day. Once the horses are fed, the stables are cleaned and the men have left, you do what you want with your time.

If you want to split the rest of the work between the morning and afternoon, that's fine.'' He remembered the dark, empty kitchen. "I forgot to tell you last night there's a coffeemaker in the kitchen. Since you have to get up so early and breakfast isn't until six, feel free to make coffee and have something to eat. There's plenty of food. Help yourself.''

"Okay, thanks.''

He nodded toward the stalls. "I checked Casper and I agree with your notes. Start him on light exercise today. If he continues to improve, you should be able to ride him by the beginning of the week.'' He returned his attention to her. "You were very thorough. I appreciate that.''

Despite faint color staining her cheeks, she met his gaze. "I'm glad. This job is important to me, Brady. I know you took a chance on an unknown quantity, and I don't want to let you down.''

He found himself not wanting to be let down. He wanted Rita to be one of the good guys so he would have a reason to believe in her. Unfortunately, life wasn't that tidy.

"So far, so good,'' he said. "The vet should be by today to check on a pregnant mare.'' At her look of confusion he nodded. "I know what you're thinking. It's August. It's not good having a mare ready to foal in a couple of months. Let's just say we had an interesting accident with one of our stallions.''

"You should be a more responsible parent,'' Rita teased. "It's important for you to explain about protected sex to your horses.''

"Tell me about it. Anyway, when the vet comes out, make a note of any problems. So far the mare's doing great. This is just routine.'' He thought for a moment. "I guess that's everything. Keep up the good work.''

At that moment, Tex rang the bell hanging outside the dining room in the bunkhouse.

"Breakfast," Brady said. "After all the work you've done this morning, you must be hungry."

"Starved. You think if I have three servings of everything, Tex will start to like me?"

"Uh-huh."

She glanced at him and grinned. Brady found himself grinning back. He knew better than to risk getting involved, yet he waited while she led the gelding back to its stall, then walked with her to the bunkhouse. As she chatted about the various horses, he wondered about her past.

Last night she'd mentioned a brother. Was there other family? Why didn't she put them down as references? Did they know where she was? And most important, why was she on the run? He'd known drifters all his life. A ranch like his attracted them. Men worked for a few months, then moved on. He'd learned how to read the restlessness in their eyes when it was near their time to go.

Rita wasn't like them. Not only because she was a woman, but because everything about her screamed "home." She'd obviously grown up somewhere, had been educated. Life on the road was the exception, not the rule.

All of which didn't mean she was safe. So he was going to ignore the fire licking up his belly and remind himself he was nothing more than Rita's boss. When whatever had chased her from home was gone, she would return. Even if she didn't, she wasn't going to want to make her life on the ranch, so there was no point in wishing for the moon.

They walked toward the bunkhouse. A familiar shape moved out of the shadows of the barn and headed toward them. "That's Princess," he said, pointing at the multi-colored, long-haired dog. "She's an Australian shepherd. I thought she might be interested in helping with the cattle, but she seems to prefer cats."

Rita peered at the dog. "She's got something in her mouth. Oh, no! It's moving! Is she killing it?" She started for the dog.

"Don't worry," Brady said, catching up with her and grabbing her arm. "Princess wouldn't hurt anything. She's taking care of her cats. Come here, girl."

The dog trotted over and set down the object in her mouth. It turned out to be a kitten, maybe ten or twelve weeks old. The furry baby, all black except for a white patch on its nose, meowed plaintively. Princess swiped at the kitten with her tongue, then looked up and gave a doggy grin as if to say "Look at what I have. Aren't you impressed?"

Brady sighed. He wasn't the least bit impressed or amused, but he wouldn't tell Princess that.

Rita crouched down and let Princess sniff her fingers, then she patted the dog. "I don't understand. She has cats? Like pets?"

"They're more of a commune. People drop off strays, she finds them and brings them home. We feed them, but otherwise, she takes care of them."

Rita turned her attention to the kitten, rubbing under its chin and making it purr loudly. "What do you mean?"

"She keeps track of them, makes sure they don't fight. During the day, she herds them from shady spot to shady spot."

Rita stood up and laughed. "She herds them? You mean, she makes them move around in a group?"

"I know it sounds weird. You'll see it today. I'm not sure why the cats don't just run off, but they do what she says. When there are kittens, she helps baby-sit. If another dog strays onto the property, she chases it off. Basically, caring for her cats keeps her busy.''

Rita tucked a few loose strands of dark hair behind her ears. "How many cats are there?"

Brady shuddered. "I don't know and I don't want to know. Probably close to twenty. Tex feeds them, and I've told him to keep the exact number to himself."

They paused in front of the bunkhouse. Brady could hear the other men inside, already starting breakfast. Rita moved to the outdoor sink and began washing her hands. "Have you given any away?"

"A few. There are plenty of people around here who want barn cats. They take care of pests, and sisters from the same litter often hunt well together. Also, some of the ladies in town want house cats. I should do more to find them homes, but I don't have the time."

"Of course, you don't secretly like the cats yourself, right?" she teased.

"Never that."

She dried her hands on a towel Tex left by the sink. With her head tilted to one side, she fixed her gaze on his face.

"What?" he asked, suddenly feeling self-conscious, as if he'd forgotten a spot when he shaved.

"I was just wondering when you lost control of this ranch, Brady Jones. You've got a bunkhouse full of drifters, a dog who collects stray cats, and Lord knows what else going on."

He grinned. "There are days when the ranch runs me," he admitted.

"You wouldn't have it any other way, would you?"

"Not for a minute."

* * *

Randi carried a dish-laden tray into the kitchen. The men had already inhaled their breakfast and left to start their day. About half of them used trucks to get to the far reaches of the ranch, the other half saddled up, just like cowboys had been doing for a hundred years. She'd watched it all, feeling as if she'd just stepped back in time.

The kitchen reminded her this was very much the present. The huge room was bright with white counters, floors and walls. Stainless-steel appliances reflected the light. The stove was the biggest she'd ever seen, with eight burners and a grill in the middle. There were triple sinks on both sides of the room, a bay window and a planter filled with what looked like fresh herbs.

Tex came in from the pantry just as she set the dirty dishes on the counter. He paused when he saw her. "You got your own responsibilities, missy. There's no reason to help me."

"So my eating that last biscuit made a difference?" she asked, her voice teasing.

The older man grumbled something she couldn't hear.

"Was that an 'uh-huh' I heard?"

He glared at her, pale blue eyes piercing her like steel blades. She met his gaze and didn't dare blink. If this was a test of wills, she was determined to, if not win, at least earn his respect.

Tex was in his late forties and had the permanent tan of a man who spent most of his life outdoors. He sported a trimmed mustache. His receding hairline had reached his crown and the hair that remained was trimmed regulation short. Once a marine, always a marine.

He looked away first. "If you have enough time to be mouthing off with me, you might as well help me feed Princess and the cats. Their bowls are in there." He motioned to a lower cupboard under the counter next to the sink.

She pulled open the door and saw a half-dozen medium-size stainless steel bowls stacked inside of one another.

"We need 'em all," he told her, then walked into the pantry. He returned with two large cans of cat food and a smaller one of dog food. "Take three into the pantry. There's a barrel full of dry food for the cats. Fill 'em with that and set 'em out. You can change their water while you're at it."

"Sure," Randi said, resisting the urge to add "sir." Tex didn't strike her as a man who would have been an officer, and no doubt he would bite her head off for calling a noncom "sir."

She did as he ordered, scooping out the fishy-smelling dry food. The back door was partially open. She nudged it wider and prepared to step outside. Instead she paused, staring openmouthed.

The animals obviously knew it was feeding time. A group of maybe fifteen or twenty cats scampered toward the kitchen. Princess brought up the rear, jogging in step with her cats, moving to the left or the right to keep them in formation. A calico dashed ahead. A quick bark from Princess brought the feline up short.

Randi laughed. "I'm looking right at them and I can't believe it."

"Princess knows her business and the cats listen. You gonna stand there or are you gonna feed them?"

"I thought I might do a little of both," she said, giving him a smile over her shoulder, then stepping onto the porch and setting down the two bowls she held. She waited for Tex to follow her out before she returned for the third bowl of dry food.

He could carry more than she could, and he held three bowls of canned cat food in one arm. Princess's dish was in his other hand. The animals swarmed around. Rita set down the last of the dry food, then cleaned out water bowls and refilled them. By the time she'd finished, Tex had settled on the top step and was lighting a cigar. He waved it at her.

"I know it's smelly and not good for me, so there's no point in you mentioning the fact."

"Okay, I won't." She plopped down next to him, figuring if he hadn't wanted company he would have sat in the middle so there was no room for her, instead of off to one side. She turned her head to watch the cats. "I think there's more food than they can eat."

"Yup. The dry food will stay out all day. I take it in at night because we don't want pests around the place."

"Don't the cats take care of that?"

"Not the big pests. They could hurt the cats. Princess, too, if she decided to play protector. And she would."

He blew smoke. Randi had never cared for the smell of cigars or pipes, but she wasn't about to tell Tex that. Not that he would care or listen. She was the outsider here; it was up to her to fit in with everyone else.

"You were up early," he said after a while.

"So were you. I saw the lights on in the kitchen."

He nodded. "I made coffee, if you want some."

"Thanks, but Brady said I could make some there. I don't want to be a bother."

"No bother. If it was, I wouldn't have offered."

"What a gracious charmer," she said without thinking. "You must be really popular with the ladies."

Instead of snapping at her, he grinned. "As a matter of fact, I am."

"So, you just pretend to be a cranky old man?"

"I'm not so old."

Rita glanced at him. "It's all an act, isn't it? This tough-guy thing."

"I can be tough."

"That's right. I bet you were a marine. How long were you in?"

"Twenty years. I was in 'Nam when you were born, little girl."

She pulled her knees close to her chest and wrapped her arms around her legs. The morning was already warm, and the afternoon would be sweltering. But for now, it was pleasant. The smells from the barn took the edge off the scent of the cigar. It wasn't as horrible as she would have thought.

"After twenty years with the marines, how did you end up here?"

"Just like everyone else. I had nowhere else to go." He bit down on his cigar. "Brady's daddy hired me. I needed the job, so I agreed to take it for the summer. That was ten years ago and I'm still here."

"Do you have any plans to move on?"

"Nope. I like it here. First place I've ever called home. Except the Corps. What about you?"

As she'd asked questions about him, it was only fair that he got to ask a few about her. Randi stared out at the yard as, one by one, the cats finished with breakfast and strolled off for their post-breakfast grooming.

"I'm not from around here," she began tentatively.

"You don't say."

She shot him a glance and smiled. "I've never been a marine."

"Shoot, you probably don't have any tattoos, either."

"Not a one."

He shook his head. "Guess there's no hope for you."

"Oh, I don't know. I learn quickly."

"Have any plans to move on?" he asked, repeating the same question she'd asked him.

Their answers were going to be different. "Yes," she said simply, then waited for him to ask her when.

He didn't. He puffed on the cigar for a few minutes, then said, "You might want to think about staying around long enough to meet Brady's folks. They're good people. You'll like 'em. They're a close family with big hearts. They make all of us feel like part of the group, especially at the holidays. Vi cooks up a big turkey. Won't let me help with anything. I make a few pies the day before, but that's it."

"They sound nice." Different from her own family, she thought. Her mother would never invite the help to the table. She never even thought to give them the day off. Holidays were a time to entertain, to be seen at the correct parties, to give the correct gifts. That was somewhere else Randi had always fallen short. She refused to let go of the belief that gifts should come from the heart instead of from a certain store or catalog.

Princess strolled over and sat next to the stairs. Randi bent over and let the Australian shepherd sniff her fingers. When Princess gave her a quick lick of approval, she began stroking the dog's head and rubbing her ears. In the shade of the trees, stretched out in the sun or sitting in flower beds, the cats all groomed.

Randi pointed to a gray-and-black tabby. "Either that one's really fat or you're going to have a litter of kittens pretty soon."

"She's pregnant. Brady tries to get them spayed or neutered as soon as Princess rounds them up, but sometimes we miss one."

"He said you try to give them away in town."

"It's time to make more of an effort. Costs money to feed this many cats."

"Maybe the next time I go to town I'll ask around," she volunteered. It was the least she could do after Brady had been willing to give her a chance.

"You do that. I've never had much luck at it, but maybe you'll have better."

She chuckled. "Why do I think you ordered people to take cats and were shocked when they refused?"

Instead of answering, he puffed on his cigar. Still, she could have sworn she saw the corner of his mouth turn up in a smile. Tex was all gruff talk, but underneath he was a marshmallow. However, she must remember never to tell him that. Not if she didn't want her head chewed off.

They sat in companionable silence. A couple of the cats got up and stretched, but none of them moved out of the area. Then, without warning, Princess barked. One by one the cats stood up and started for the barn. When the pregnant tabby fell behind, the shepherd moved next to her and yipped. The cat hissed. Princess swiped at her with her tongue. The tabby rubbed her face against the dog's front left leg, then trotted to the barn.

"Amazing," Randi said. "They really listen to her."

"Too bad women don't listen to men the same way."

"If men were as sensible as Princess, they just might."

"Uh-huh."

She laughed. "I like it here, Tex, and I like you."

He blew a smoke ring. "Brady's a good man."

She stared at him. Had she missed a transition in the conversation? "He seems to be."

"He's had his share of trouble, but he's gotten through it. Things are going well for him. Would be a shame if that changed."

"I'm sure—" She clamped her lips together. Okay, she got it. He was warning her off. Brady didn't need trouble and that's how Tex had pegged her. Surprisingly, his assessment hurt. She wanted to tell him he was wrong about her, that she wasn't the type to make trouble, but was that true? She'd shown up with little luggage, no past, and was obviously on the run from something. People didn't usually run away from good stuff in their lives.

She stood up. "I have my reasons for being here," she said. "I'm not going to explain them except to say that they have nothing to do with anyone else. You don't have to worry. I'm not going to mess up Brady's perfect life." She brushed her hands against her rear and walked down the steps. "I have some work to finish up in the barn. I'll see you later."

She headed around the building without waiting for him to respond or looking back to see if he waved. The comfortable mood had been broken.

When she reached the barn, Princess had the cats lying in a nearly perfect circle. Some were still grooming, but most had already stretched out for their morning nap. She thought about the dog's odd behavior and the cats allowing it. Was it any stranger than Brady's collection of strays?

She remembered a Christmas special on television when she was growing up. The title eluded her, but the show had been about a land of misfit toys. That's what they were here on the ranch. Misfit people, and Brady was their leader. Oddly enough, she sensed she could feel safe here. At least until it was time to move on.

If she was smart she would use her time here to figure out a plan. At some point she was going to have to go home and face Hal. A twinge of guilt flickered in her chest. Maybe she should have called him. But what was there to say? Abandoning him at the church was a pretty clear message. She doubted he was expecting or hoping for a reconciliation. Hal was the consummate politician—he knew when to cut his losses. No doubt he was relieved. Her behavior proved she wasn't cut out to be a politician's wife. Not getting married was better for both of them.

Randi grabbed a halter and headed toward Casper's stall. She might as well exercise the gelding before it got too hot.

As she led the horse outside, her thoughts strayed back to Grand Springs. Even though not marrying Hal had been the right thing to do, she was embarrassed by her behavior. She was twenty-four-years old. When was she going to stop running out on her problems?

At least she could be confident that she was finally growing up. Life on the road had a way of wearing away at a person's pretensions. Over the next few days and weeks she would figure out the best thing to do. After all, there was more than Hal to worry about. There were the men with the guns.

She stepped into the center of the ring and urged Casper to walk. As she monitored the horse's gait to make sure he wasn't favoring his healing leg, she wondered if it was too late to call the police. Would they believe her? She shook her head. No doubt they would think she was trying to excuse her behavior so she wouldn't look like such a flake for running off.

But the men were real, and their guns had been more than water pistols. Why would someone want to kill her?

The fear returned, and with it a coldness that made Randi's limbs go numb. She shook her head to force the thoughts away. No one was going to find her on the ranch. She didn't have to make a decision today. She didn't even have to think about what had happened. All she had to do was finish her chores.

The steady sound of hooves caught her attention. She glanced up and saw Brady riding back to the barn. His cowboy hat hid his face from view, but her memory supplied a picture of his handsome features. He moved with the confidence of a man who has spent a large portion of his life in the saddle.

He was about as different from Hal as denim was from silk. After being gone for nearly two months, Randi couldn't figure out why on earth she'd allowed herself to be railroaded into the engagement or the wedding. Ten minutes before the ceremony she hadn't been sure she'd liked Hal, let alone loved him. Now she knew she'd been right to worry. Her only lingering feeling about him was relief that she'd gotten away in time. The thought of marriage made her shudder. She couldn't think about kissing him without grimacing. Thank goodness they'd never made love.

Brady rode closer. Maybe it was her imagination, but the sun seemed to shine a little brighter on him. She hadn't needed Tex to tell her Brady was a great guy. But if he were so wonderful, why wasn't he married? Was there a hideous flaw she hadn't discovered, or some dark secret from his past? And why was it suddenly so important for her to know?

Four

"Chow's on," Randi called as she set down the cat food dishes. Unlike Tex, she could only carry two bowls at a time, and she had to hurry back into the kitchen for another set. In a matter of minutes, all the cats were eating. Princess had started her dinner, as well.

Randi settled on the porch steps and breathed a sigh of contentment. It was late afternoon, and a rainstorm had blown through earlier, dropping the temperature to the low seventies. The ground was damp and the horses would be muddy, but it was a small price to pay for relief from the heat.

Princess finished eating and came over to get her nightly attention. They were all settling into a routine. Even though feeding the cats wasn't one of her responsibilities, Randi had taken over the chore from Tex. When the older man had protested, she'd explained that she liked spending time with the animals. She was starting to learn the different personalities of the cats and even to name them, although Tex had warned her not to let Brady know she was making pets of them. The rancher tolerated the cats, but he didn't actually like them.

She rubbed Princess's ears and smiled. "Brady talks tough," she said aloud to the dog, "but I think he's faking it. He likes you and your herd of kitties, doesn't he?" Princess thumped her tail against the wooden porch.

The pregnant tabby finished her meal and jumped up

onto the porch. She settled next to Princess and began licking her front right paw. When it was clean, she began the intricate process of grooming her face.

"How are you feeling, Pokey?" Randi asked. "If that belly of yours gets much lower, it's going to drag against the dirt."

Pokey ignored her criticism and concentrated on the task at hand. The cat worked in a rhythmic, circular motion, licking her paw, then swiping it across the side of her face, then licking the paw again. First she cleaned her muzzle, then her cheeks, the area around her eyes, her forehead and finally behind her ears.

Randi watched, amazed at the patience and thoroughness involved. "See that," she said, pointing to the cat. "If you learned to do that, Princess, you wouldn't have to get a bath every couple of weeks. You're a great dog, but I have to tell you, you smell."

Princess grinned her doggy grin, obviously unconcerned about her odor problem. Peter, the eleven-week-old black kitten, climbed up the stairs and into Randi's lap. Once there, he purred loudly and stared at her with his big yellow eyes. When she didn't move to pet him right away, he butted her stomach with his head.

"Impatient little devil, aren't you," she said, scratching him behind his ears. The purring rose in volume as tiny paws kneaded her belly and incredibly sharp claws poked through denim.

She endured the slight pain. In a few minutes Peter would sink down onto her lap and doze off. In this time before dinner, she liked to enjoy the quiet of just her and the animals. Maybe it was because she'd never had a pet as a child. Her mother wouldn't have allowed one in the house. After all, a wild creature couldn't be trusted around expensive rugs and priceless antiques. It had been hard enough to control two children. Randi grimaced. Who was she kidding? Noah hadn't been the problem; she had.

One of her earliest clear memories was of standing next to a broken vase, crying. Her mother had been screaming at her. Not only because of the value of the destroyed piece, but because Randi had cut herself and was dripping blood on the rug. She remembered holding out her hand, trying to show her mother that she was still bleeding, that the cut hurt. Her mother had shoved her away and told her to drip over the hardwood floor. Eventually Noah had found her sobbing in her room and had taken the time to bandage her small wound.

Randi pushed that memory away. She didn't want to think about her mother or Grand Springs. For the first time in a long time, life was good. She'd put in a hard day's work, she could smell Tex's delicious cooking, and Peter's tiny, trusting kitten body warmed her.

Footsteps coming around the bunkhouse broke the solitude. Princess turned toward the sound. Peter raised his head to watch the newcomer.

Randi found herself leaning forward, her heart suddenly thudding louder in her chest. Anticipation surged through her. *You're being a fool,* she told herself. It didn't help.

But the man rounding the corner of the bunkhouse wasn't her boss. Instead, Ty stepped into view. Randi told herself she was silly. What did it matter if Brady sought out her company or not? But the logic didn't ease the pinch of disappointment.

The tall, dark-haired cowboy paused at the bottom of the steps and leaned against the railing.

"'Evening," he said. With his hat pulled low, it was impossible to see his eyes. Not that it would have mattered if she could. She'd seen Ty enough in the dining room to know that he kept his expression unreadable, his feelings hidden.

Technically he was better-looking than Brady. There was something about him that should have called to her. No doubt when he went to town, the ladies lined up for miles. Maybe it was the air of danger he wore like a familiar coat. Maybe it was the hint of sadness in his straight mouth. Whatever the appeal, while she could intellectually admit he was as handsome as any media heartthrob, he didn't do it for her. Her life was messed up enough without dealing with a mysterious stranger.

Brady, on the other hand, made her feel comfortable. With him around, she could relax enough to enjoy life. He was the kind of man who made women smile and feel special.

"The last groom preferred working with larger fourlegged critters," Ty said, jerking his head toward the cat on her lap.

"I like them in all sizes," she said.

"Me, too." As if to confirm his words, Percival, one of the larger male cats, strolled over to Ty and rubbed against his calves. Ty bent down and picked up the cat, holding him in his arms and stroking him.

Randi stared. "I can't believe that. I tried to touch him a couple of days ago and he spit at me."

"This old cat and I understand each other." Ty's slow movements made Percival purr loudly.

Interesting, Randi thought. Who was this man with his unreadable eyes and a way with cats? What was his story? She returned her attention to the kitten on her lap and reminded herself to mind her own business. Out here everyone had a story, even Brady. Everyone had secrets. If she wanted to keep hers, she'd better not snoop into anyone else's.

"We're two of a kind," Ty continued.

She realized the cowboy was right. Princess might rule the cats, but Percival staked out his own territory and he defended it with teeth and claws. Ty was similar, maintaining a physical distance from the other men. He moved in a way that left no doubt he would fight for what was his. Controlled danger. Something she was trying to avoid in her life.

"Evening, R-Rita."

She glanced up to see Ziggy and Quinn approaching. "Hi, guys. How was your day?"

"Not bad." Quinn nodded at Ty, then reached down and patted one of the cats. Randi noticed that he kept his left hand tucked in the front pocket of his jeans. She'd watched him at the table and had realized he could barely use his hand or arm. Yet his physical limitations didn't seem to interfere with his ability to get his work done. Brady often mentioned how well Quinn performed. But how many employers would have given Quinn a chance to prove himself in the first place?

"This one looks ready to pop," Quinn said, reaching over to pet Pokey.

"Don't tell Brady," Randi said quickly. "The last thing he wants to know about is more cats."

"He's all talk." Ziggy managed the short sentence without stuttering.

"Maybe, but I've been thinking of trying to find homes for some of them." Randi stroked the kitten on her lap. "They're certainly well-trained animals."

Conversation continued as they waited for Tex to ring the dinner bell. Randi participated, but part of her attention focused elsewhere as she strained to hear another set of footsteps...those belonging to a man she had no business thinking about.

When the bell rang, Princess barked twice and the cats stood up. They began their evening journey back to the barn, where they would settle for the night.

Randi walked around to the front entrance to the dining room. When she crossed the threshold, she found Brady already inside. How long had he been there? Why hadn't he joined the other men and come to see her and the cats?

Don't even think about that, she ordered herself as she took one of the empty chairs halfway down the table. Ziggy immediately sat next to her and she gave him an absentminded smile.

Brady was just her boss. Just a guy who had hired her. He wasn't special, and even if he was, he wasn't for her. In a few weeks, when she'd figured out what she was going to do with her life, she was moving on. Until then, she would do a good job, collect her pay at the end of the week and stay out of trouble.

Despite that excellent advice, as Tex brought out the food, Randi found her gaze straying again and again to the far end of the table.

The men all showered after they finished their work, but none of their still-damp hair or fresh shaven faces affected her the way Brady's did. She didn't want to touch their skin or say something funny so they would smile at her.

Consciously, she forced her attention away from Brady and onto the conversation at the table. As bowls of food were passed to her, she took a serving for herself. Once, when she forked two pork chops onto her plate, she caught Tex looking at her and she winked. The ex-marine grinned.

Contentment stole over her, surprising her with a sense of warm belonging. She could fit in here. More important, she *wanted* to fit in.

"I heard you found a couple of steers in a mud hole this afternoon, Ralph," Brady said.

The older cowboy nodded. "Got 'em out, boss."

"I know. I checked on them. You did a good job. Thanks for checking that dry pond. I'd forgotten all about it."

Ralph mumbled a reply.

"Ziggy and Quinn, that fence is going up faster than I'd expected."

"Some of the main posts aren't rotted, so we're reusing them," Quinn said.

Brady's style of management was very hands-on. About the second or third night, Randi had noticed he made it a point to find something to praise about each employee nearly every day. No wonder even the drifters stayed.

"Rita."

She looked up when he said her assumed name. An unexpected attack of nerves made her fork slip out of her fingers and bang against her plate. She picked it up and cleared her throat. "Yes?"

He continued to smile as if nothing was wrong. "I'd like to see you in my office after dinner."

"Um, sure."

"You rode Casper today?"

"Yes. There's no hint of the injury. You can put him back to work tomorrow."

"Great. You've been patient with him. I appreciate that."

"No problem."

She forced herself to cut off a piece of pork, but instead of eating it, she chased it around her plate. When Ziggy handed her the bowl of biscuits, she passed them on without taking one.

He wanted to see her in his office. She knew what that

meant. After only a week, she was out on her butt—just like that.

She couldn't remember making a mistake. Damn. The irony was, she had barely gotten used to being here and now she was going to be asked to move on. Just when she'd realized she would very much like to stay for a while.

The motel's window air conditioner fought a losing battle against the early evening heat, but for $19.95 a night, neither occupant expected luxury.

"Yes," the bald man said into the phone. "I understand, but without any clue as to where to look for her—"

The caller cut him off with a sharp word. The bald man frowned his impatience, but didn't say anything aloud. He was too fond of his job...and his life...to complain.

His companion, a dark-haired man wearing a White Sox baseball cap, tossed a full pack of cigarettes into the air and caught it. He repeated the action, not paying attention to the phone conversation. There was no point in worrying. They would get their instructions and they would follow them. End of story.

"I understand your concern," the bald man said. "It's also mine. But it's been two months and the trail is cold. If my associate and I had been tracking her from the beginning, she would already be taken care of."

"Take care of her now," the caller said. "I can't stress the importance enough."

The bald man nodded. He knew what that meant. Find Randi Howell or else. "Is someone watching the police station?" he asked. "She could be caught on her way in or out."

The caller's voice sharpened with annoyance. "If she speaks to the police, there's no point in worrying about her. Understand? Another murder would make everyone suspicious and we don't want to take that chance unless we have to. Now, I just want to know where she is and what she's doing. Then we can decide the best way to make sure she doesn't talk.''

"She hasn't called the police with the information?"

"Not yet. It's been so long now, she may think they wouldn't believe her. The broad's been on the run for a while. She's alone and scared and probably doubting what she saw. She'll get careless about her whereabouts. You be there to take advantage of that.''

The caller hung up without saying goodbye.

The man in the baseball cap looked at his associate and raised his eyebrows.

"Bad,'' the bald man said. "We have to find her before she talks to the cops. It's important.''

They stared at each other and ignored the fear. Important. As in they would pay with their lives if they failed.

"We found the trucker who dropped her off in Phoenix," the bald man continued. "We've checked west and north. It's time to go east. We'll check the small towns. A newcomer looking for work should be easy to remember. She's gotta work. She couldn't have had much cash on her, and she hasn't used her bank card to get any.''

The second man tossed the cigarette pack in the air again, caught it and grinned. "I know where she is," he said.

"Where?"

"It's in her file. You said she needs a job. She only worked in one place while she was in school. According to the information, she loved it. A stable. We should start checking ranches.''

The bald man nodded. "Good idea.'' He picked up the phone and dialed a familiar number. When it was answered, he said, "Yes, it's me. We have an idea about where she might be." He explained about the ranches. "I think it might work, too. Also, she may try to contact someone, using a rodeo or horse show for a cover. We'd like you to let us know if anyone in Grand Springs leaves to attend either."

He listened for a minute, then hung up. "They like it," he told his associate. "They're pleased."

Good news for both of them. Now all that was left was to get the girl.

Brady straightened the papers on his desk. They didn't need straightening, but he ignored that fact, just the way he ignored the faint tension in his gut that told him he was nervous. Hell of a state for a man to find himself in.

She's just an employee, he reminded himself. If he treated her like everyone else, he would be fine.

Yeah, right, he thought grimly. Who was he trying to kid with that line? He couldn't think about her like everyone else, because he couldn't stop thinking about her at all. He could easily dismiss the cowboys from his mind, but Rita got under his skin.

A brief knock caused him to look up. She stood in the doorway.

"Come in," he called, feeling like an adolescent with his first crush for being so pleased to see her.

She brushed her palms against her jeans-clad thighs, then did as he requested.

In the evening she usually let her hair loose of its braid and simply tied the riot of curls back at the base of her neck. Lamplight made them gleam as a few wayward strands danced around her neck. Her pale, much-washed T-shirt emphasized her strong arms and well-formed breasts.

He told himself to look away. Her feminine attributes were none of his business. She was his employee, nothing more. But as she walked toward him, her hips swaying with each step, he found himself wanting her. As he swallowed against rising desire, he wished he were the kind of man who could simply scratch the itch with whomever was handy. A night in town could take care of his need.

But he wasn't that kind of man. He needed to trust and care before he participated in an intimate relationship. It was a flaw in his character, at least his rodeo buddies had told him so when he'd refused countless invitations by attractive and willing buckle bunnies.

As he wasn't going to get involved with Rita, who was both an employee and a woman with a past, he had no choice but to live with the itch. In time it would go away. It always did.

She gave him a tentative smile. He returned it and motioned to the chair across from his desk. Days in the sun had given her skin a honey-colored glow and brought out a few freckles on her nose. She was bright-eyed and young. Too young for him. There were nine years between them. While he wrestled with his lustful thoughts, she probably saw him as an old man. Someone to be respected, like an older brother or an uncle.

Hell, she would be disgusted if she knew how he'd imagined them together, bare and touching, bodies—

With a supreme effort of will, he forced his mind to the matter at hand. Rita and her job performance. Was it hot in here or was it just him? He tugged at the collar of his shortsleeved shirt and cleared his throat.

"You've been here a week," he began, only to notice that she fidgeted in her seat. She crossed and uncrossed her legs, she clenched and relaxed her fingers, her gaze wouldn't meet his.

"What's wrong?" he asked.

"Nothing." She pressed her lips together, then blurted out, "You're going to fire me and I don't even know what I've done wrong. I've followed the rules. All of them. The horses are in good shape, I'm up early, I work hard." She straightened her spine and stared at him. "I'm quiet in the house, I haven't made trouble with the men. I even clean the bathroom every afternoon after I shower. I just can't think of a single thing I'm doing that you wouldn't like."

The vulnerability in her eyes called to him. Before he could stop himself, he half rose out of his chair. Don't even think about it, he warned himself as he slowly resumed his seat.

"I'm not going to fire you," he said. "We agreed to a one-week trial, Rita. The week is up. I want to talk to you about your job. You do great work and I'd like you to stay on. I asked you here so we could talk about that. Nothing more."

Her mouth opened. Color flooded her face, then faded. "Really?" Her voice squeaked. "I thought—" She shook her head. "I guess I overreacted, huh?"

"Just a little. But under the circumstances, it's understandable. Now I know why you turned down dessert. When we're done here, why don't you go explain it to Tex. I'm sure he's got some peach cobbler left over. He'll be wondering why you didn't have your normal two or three servings. We can't afford to have our cook sulking, now, can we?"

She laughed. "I promise I'll go speak to him." She leaned forward and placed her hands on his desk. "I like my job, Brady. I'm enjoying the ranch. If you want to keep me around, I'd like to stay."

Pleasure heated his belly. He ignored the sensation, just

as he ignored the impulse to lean forward as well and capture her hands in his. "Great. I'm going to raise your salary thirty dollars a week. Can you give me any kind of time commitment as to how long you'll be staying?"

He always asked that question of new employees, but this time his interest in her reply was personal. Shadows moved across her face. She withdrew her hands to her lap and shook her head.

"Not really. A couple of months. Maybe."

"I see. Well, we're happy to have you here as long as you want to stay."

The disappointment was sharper than the pleasure had been. He'd wanted more. Trust, maybe? It was too soon to expect that. She might never trust him. Could be life had taught her it was too dangerous. After all, he'd had his own lessons. He'd learned it was safer not to give away his heart.

"If anything changes and I find I can stay, I'll let you know," she said. "But I can't promise more. Not without knowing if I can keep my word. It wouldn't be fair."

"I understand."

There was an awkward pause as the room filled with unasked questions. Questions about her past and his, about a future that was never going to be.

"That's all I had to say," he said, dismissing her. "Your raise will be in your next paycheck."

"Thanks." She rose to her feet and gave him a quick smile, then moved to the door.

He watched her go, telling himself the emptiness inside had nothing to do with her, or with feeling lonely. He wished it could have been different. He wished he could have fallen in love with someone who wanted what he wanted. But he hadn't. Instead he'd learned a hard lesson.

Love was a rare and elusive gift. Once given, there was no guarantee it was going to be enough to make the relationship work. He had the scarred heart to prove it.

Five

Randi leaned against the window frame and inhaled the soft smells of the night. It was getting late, and she should think about going to bed. After all, 4:00 a.m. came pretty early. But she couldn't seem to settle down. Her body was pleasantly exhausted from a hard day's work, but her mind was restless.

Thoughts flitted around like butterflies in a meadow. She was pleased that Brady wanted her to stay, proud that he thought she was doing a good job. She wondered about Grand Springs, then questioned what it meant that she no longer thought of that place as home. She missed Noah, if not her mother. She tried to imagine her future and couldn't picture herself in any one place. Or with any one man.

She stared through the trees. Brady had wanted to talk about her past. She'd read it in his eyes. He had questions and she couldn't blame him. What must it be like to hire someone with no references, no experience? Why had he given her a chance?

It would be so easy to confess everything to him, to tell him about the wedding and her near escape, to explain about those two men with guns. She sighed, knowing he would despise her for the former and disbelieve the latter. She couldn't even make it sound better by saying she ran *because* of the men with guns. The truth was she'd been on her way out when she'd seen them. As much as she would like it to be otherwise, they had nothing to do with why she'd left Hal at the altar. So she wasn't going to let on even a single whisper about her past.

If the last week had taught her only one thing it was that Brady Jones was an honorable man. Her first assessment of him had been right on the mark. If this was a 1950s western, his part would be played by John Wayne. Brady was an all-American hero. She was just a woman who'd run out on her own wedding and didn't know what to do with her life. She thought he was wonderful; he probably didn't think about her at all. They had nothing in common.

He spent his life helping out strays and others in need—she waited to be rescued, first by her father, then by Noah. Sure, this time she'd decided to take care of the problem herself. She might be making progress and growing up, but it wasn't enough for a man like Brady.

A cool breeze blew into the bedroom, calling her, tempting her. Finally she gave in. As there was no way she was going to sleep for the next couple of hours, she might as well enjoy the night.

After slipping off her boots and socks so she could walk quietly and not wake Brady, she tiptoed down the hall and the stairs before crossing the hardwood floor and moving to the front door. She pulled it open slowly, wincing at a faint creak. She stepped onto the porch and pulled it shut behind her.

"Great night."

The unexpected voice made her jump. She peered toward the sound and saw Brady sitting on the front steps.

"I, ah—" She didn't know what to say. Obviously she hadn't been the only one tempted by the night. "Sorry. I don't mean to intrude." She turned to go back inside.

"If you came out to enjoy the night air, there's plenty for both of us."

She glanced at him. He slid over on the step and patted the wood beside him.

"I don't bite," he encouraged.

She relaxed. "But as a former rodeo cowboy, you can probably hog-tie me in less than four seconds, right?"

He grinned and raised his hands. "Yup, but I don't have my trusty rope, so you're safe."

She crossed the porch and sank down on the top step, taking care to sit as far from him as possible. It wasn't that she didn't trust him. Quite the opposite. After comparing the goodness of their respective souls, she was feeling a little lacking and out of her league.

"You work hard enough to be asleep," he said. "So it must be a guilty conscience keeping you up."

She jumped at his words and stared at him. Dear Lord, how did he know?

Brady shook his head. "It was a joke, Rita. Relax."

"Okay. Sorry. I don't feel guilty. Just sort of restless. Mentally, not physically," she added quickly. "I like it here at the ranch and I really appreciate the raise."

"I'm glad you're staying."

"Yeah?"

The porch light allowed her to see his features. His eyes were dark and beckoning. She let her gaze lock with his, feeling drawn toward something she couldn't quite define. Maybe it was supposed to frighten her, but it didn't. Quite the opposite—it made her feel safe.

"My daddy always taught me to pay good help well and they'll be loyal in return," he said.

"Your father sounds a lot like mine." She brought her knees to her chest and wrapped her arms around her legs. "A good man, right?"

Brady nodded.

"Mine was, too. He died when I was pretty young. I miss him. I'm sure you won't be surprised to hear he spoiled me. Some days I miss being his little princess."

"You still are, in your memories."

"I know, but I'd prefer it in real life." Not that she would want him to rescue her this time, Randi reminded herself. She was supposed to be getting herself out of this mess alone.

She shook off her thoughts. "Where are your folks? Somebody said something about them traveling?"

"They bought an RV and are using it to see the world. Or at least this part of it. They're strange, but I love them." He reached into his shirt pocket and pulled out a folded postcard. After smoothing it, he handed it to her.

She held the picture up to the light. "Rio?" she asked disbelievingly. "Your parents are in South America?"

"I know it's crazy, but that's where they are. They wanted to explore as much of the world as they could, so they drove to the tip of South America and are working their way north. They wanted to hold off on the States and Canada until they were older."

"Rio." The postcard showed a stunning aerial view of the city from the top of Corcovado Mountain. The shadow cast by the famous Christ the Redeemer statue was in the foreground.

"You can read what they wrote. Like I said, my folks are a little odd, but nice people."

She turned over the postcard and held it up to the light.

We love Rio. Wonderful food, friendly people. Lots of stray cats, which makes us think Princess would enjoy it, too. I wanted to send you a postcard of the topless girls on the beaches, but your father got embarrassed at the gift shop so I couldn't buy it. We are having a wonderful time, and we miss you and love you very much.

"They sound terrific," she said. "Are you disappointed about the postcard?"

He chuckled. "Knowing Mom, she'll find a way to buy one without my dad finding out. At least the mail carrier is an old friend and I won't have to do any explaining."

She handed him the postcard and wished her mother had been half as affectionate. While her father had obviously loved and cared for his children, he'd been gone a lot. Her mother had been the one at home, and the one to find fault all the time.

"I envy you them," she said lightly, hoping he didn't hear the loneliness in her voice. It wasn't that she missed what she had, but instead she felt a sense of loss for the potential of what should have been.

"Does your family know where you are?" he asked.

She stared at him.

Brady shrugged and tucked the postcard into his shirt pocket. "That first night you mentioned a brother, so you must have some family."

She thought about changing the subject, then figured she owed Brady better than that. "Noah knows that I'm safe. I called him. But no, he doesn't have any specific information on my whereabouts. I'm sure he passed the information along to my mother. She's not someone I'm anxious to have a conversation with right now." There was an understatement. When Randi thought about the spoiled wedding, the scuttled plans for the reception, the wasted food, she cringed.

"I'm not ready to be in contact with them," she continued. "I have a few things to work out."

"The ranch is a good place to do that," he told her. "When I need to think things through, I get on one of the horses and ride. Speaking of which, if you want to explore the ranch, go ahead. I saw you on Casper and you know what you're doing. Any of the horses that aren't being worked need the exercise, anyway, so help yourself."

"Thanks. I might do that." She paused, wondering if he was judging her. "It's not as bad you think," she added, even as she told herself it was too late, not to mention futile, to try to tip the scales in her favor. "My being on my own. I just—"

"Rita, you don't have to explain," he interrupted gently. "People get into different situations, and sometimes they need to take a break from that. My only assumptions about you are based on the job you're doing right here, the same as the rest of the guys. Everyone has secrets. As long as yours don't get in the way of the work getting done, you're welcome to them."

He was right about everyone having secrets. What were his?

She reminded herself she didn't have the right to ask. Besides, there was no way his were as bad as hers.

In the distance night creatures called to one another. "I've seen the topographic maps in the barn," she said. "The ranch goes on for miles. You ever get lost out there?"

"Not since I was a kid. I used to camp out in the summer. Eventually I would find my way home, or one of the cowboys would come after me. I like it out here."

"It's different from anything I'm used to," she said. "The landscape's forbidding."

He leaned against the railing and angled toward her. "*Barren* is the word you're looking for. West Texas isn't exactly the breadbasket of the world. It was the last part of the state to be settled. Some people think it's still being settled.''

"The wide-open spaces are a little intimidating. I can understand why those early pioneers kept on going."

"Me, too. Hot as hell in the summer. Freezing in the winter. We get storms coming in all directions, tornados, remnants of gulf hurricanes.''

"Sounds like paradise," she teased.

"It is to me. I've traveled a lot, and this is where I belong. It's not for everyone, though."

She gazed up at the star-filled sky. "Maybe not, but I understand the appeal. There's no one around telling you what to do. No pressure. I'd forgotten what it was like to do physical work, something with my hands, to have something to show for a day's work."

"I wouldn't have picked you as an old-fashioned girl."

"Me, neither. I'm still figuring things out." She looked at Brady. Ruggedly handsome, she thought with a sigh. A perfect, romantic cliché. Too bad she wasn't in the market for a cowboy. He was a hundred percent fantasy material.

Broad shoulders filled out his shirt, stretching the material just enough to make a woman sit up and take notice. She'd seen him calming his horse. He spoke gently, moving his hands with a sureness that made her wonder what else those hands would do as well. What other tasks did those long, strong fingers move into easily, confidently? Wasn't there an analogy about women and horses being similar—unpredictable to tame but worth the effort? Or was that just wishful thinking on her part?

"How long have you run the ranch?" she asked.

"Five years."

"I'm surprised. You must have been a baby."

He grinned. "Twenty-eight. I've aged quickly. Now I'm an old man like Tex."

"Thirty-three isn't old."

"It's nine years older that you, Rita."

She stiffened and stared straight ahead. "I'm not a child."

"Agreed. You're more of a youngster."

Randi knew he was teasing her, but oddly enough, she found it difficult to smile in return. She didn't want Brady to think of her as immature—not when she was a grown woman. But defending herself would only prove his claim of her youth. She would have to find another way to point out that he should take her seriously.

She would also have to keep her past from him. Running out on a wedding was not the act of a mature adult.

"Being the baby of the family made it hard to grow up," she admitted. "Things are different now. Time on the road changes a person."

"How long have you been on your own?" he asked.

"Two months. It's been hard, but in a good way. I'm learning to depend on myself rather than letting other people take care of me. I guess I'm becoming responsible."

"That's a hard lesson to learn."

She wrinkled her nose. "Not for you. I'll bet you were born responsible."

"Are you saying I'm boring?"

"Not at all." She glanced at him. "Responsible isn't boring. The world needs more responsible people in it. Otherwise the rest of us would be in trouble."

"You're doing okay. Taking care of the horses is a challenging job. People think it's all about mucking out the stalls, but there's more to it. You have to learn about the animals, understand them, so you can see if they're healthy. You connect with them."

His compliment pleased her. "Thanks. I guess you got lucky, huh? I could have been a complete flake."

"A flake wouldn't have worried about getting up on time that first day."

"Maybe." She wrinkled her nose. "You don't have to answer this, but...why did you hire me?"

Brady surprised her by turning away. She might be crazy, but she would have sworn the question made him uncomfortable.

Silence stretched between them. Randi wondered if she'd crossed some invisible line between employer and employee. "I'm sorry," she said. "I shouldn't have asked."

"It's not that," he told her. "I'm trying to work up an answer that doesn't sound nuts. The truth?"

She nodded.

"I hired you because my gut didn't tell me not to. I get this feeling about people, and I've learned to listen to it. If my gut said you were going to be bad news, I wouldn't have offered you the job."

She had thought his answer would make her feel better, but it didn't. She felt worse because his gut had been wrong about her. She *was* bad news.

"It turned out right in the end," he said, and leaned forward to capture her left hand. She was too surprised to stop him, and once he'd taken her fingers in his, she didn't want to.

He held her gently, almost impersonally. After turning her palm to the light, he ran his thumb across the bumps at the base of her fingers.

"New blisters," he said. "Thicker calluses. A few more months of this and your hands are going to look like mine." He turned his wrist so his palm faced up. With his free hand he pointed at the marks on his skin. Several

fingers were scarred; there was a healing cut by his thumb.
"See what hard work can do."

He was bigger than her, his fingers longer, his palm
broader. Maybe his strength should have frightened her,
or at least pointed out how vulnerable she was with him.
Instead, she found comfort in his physical power, sensing
he would use it to protect rather than threaten.

"I've seen the rewards of hard work," she said, raising
her gaze to his face. "The ranch is wonderful. You should
be very proud of yourself."

Dark eyes blended with the dark night until she
couldn't read his thoughts or emotions. She desperately
wanted to know if he felt the same things she did, if her
touch affected him with the same intensity that his did
her.

There were no overt sparks, no conflagration of instant
desire. Instead she felt a steady glow, similar to that given
off by a well-built fire. Instead of flash and smoke, there
was security, as if the heat would last a long time.

He released her hand. "The ranch was already a suc-
cess when my father left it to me. I've followed in his
footsteps. I'm lucky—he left me a clear path."

Randi drew her fingers into her palm as if the action
would allow her to hold on to the sensations he'd created
with his touch. Her belly tightened as if she was nervous,
but she wasn't, at least she didn't have reason to be. What
was going on? She'd never felt this way before—content,
yet unsettled.

It wasn't like when she'd spent time with Hal. She
frowned, trying to remember what her ex-fiancé had
looked like, and realized she couldn't force his image into
her mind. She couldn't remember the color of his eyes,
or the shape of his mouth when he smiled. She certainly
couldn't remember being with him. How strange. A man

she'd considered marrying had disappeared completely from her mind.

A fast-moving shadow caught her attention. She squinted to see in the dark. "What is that?" she asked, pointing.

"Princess. She makes one last round about this time. Just in case."

"How often does she find cats?"

"We can go a couple of months without anyone leaving any, then we might have three additions in a week." He muttered something that sounded like "damned felines," but she wasn't sure.

Tilting her head so he wouldn't see her smile, she said, "I've been thinking about talking to some people the next time I'm in town. You know, maybe find a few homes."

"That would be great. At this rate, I'm going to have to get licensed as a zoo or something."

She laughed. "If they don't make you do that for all the steers you have, they're not going to make you do it for the cats."

"I guess. At least the steers are money on the hoof. What good are the cats?"

"They're great hunters. I'll bet you don't have a bug or a small rodent within a mile of the house."

He grumbled low in his throat, but didn't respond.

"You talk tough, but I've seen you petting them," she said, rising to her feet. "Especially Peter."

"Who the hell is Peter?" He stood up and glared at her. "You're not going to start naming them. Over my dead body. Next thing you know you'll be attached to them and won't want me to give them away. No names."

"Peter is the black kitten with a white patch on his nose. You were holding him. I saw you, so don't bother denying it."

"I was not. I was checking to see if he had something in his paw. I thought he was limping."

"Sure. It's a good story, Brady. You *might* get someone to believe it. Just not me."

He glanced around as if checking to make sure they were alone. "All right," he said, his voice low. "Maybe I was petting that one, but I still don't like cats."

"You're right. You adore them."

She laughed and he joined in. He made a move toward her, as if to deliver a mock blow. She raised her hands in a gesture that was two parts protection, one part surrender. Not sure if she'd stepped forward or if he'd been the one to close the distance between them, she found herself in his arms.

As hugs went, it wasn't especially romantic. He held her lightly, his hands barely touching her back. Yet there was a rightness, as if they'd been created to fit together. Her body heated unexpectedly. Her thighs began to tremble, as did her arms.

After a brief squeeze, he released her. Slowly, she let her arms drop to her side, oddly reluctant to move away. Nerves tingled where her fingertips had rested on his shoulders.

"Thanks, Brady," she said, wondering if he could hear the shaking in her voice. What was wrong with her? It was just a hug. "I mean, for the job and the raise. And for trusting me. I won't let you down."

"I know you won't. Good night, Rita." He bent over and brushed his lips against her cheek.

Her heart lurched in her chest and her breath caught. She spun on her heel and walked rapidly to the front door, calling a quick "'Night" over her shoulder as she ducked inside.

By the time Randi made it back to the safety of her

room, she still hadn't been able to slow her breathing. She pressed her hands to her cheeks and was shocked to feel heat. Was she blushing? She wasn't embarrassed, she was stunned.

"Calm down," she told herself as she paced from the door to the window. "Deep breaths. It's not a big deal. Just a hug and a kiss on the cheek. Just like Noah does all the time."

Maybe the actions looked like the same brotherly affection, but her reaction couldn't have been more different. With Noah, she felt a sisterly love. With Hal, she never felt anything at all. But in Brady's arms—

"Don't think about it," she said. "Remember who you are and what you've done. Brady isn't going to be interested in a woman like you."

Maybe. Probably. Certainly. But that knowledge didn't stop her from pressing her fingertips to the cheek he'd kissed. Nor, when she was in bed and staring at the ceiling, could she stop reliving those brief seconds in his arms. Her body hadn't reacted that strongly to the passionate kisses she'd received from the young men she'd dated in college. And all Brady had done was kiss her cheek.

A noise downstairs caught her attention. She heard measured steps on the stairs and knew Brady had returned from his final check of the ranch. Every night he walked around the barn and the bunkhouse, making sure all was well. He guarded his domain much as Princess guarded hers.

Randi turned on her side and pulled her knees up to her chest. Longing filled her. Longing for a home and a place to belong. If only... What a useless phrase, she thought. If only she could belong here. Isn't that what her first week had taught her? That she wanted to stay here awhile. On the ranch.

But it wasn't the ranch that appealed to her. Oh, she liked the wide-open spaces and enjoyed her work. The cowboys were fun, as were Princess and the cats. But the real appeal was currently getting ready for bed in a room down the hall from her. She hadn't seen it before. It would have been easier to pretend she'd never seen it.

She could ignore the truth if she wanted. She could play games and imagine what it would be like to stay with him. She could relive his impersonal kiss and thank God he didn't know how much he'd affected her. In the end, none of that would matter. She couldn't escape who she was and what she'd done.

She could let herself believe Brady might be the man for her—and all she wanted. That didn't change a thing. The truth was, with her past, she wasn't the woman for him.

Six

"Cooperate, damn you," Brady muttered when the large gelding took an unexpected side step and bumped him. Brady scrambled back to keep from falling on his butt. "I *own* you," he reminded the horse. "Keep this up and I'll sell you for glue. Or dog food."

Rita laughed. "That's telling him, boss. Remind him who's in charge and how you hold his life in your hands." She stroked the horse's head. "Are you scared, big fella? Don't be." She lowered her voice to a whisper. "He's all bark and no bite. Yes, it's true. Cheap talk. Can you say cheap?"

The horse snorted.

"She's got a way about her, that one does," McGregor said as he finished shaping the shoe and returned to the horse's side. "Come on, laddie. Don't be givin' an old man trouble."

The farrier bent over and deliberately bumped the gelding's right front shoulder. The horse obligingly shifted his weight to the other three legs and allowed the man to pick up his hoof.

"Good boy," the Scotsman crooned. "Stay steady just a wee bit longer. We'll be gettin' you a nice new shoe. The ladies will be impressed." He set the shoe over the hoof and grabbed a handful of nails from a pocket in his oversize leather apron.

A few minutes later the shoe was in place, the edges

filed to insure a perfect fit. McGregor released the hoof and straightened.

"I do fine work, if I say so myself. No doubt you'll be thinkin' the same, Brady."

"You're the best, McGregor. I appreciate you taking the time to see to my horses."

Rita giggled. Brady shot her a quick look and winked. The old Scotsman was the best farrier in the business. He was also the only one close enough to come by on a moment's notice. The gelding had thrown a shoe the day before. Until it was replaced, he couldn't be worked.

The horse stamped his foot as if checking the fit. He tossed his head, then blew out air.

"See," McGregor said. "He approves. You'll be wantin' me to look at the other three?"

Brady nodded. "I think that back shoe is coming loose."

"Shoddy workmanship, and not mine. Who have you had around pretendin' to shoe these horses?"

"Your nephew. Remember? You took off for a cruise."

"Aye. I remember." McGregor looked at Rita and smiled. "The Caribbean, it was. Very lovely. You ever been?"

"No. I haven't."

"You'd like it. Lots of pretty girls, but not as pretty as you."

"Aren't you sweet?"

Brady held in a sound of disgust. Not only was McGregor old enough to be her father, but his lines weren't that good. Yet women everywhere always fell for him. "It's the accent," he muttered under his breath.

"What did you say?" Rita asked, but the glint in her blue eyes told him that she'd heard his comment.

"Nothing."

"Gee, I could have sworn you said—"

"Rita." Brady cut her off with a look designed to remind her he was her boss. She wasn't the least bit intimidated, either.

She turned her attention to McGregor and said, "I adore your accent. It's very charming."

"Accent? Me?" McGregor moved around the gelding and lifted his left rear hoof. "You're the one who sounds funny, lass." He tapped at the shoe. "This one's loose, like you said. I'll be havin' a talk with my nephew. I taught him better than this. The boy's lazy. You know how young men are. Still, that's a lame excuse for bad work." He smiled at his pun, then set the hoof down and headed for his truck. "Let me get another shoe and I'll replace it."

The gelding shifted, again bumping into Brady. He pushed back. Unfortunately, the horse didn't budge. "What's your problem?"

"He's establishing dominance," Rita said.

"I thought we'd taken care of that already."

"Not really." She lowered her voice to a whisper. "I think the basic problem is that he doesn't understand enough English to know that you're threatening him. Otherwise, I'm sure he'd be terribly respectful." She spoke seriously, but the corners of her mouth twitched.

"Right," he said, fighting a grin of his own. "Sort of like you."

"I'm very respectful."

"To whom?"

She laughed.

The gelding took another step. Brady saw it coming and ducked under the animal's head. The horse was just as quick. He shifted back, catching Rita unaware, pulling her forward and making her stumble. As Brady moved to keep her from falling, the gelding stepped between them. Rita hit the ground, knees first.

Her shoulders were shaking. Fear darted through his chest. Had she hurt herself? He grabbed the halter and forced the gelding back two steps, then crouched down beside Rita.

"Are you okay?" he asked.

She rolled onto her rear, and looked at him. Tears streamed down her face, but they weren't from pain. She was laughing. "He's so bored," she said, motioning to the horse. "He's been bugging me ever since you brought him in. I think he hates not being outside with the cattle." She brushed the moisture from her face. "No horse has caught me so off guard since I was fourteen."

Her reaction surprised him, then he reminded himself that it shouldn't. Rita wasn't like other women he'd known. She was tough and sensible. Competent, not that she would consider his assessment much of a compliment, however he might mean it that way.

"You fell pretty hard," he said, and touched her left leg. "Are you sure you're not hurt?"

He squeezed her knee, trying to feel for swelling or tenderness. As he slid his hand a few inches down her shin, then up her thigh, he watched her face, looking for a hint of pain. He ignored the pleasure touching her brought. This wasn't about desire, it was about making sure she was all right. Even so, it was difficult not to let his hand linger on her knee.

When he paused in his actions, she shrugged. "It's a little sore from the fall, but I'm fine. I'm tougher than I look."

"I know." He stood up, then held out his hand to help her to her feet.

As she straightened, they were standing very close. He

was once again reminded of their brief hug last week. He swore under his breath. Every time he was close to forgetting that incident, along with the kiss he'd stupidly given her, something happened to make him remember. He didn't want to remember. He wanted to take the whole thing back. It had been inappropriate behavior, and not his style at all. He'd had female employees before and had never once been tempted.

He couldn't explain the impulse that had made him kiss her, and he couldn't forget.

Rita didn't seem to be having the same problem. She stepped up to the gelding and took his large face in her hands. "Don't do that to me again," she told the animal. "You know better."

The horse snorted gently, as if apologizing.

"Like I believe that," she said.

"Believe what?" McGregor asked as he entered the barn.

"Anything a man says to me. You all tell wonderful stories that don't have a lick of truth."

"I'm wounded, lass. At least let me share a story or two before you start accusin' me of somethin'. In fact, I'll think up a good one to tell you at the barn dance next week. What do you say? Surely an old gent like myself deserves a wee bit of your time."

Rita blinked in surprise. "I didn't know about any dance, but I don't think—"

McGregor made a noise of disgust and glared at Brady. "Did you mean to be keepin' the lass to yourself?"

"No. The subject never came up in conversation."

"Typical. These young men. They don't know what's important in life." McGregor moved to the gelding and lifted the animal's rear hoof. "Next Saturday night there's a barn dance in town. Everyone's invited. It's at the lodge, so it's not really a barn, but it's called that. There's lots of music and food. Perhaps a wee bit of drink, too.'' He held the metal shoe against the hoof, then lowered the animal's leg.

Brady, who hadn't been to one of the town dances in months, found himself suddenly eager to go. To dance. Specifically with Rita. *Down boy,* he warned himself.

"They're a lot of fun," Brady said, hoping he sounded casual. "You'll know a lot of people there." At her questioning look he added, "The cowboys all go. Even Tex. You don't need a date."

"But you will need a few dancin' partners," McGregor said, then pounded the shoe into the right shape. "I believe I'd like to claim one dance for myself."

Rita bit her lower lip, then nodded. "I'd like that," she said, sounding hesitant.

Brady wondered why. Was it going to a place where she didn't know many people, or was it attending the dance itself?

"A two-step?" McGregor asked.

Rita smiled. "Perfect."

Brady turned away, annoyed to find himself wanting to claim his own dance. Dammit, he wasn't jealous of McGregor, he wasn't jealous of anyone. He had no claim on Rita. She was just an employee. A *young* employee, he reminded himself, thinking of the nine years between them.

"And maybe a waltz," the Scotsman teased.

Brady stepped around the gelding and headed for the back of the barn. "I'll write you a check for the shoeing," he said.

"Just for the one," McGregor called after him. "The second one is repairing a bad job. No charge for that."

Brady grunted in reply. He knew what the problem was,

but knowing it and fixing it didn't seem to be the same thing. If he was jealous of someone who wasn't the least bit interested in Rita, what would happen if someone who was came sniffing around?

He crossed to his desk and jerked open the upper right drawer. His checkbook lay on top. As he sat down, he told himself to get over it and fast. So what if Rita got to him in a way that left him hard and wanting? So what if no one had affected him like that in years? So what if she wasn't Alicia? She was still a woman with secrets. A woman with a past, and he of all people knew the danger in that.

He scrawled out the amount, then signed the check. Ten minutes later, the farrier came in to collect it. They chatted for a short time. When McGregor left, Brady tried to ignore the sounds from the barn. He didn't want to think about Rita with the horses, of her doing her chores, of the way she would look bending over to spread straw or raising her arms high to grab a feed sack.

He rested his elbows on his desk and rubbed his temples. He had it bad.

"Brady?"

He glanced up and found Rita standing in the doorway to his office. Her long braid hung over one shoulder and down the side of her right breast. He forced his gaze to her face. Some dark emotion flickered in her eyes. "Yes?"

"I, um…" She twisted her hands together in front of her waist. Worn jeans emphasized her round hips and shapely thighs. He told himself not to notice. "Would you rather I didn't go to the dance?"

He leaned back in his chair and motioned for her to take the seat across from his. "No. Why?"

She sat down. "I'm not sure. You seemed a little put

out by my conversation with McGregor. He was just jok-
ing. I knew that. I don't want you to think I took his
flattery seriously.''

Brady winced. Bad enough to act like a jerk, worse to
be caught. "I'm sorry, Rita. That wasn't it at all. You're
welcome to go to the dance or anywhere else. Your free
time is just that. Yours. I think you'd have fun, so I hope
you'll go. McGregor is a great dancer, if you don't mind
some theatrics along the way."

"Are you sure?"

"Positive. I might even claim a dance myself, seeing
as you have this thing for old men."

That earned him the smile he'd been waiting for. As
her mouth curled up, her eyes began to sparkle. "I consider humoring the elderly my good deed for the day."

"When have you humored me? Weren't you the one
encouraging insurrection with my horse just a few minutes
ago?"

"Hardly." Her humor faded a little. "Are you or Tex
going into town in the next few days? If either of you are,
I need a ride. I have to buy a couple of things."

"Yes, of course. I'm sorry, Rita. I should have thought
of that. You've been trapped out here on your afternoons
off."

"I don't mind," she said quickly. "I like being on the
ranch. A couple of the cowboys have invited me to ride
in with them, but I didn't feel comfortable doing that.
Until now, shopping hasn't been an issue, but I'd like to
buy something for the dance."

So much for being a thoughtful employer, he thought
grimly. He paid her in cash, as he did all his employees.
The people who worked for him often didn't have bank
accounts. But he hadn't considered that she might want
to spend some time in town. And maybe not alone.

He'd told her not to make trouble with the men and she'd listened. "You don't have to avoid all social contact with the men," he said, careful to keep his voice neutral. "If you would like to see one of the cowboys off the ranch, no one will interfere. What I'm trying to say is when you're on your own time—"

She cut him off with a wave. Faint color stained her cheeks. "I know what you're saying. That's not what I meant. There's no one that I want to see that way. I mean, they're all very nice men and I appreciate the time they've taken to befriend me, but it's not anything else."

Did that include him, too?

The thought came out of nowhere, and Brady wished it back to that spot. "Okay," he said slowly. "That's clear. I have to go into town day after tomorrow. You're welcome to take the afternoon off and ride in with me. My business will keep me busy for a couple of hours. Is that enough time?"

"More than enough." She rose to her feet and smiled. "Thanks, Brady."

He watched her walk out of the office, trying to ignore the sensation of being sucker punched. It had just been a smile. Nothing more. So why had it hit him like a blow to the gut? And lower?

Randi tried to dispel the butterflies dancing in her stomach, but however much she imagined calming pictures and words, those darned butterflies just kept acting up. It was as if they moved to a wild music only they could hear.

Nerves, she thought in disgust. When would she be able to control her emotions? They were just going to town, yet she was as tense and nervous as she'd been when she'd first run away.

Maybe it was that all small towns looked alike, she

thought as she stared out the side windows at the stores lined up on the single main street. This one could have been any of a dozen she'd driven through as she'd hitched rides to escape from Grand Springs. Familiar yet unfamiliar, reminding her that she'd chosen to run instead of stand up for what she wanted.

Don't think about that now, Randi told herself. She didn't want to ruin her afternoon. So as Brady pulled the truck into a parking space, she took a deep breath and tried to clear her mind.

"Everybody knows everybody," he warned as he turned off the engine. "You're going to get a lot of questions and be the favorite topic at dinner for the next couple of days. Think you can handle that?"

"As long as what they're saying is nice."

"A pretty girl like you? What else would they say?"

She laughed. "You're as bad as McGregor. All hot air and flattery. Here I was thinking you had substance."

He winked. It was all just a game. Harmless conversation. Yet she couldn't help but be pleased by his words. No one had ever told her she was pretty, not even in jest. Whether or not Brady meant the compliment, she was going to hang on to it with both hands.

She slid out of the seat and slammed the door behind her. Brady paused on the sidewalk and pointed up the street.

"We have a general store on the corner. Some folks call it a department store, but that's stretching things a little. There's clothes, shoes and other female kind of stuff."

"Gee, what would that be?"

Confident Brady looked uncomfortable all of a sudden. "You know. Creams and junk."

"Makeup?"

"That, too."

"Creams and junk. What a way you have with words."

He shoved his hands in his front pockets. "Just because I've brought you into town doesn't mean you have the right to say anything you want to me."

"Sure it does. Here you're not my boss. You're just a guy who's terrified of female stuff."

He rocked back on his heels. "I'm not afraid."

Wondering what it was about this man that made her want to have fun, she stretched out her hand and touched his cheek. "You ever have a facial, Brady? You could use something to tighten those pores."

He jerked his head away as if she'd burned him. "My pores are just fine."

"And those little lines around your eyes. They have stuff to prevent that."

He turned toward the storefront next to them. The large plate-glass window reflected the street. Brady frowned, then smiled, as if checking his wrinkle quotient.

Randi covered her mouth to hold in her laughter. Who would have thought this big, tough cowboy would be so easy to tease?

"I don't know what you're—" He glanced at her and drew his eyebrows together. "You're laughing!" His voice accused her of an unforgivable crime.

"No, I'm not." She swallowed hard and forced her expression to stay neutral.

"You're mocking me. I don't have a problem with my pores, or my eyes."

She gave in to humor and chuckled. Brady grinned. "I've been had," he complained. "You should warn a man when you're going to take advantage of him."

"You love the attention."

"Hey, I'm the strong, silent type. You want to continue to make fun of me, or do you want to shop?"

She folded her arms over her chest. "Tough decision. Can I really pick either one?"

"Why do I put up with you?" He placed his hand on the back of her neck and pushed her forward.

"Because there isn't another alternative."

She was proud of herself for managing a relatively long, coherent sentence. It was hard enough to keep breathing, let alone talking, while Brady was touching her neck.

She told herself it was an impersonal gesture at best. That it didn't *mean* anything. He was treating her like a little sister. Funny, though. She didn't feel like his little sister. She felt strangely alive and happy. Being here with him—she couldn't explain it, it just felt so right.

When they reached the store, he released her neck and grabbed the door. As he pulled it open, he motioned for her to go first. Polite, charming, funny, sensitive, amazingly good-looking. Her original question still stood. Why wasn't he married? Were all the women in the county blind, or was there something she couldn't figure out? Some flaw he'd kept hidden, or maybe something from his past?

He placed his hands on her shoulders and turned her toward the center aisle. "Female clothing to your right. Creams and junk to your left. Shoes are upstairs. I have a meeting with my banker, so I'll be gone for about an hour and a half."

She turned her head so she could see him. "I've shopped before. Amazingly enough, on my own. So far I've avoided major disasters and shoplifting. I'll be fine."

"You have enough money?"

The question touched her, mostly because his concern was involuntary. He was the last of the good guys.

"My boss just gave me a raise. I've got plenty."

"Have fun."

He disappeared out onto the street. Randi looked over the store, then started toward the racks of dresses against the far wall. She needed something for the dance. Maybe she would pick up another pair of jeans and some T-shirts, too.

An hour and fifteen minutes later, she stepped onto the escalator to the ground floor. She'd bought a simple summer dress, on sale, along with a pair of jeans and two shirts. In the shoe department, she'd found an inexpensive pair of pumps. Everything she'd purchased had cost less than the cheapest dress in her closet in Grand Springs. If it didn't have a designer label on it, her mother didn't want it in the house.

Those clothes weren't her, she thought as she moved down the center aisle, glancing left and right, looking for Brady. It had taken her a long time to finally figure out she didn't care about who made the clothes as long as they fit and were comfortable. Keeping up with the latest styles didn't interest her, nor did she worry about a trendy haircut. Thank goodness, because with her unruly curls, she was destined to always look a little messy.

She reached the front door, then turned back to face the store. On the far side, in the middle of the "creams and junk" department, she saw Brady talking with an older woman. From the way they chatted and laughed, they must be old friends. That made sense. Growing up near a town this small, Brady probably knew just about everyone.

As she crossed the store, she tried to ignore the flickering in her stomach. The butterflies had returned. She sighed. She wanted her nerves to be about coming to town, not about Brady. While he was nice and handsome and a lot of good things, he wasn't for her.

She paused in the middle of the teen department and stared at him. He was so different from Hal. Not just in looks, but in temperament and style. Hal was the kind of man who measured every action based on how it would look and how many votes it was worth. Brady acted a certain way because he believed it was right, regardless of who might or might not be watching. Hal was a politician down to his bones. Brady was just a man.

She'd known her ex-fiancé for years, yet, looking back at their courtship, she could easily admit she'd never known him at all. Brady had been in her life two-and-a-half weeks, yet she felt that she understood him and the code by which he lived.

Brady looked up and saw her. "You about finished?" he asked.

She nodded and held up her bags. "I've bought as much as I can carry. That's when it's time for me to leave."

He walked over and relieved her of most of her purchases. "I thought we might stop at the ice cream shop on the way out of town. I've got a taste for a hot fudge sundae."

Randi raised her eyebrows. "It's nearly four o'clock. You'll spoil your dinner."

"I know. You have to promise not to tell Tex."

Ice cream and hot fudge? How could she resist? "I'd love to join you," she said. "If we try really hard, I'll bet we can eat just as much dinner, too."

"Deal."

They shared a conspiratorial glance, then headed toward the street. Even though it was a temporary situation,

Randi enjoyed fitting in. Brady was different off the ranch. Freer. Or maybe it was both of them. She'd been worried about coming into town, but she was having fun. Somewhere in the past couple of weeks, Brady had become a friend. Even if he didn't know the truth about her, even if she needed to keep her secrets, she believed that he would be there for her if she ever needed him.

For the first time since running away, she didn't feel alone.

Seven

Randi stretched and rolled over to look at the clock. It was nearly one in the afternoon. She would feel decadent at being in bed this late in the day if she hadn't already worked six hours in the barn. Her late-morning nap was what allowed her to stay up until ten at night and still be able to function at four in the morning.

She'd been at the ranch three weeks today. It was the longest she'd been anywhere since leaving Grand Springs. Before, she'd always felt a restlessness after a few days, a nagging sensation that she had to keep moving. It was the only way to feel safe. But here that wasn't necessary. If anything, she was going to have to force herself to press on. It would be far too easy to make this a permanent home.

She stood up and reached for her clothes. After slipping on jeans, a T-shirt and boots, she walked into the bathroom to wash her face and tame her hair. As usual, the braid looked tidy for about thirty seconds before the curls worked their way loose.

She went downstairs, then stepped outside to head for the barn. The men came in for their midday meal around eleven-thirty. Tex packed a lunch for anyone working too far away. For the first couple of days, she'd joined the cowboys, but she'd found it difficult not to nod off during the meal. Tex had taken pity on her and offered to keep a plate warm until the early afternoon.

Peter, the littlest kitten, sat on the porch railing. When he saw her, he meowed.

"What are you doing out here?" she asked, and picked him up. He curled against her shoulder and began to purr. "Is Princess taking the afternoon off? Or did you sneak away from her?"

Usually Princess herded her charges into the shade of the barn for their afternoon nap. Playtime didn't start until around four.

"You want to join me for lunch?" she asked the kitten. "I bet Tex would give you a treat."

The kitten kneaded her shoulder, his eyes closed in contentment.

She walked into the dining room, crossed the linoleum floor and moved toward the kitchen. Tex sat at the small table in front of the window. There was a mug of coffee in front of him, along with a slice of strawberry pie. Across from him was a single place setting. Two sandwiches under plastic wrap, a green salad, some cut-up raw vegetables.

She set Peter on the floor, then headed for the refrigerator. After grabbing the pitcher of cold water on the top shelf, and a bowl with a single, albeit generous, serving of potato salad, she walked to the table and took her seat.

Tex looked up from the paper he read. "'Afternoon."

"Hi." She glanced at her plate, then at him. "Tuna sandwiches and raw veggies? Why do I know you didn't feed the guys that?"

He grinned. "Five-alarm chili. I didn't think you'd want any."

She pressed her hand to her stomach, remembering pain from the last time she'd indulged. There weren't many things that upset her stomach, but that was one of them.

"While I appreciate the thoughtfulness, you didn't have to make me a special lunch."

He shrugged. "No bother."

"You guys are all alike. Tough on the outside, and complete marshmallows on the inside."

Peter stood up on his hind legs and pressed his front paws against Tex's shin. The kitten meowed plaintively. "Damn cat," the former marine muttered as he picked him up and set him in the crook of his arm.

Randi spread her napkin on her lap and laughed. "I believe that proves my point."

"Uh-huh."

She unwrapped her sandwiches and pulled the cover off the potato salad. "Tell me about this dance Saturday. Do you go?"

"Sure. Everyone's there." The older man grinned. "They'll dance your feet off."

"Fortunately I bought comfortable shoes when I was in town yesterday."

Tex frowned. "You two thought I didn't know you stopped for ice cream, but I could tell."

Randi had raised the fork halfway to her mouth. She froze. "How'd you figure that out?"

"You both looked so damned guilty. Like kids caught stealing from the cookie jar. I hope you had a bellyache from all the supper you ate, hoping I wouldn't notice."

"Sorry, no." She chewed the potato salad and swallowed. "I have the most unladylike appetite. At least that's what my mother always told me. She ate little tiny portions of everything. It made me crazy. I can stand just about anything but being hungry. Heaven help me if I ever have to go on a diet."

"You're strong. All that muscle needs fuel."

"A nice way of saying I'd never make it as a model."

"Why would you want to?"

"Why indeed." She thought about Brady. About how he'd made her heart beat faster and her stomach quiver with nerves. What kind of woman did he find attractive? Skinny blondes with big boobs? Sultry redheads? She doubted he had a thing for sturdy women with uncontrollably curly hair. Just once she would like someone to think she was pretty. Her father had been kind and generous with compliments, but they hadn't been enough to counteract her mother's brutal honesty.

She still remembered dressing for a dance when she was sixteen. She hadn't wanted to go, but her mother had arranged for a friend's son to be her escort. A mercy date. She'd been standing in front of her mirror, trying to convince herself she didn't look horrible when she'd heard her parents in the hall. Her father had been excited about taking her picture, but her mother had stopped him.

"She's nothing to look at. Why do you want to remember that?"

"She's my daughter," her father had protested. "She's beautiful."

"Oh, please. Randi's plain at best. That hair. I'm at my wit's end with it. At least she has decent skin. With those features, if she had blemishes, too, we'd have to put a bag over her head."

Eight years later, the words still hurt. She knew she wasn't pretty, but she'd come to grips with that. Some days she thought she was actually okay-looking. Time had taught her that her mother's overly critical remarks had little to do with physical appearance and more to do with the older woman's general dissatisfaction that her daughter wasn't a perfect clone. The two of them had nothing in common, save a blood relationship.

"You gonna eat that, or are you just going to stare at it?" Tex asked.

Randi glanced down and realized she was holding half a sandwich in her hands, but hadn't taken a bite. "Sorry, I was lost in thought."

"Judging from the look in your eyes, somewhere far away."

She glanced at the cook. "Sometimes you're too observant, Tex."

He grinned. "Part of my charm. It's one of the reasons they've kept me around for so long."

"What are the others?" she asked, pretending innocence.

"My cooking, and don't you say another word about it."

She took a bite of her sandwich and chewed. Peter raised his head and sniffed the air. He glanced up at Tex and mewed hopefully.

"Don't even think about it," the cook told him. "No tuna for you."

Peter blinked, then collapsed back into the crook of Tex's arm. He yawned, leaned against the large man's chest and closed his eyes.

"Ten years is a long time to work somewhere," she said. "First the marines and now the ranch. You bond with large groups. What about with individuals?"

He drew his eyebrows together. "You one of those psychological types? I'm not interested in being analyzed."

"Just curious. You're a great guy. Why aren't you married?"

Tex cleared his throat. "Never met anyone I cared about that much. The marines kept me moving around. Not many women want to put up with that."

Randi swallowed and took a sip of water. "Not to mention the fact you loved being a bachelor."

He grinned. "That, too." His grin faded. "I've got what I want here. A home. These are good people to work for."

"I agree."

His pale gaze settled on her face. "Brady's a good man, too. He deserves some happiness in his life."

"I'm sure he does."

His gaze narrowed. "Be a shame for him to get hurt, wanting something he can't have."

The mouthful of sandwich dried up. Randi kept chewing, but she had to take a sip of water before she could swallow. Her appetite fled, and with it, her good mood.

She pushed her plate away. "Don't be subtle, Tex. Just come right out and warn me off. But before you do, I want you to know I admire and respect Brady. He's my employer. That's as far as it goes. There's no need for you to worry about anything else."

She told herself she wasn't lying. Just because she had some serious chemical reactions when Brady was around didn't mean he returned her feelings. In fact, she would bet money he barely thought of her, and when he did, he considered her a kid sister. That was hardly a basis for romance.

She slid the chair back and stood up. After grabbing her plate, she crossed to the sink and dumped the rest of the food down the drain. The roar of the garbage disposal couldn't drown out the disappointment she felt.

Not because Tex thought she was inappropriate for his boss. She was a drifter with no past—why would anyone want to risk that? Tex was only looking out for someone he cared about. What hurt the most was that she'd allowed herself to think she'd found a place to belong.

She turned off the disposal and rinsed her hands. When she turned around, Tex was standing behind her, the kitten still in his arms.

"I didn't mean it like that," he said awkwardly.

"Yes, you did. I can't blame you. You don't know anything about me, right? Who knows what secrets lurk in my past. You're being cautious, and I'm sure Brady appreciates that."

She walked out the back door and headed for the barn. Maybe she should just leave. That would solve everyone's problem. Except she'd promised herself to stop running. She wanted to grow up enough to stay in one place and find solutions. But did it have to hurt this much?

"I thought I'd found a home here," she told Pokey as she paused to bend down and pet the pregnant tabby. "You did. Life is complicated, and I want it to be easy. Pretty stupid, huh?"

The cat purred in response.

Maybe there was a bright side. Maybe Tex was concerned because he'd sensed interest on Brady's part.

"Wishful thinking," she muttered. Brady's platonic hug and kiss on the cheek last week weren't the actions of a man smitten by overpowering passion. He'd been attentive yesterday in town, but she suspected he'd been motivated by guilt. He'd needed to make up for her having not been off the ranch since her arrival. It wasn't personal.

Randi straightened and glanced around the yard. All she'd wanted was to fit in. She didn't deserve to be made to feel she was less than everyone else. She didn't—

She frowned, her attention shifting from her personal problems to the yard. "Something's wrong," she said softly.

She took a step back and turned in a slow circle, trying

to take everything in. The barn doors were open, as they should be. A couple of the mares grazed in the pasture behind the bunkhouse. The main house looked fine. There were cats scattered all around. None of them looked alert or cautious. They were just dozing.

She snapped her fingers. That was it. The cats. They weren't neatly herded together, resting in the shade of the barn. Odd behavior, because Princess usually kept them under control. But the shepherd was nowhere to be seen.

"Princess," Randi called. "Princess, come here, girl."

As she waited she tried to remember if she'd seen the dog at all this morning. There had been the usual frenzy when she'd fed everyone, but she didn't recall seeing Princess.

She jogged around the barn, then checked up at the main house. There was no response to her repeated calls. Something wasn't right. Something had happened to Princess.

Wishing there was someone else to tell besides Tex, Randi hurried toward the bunkhouse. She stepped into the kitchen. Tex stood at the sink, peeling potatoes.

"I can't find Princess," she said. "I don't remember feeding her this morning. Have you seen her?"

"No." The older man frowned. "She keeps a regular schedule and doesn't usually go missing. Unless she'd found a sick cat on her route. Then she'll stay by the animal until help comes."

"Or she could have been hurt herself."

Tex nodded. "That's a possibility. Brady's the only one who knows all her spots. You'll have to go get him." He crossed to the built-in butler's pantry on the far side of the room and pulled open a drawer. There was a pad of paper on top. After grabbing it and a pencil, he returned to the table. He spoke as he drew.

"Take one of the horses. It would be faster to drive there, but you'll need a horse to find Princess. She doesn't keep to the main road all the time, and I doubt any of the trucks would make it on that rough terrain. Brady's working north of here. It's about four miles."

He gave her the map and detailed instructions, then ordered her to wait. Two minutes later he returned with a cellular phone, a couple of blankets and a first aid kit. "Just in case," he said, pressing the supplies into her arms. "If she's hurt and you don't think you can bring her back, call and I'll drive the truck out."

"Okay." She paused, wondering if she should say anything about their previous conversation, then figured it didn't matter. Not now.

Once in the barn, she quickly saddled Casper, grateful the strong, gentle gelding hadn't been taken out to work that day. He was the horse she'd ridden the most. She trusted him.

After loading the saddlebags, she studied the hand-drawn map for a minute. First she had to find Brady, then they had to locate Princess. She sent up a quick prayer that the dog was all right.

Brady studied the dozen steers in front of him. It always came down to the last few. Making a decision about a couple hundred seemed easier, somehow. He was gambling—trying to put together the right elements without having all the facts. He had to have enough hay to feed the cattle he kept until spring. How much stock, how much hay, how long would they be able to graze, how long the winter? Guesswork, all of it.

Ty sat on the horse next to him and waited patiently for instructions.

"Hell," Brady muttered. "Keep 'em."

"Yes, boss." The cowboy turned to give another man instructions, then glanced over his shoulder and pointed. "We've got company. I think it's Rita."

Brady frowned and raised his binoculars. Ty was right. Rita rode toward them. This wasn't a pleasure call; her expression was too tense.

He dropped the small but powerful binoculars back around his neck and urged his horse forward. His gelding broke into a trot, then a canter. He met her on a grassy slope.

"What's wrong?" he asked.

"Maybe nothing," she said, her words coming in gasps as she tried to catch her breath. "Princess is missing. I can't remember if she was at breakfast this morning. I know I haven't seen her all day. Tex said you knew her route." She reached behind her and patted the saddlebags. "I've got blankets, medical supplies and the cellular phone. Just in case."

He nodded, then motioned Ty over. Quickly he explained the situation. "Take the herd east," he said.

Ty's dark eyes clouded with concern. "I know what to do, boss. Just go find the dog."

"We will." He glanced at Rita. "You doing okay?"

"I'm fine. I hope this is a false alarm. She's probably fine. I'd hate to take you away from your work for nothing."

"You were right to come get me. Princess always keeps to her routine. If she's not at the barn, something's wrong."

He tapped his horse with his heels. The gelding broke into a trot. Casper fell into step beside him.

"You're welcome to head back home," he said. "Even if she's hurt, I can handle her on my own."

"No. I want to come with you. I feel terrible that I

didn't notice her missing before. If she's injured—'' She shuddered.

"Princess isn't your responsibility, Rita. I appreciate that you thought to keep track of her at all. It's going to be fine.''

He spoke the words calmly, but there was a knot of worry in his gut. In this terrain, anything could have happened to the shepherd. There were feral dogs, rattlers, flash floods, old wells. Princess was smart, but that wasn't always enough.

An hour later they crested a slight rise. Below them was the four-lane highway. "Her path parallels the road,'' he said, pointing to a narrow track that cut through the brush. "There isn't room to travel abreast. You'll have to ride behind me.''

"That's fine.''

"Look out for any kind of movement or tracks leading off. Also, we'll alternate calling for her. If she's conscious, she'll bark back.'' He turned his horse toward the path.

"Brady, I'm scared. I don't want anything to happen to her.''

He gave her a reassuring smile, one that belied his own tension. "She's a tough old girl. She'll be fine.''

Rita bit down on her lower lip. "I hope so.''

Oddly, her concern eased some of his worry. As if the burden was lighter because it was shared. Since his folks had started traveling five years ago, he'd been solely in charge. Often he'd wanted to share his troubles, but didn't feel he could confide in anyone. The men were his employees. He couldn't talk to them about each other. Tex listened, but it wasn't always enough.

Rita works for you, too, he reminded himself. He knew that was true, yet it wasn't the same.

"Princess!" she called behind him. He waited a few seconds and yelled the dog's name.

Only silence greeted them, broken by the odd car or two zipping along the highway. They continued to follow the path. Occasionally Brady would stop and use his binoculars to scan the area. Once he thought he saw a flicker of movement, but it turned out to be a piece of sun-bleached cardboard dancing in the warm afternoon breeze.

The path angled sharply north, heading away from the road. He yelled again. When he would have kicked his horse into a canter, Rita called for him to stop. She tilted her head.

"Call her," she said.

"Princess!"

She closed her eyes. "There!" she said, pointing east. "Can you hear it? I'm sure it's her barking."

He shook his head. "I don't hear anything." He took a deep breath. "Princess! Come on, girl," he yelled as loud as he could, then leaned in the direction Rita had indicated.

A gust of wind carried with it the faint echo of a bark. "You're right. Let's go."

He angled his horse east and gave the animal its head. Five minutes later he slowed to check with his binoculars. A rush of movement caught his attention. "There," he said, pointing. "In the shadow of those rocks. She's pacing, but she won't come. She must have something."

They rode closer, then stopped a few feet from the rocks. Princess raced toward them, obviously limping. Brady jumped off his horse and reached for the dog. Her paws were bloody.

"What the hell?" he growled. "What did you do?"

But Princess didn't stay still long enough for him to

examine her. She ran back to the rocks and yipped plaintively. Brady saw a small bundle resting against the shade.

He moved closer. A faint hissing warned him that Princess had indeed found another cat. "Hush, little one," he said soothingly, taking one step at a time. "It's all right."

The bundle turned out to be a burlap sack. As he bent over it, he saw a white cat nursing five kittens. Their damp bodies and the blood on the burlap told its own story, as did the ragged tears in the cloth.

"What happened?" Rita asked, coming up to stand beside him. "Oh, my. Kittens."

"She just gave birth. Probably this afternoon. Some bastard put her in a sack and left her out here to die."

Rita blanched. "That's disgusting. What kind of person would do that?"

"You'd be surprised." Princess came up and nudged his hand. He crouched beside the dog. "You saved her, didn't you, girl."

Princess whined. There were scratches on her face. A deep one in her cheek still oozed blood. He checked her paws. All her nails were intact, although she'd worn away patches of skin in her effort to free the cat.

"Let me get the first aid kit," Rita said.

"Don't bother. We need to get everyone back to the barn. Once they're safe there, the vet can come out and check all the cats and Princess."

"How are we going to move them? I've got the cellular and we can call Tex to bring the truck, but I don't think it will make it here."

He eyed the rough terrain. "We'd be faster just carrying them back. Did you bring blankets?"

"Sure. There's a couple."

"Good. We'll make slings."

She walked to her horse. Once there she seemed to be

having trouble with the saddlebags. Brady stood up and moved to her. "Can I help?" he asked.

She shook her head, but didn't turn around.

"Rita?"

"Damn," she muttered, and got the bags open. She thrust her hand inside and pulled out the blankets, then tossed them to him. "Here."

He caught the blankets, but didn't turn away. "What's wrong?"

"Nothing." She sniffed, then spun toward him. Raising her chin defiantly, she said, "I'm just being a typical female and dissolving into tears. Ignore me."

Just as she said, tears filled her eyes and trickled down her cheeks. Her skin was smudged, and the moisture left visible tracks.

"I know it's stupid," she continued. "And emotional. I just can't believe anyone could be so cruel. It's awful." She folded her arms over her chest and swallowed. "This is where you tell me I'm too much of a city girl to make it out here."

Without stopping to consider it wasn't a good idea, he slid his arm around her shoulders and squeezed her close. "This is where I tell you that you'll be just fine out here. Big hearts are always welcome."

She raised her head and stared at him. "You don't think I'm a sissy girl?"

He thought she was beautiful, even red-eyed and dirty. He thought she was compassionate and funny. He thought she had the kind of body designed to drive him to the edge of sanity, but doubted she wanted to hear any of those things.

"I think you're special," he said, and dropped a quick kiss on her forehead.

Her smile nearly blinded him. He was forced to turn away so she wouldn't see the shock in his eyes.

"What do you want me to do?" she asked, wiping her cheeks with the back of her hand.

"You're going to have to carry Princess," he said. "She can't make it back on her own. I don't think she's caused herself any serious injury, but those paws have got to hurt her."

Rita nodded. "Walking in the dirt will only increase the chance of infection, too. But how do I carry her?"

"With this." He took the smaller blanket and folded it into a triangle. Then he walked behind her and secured the ends, with the blanket hanging over one shoulder. "She can sit on the saddle in front of you. The blanket will hold her securely so she doesn't fall off. Can you ride back like that?"

"Of course. Are you taking the cats?"

He glanced at the burlap sack and wondered how much blood the mother cat was going to draw. "Yeah."

"Be careful. Look at what she did to Princess's face."

"I saw. Get on your horse."

While she mounted up and arranged the sling, Brady made a quick call to Tex and explained what they'd found.

"Get bandages and some of that anti-infection cream we've used on her before and call the vet." He listened to Tex. "The cream's in the medicine cabinet in the barn. Top shelf. Oh, and get a box for the mother cat and her kittens. Stick it in that rear stall. The empty one. Don't forget food and water."

"We'll be ready," Tex told him.

"Expect us in about an hour and a half." Brady pushed the End button on the cellular phone, then glanced at the sky. They were going to beat the sunset, but just.

"You ready?" he asked as he replaced the phone in the saddlebags.

"Yes."

He collected Princess and lifted the dog onto Rita's saddle. She wrapped her arms around the shepherd. When her horse sidestepped, Brady grabbed the reins.

"Hold on, boy. Stay steady."

Rita secured the blanket around Princess. Fortunately the shepherd didn't squirm. She flopped against Rita, resting her head in the crook of the woman's arm.

"How are you going to collect the cats?" Rita asked.

"Carefully," he said, tying the other blanket around him. Even if the feline was the most even-tempered creature God had ever made, her recent treatment, not to mention giving birth, was going to make her hostile.

Brady approached her slowly, speaking softly. It didn't help. The cat hissed when she saw him. As he gathered up the burlap sack, she swiped at his hand with her claws, laying open four long, deep scratches. He ignored the blood and the burning.

"I'm sorry," he said as he pulled the edges of the sack together. There was no other way for him to get on his horse.

Inside the sack, the cat began to howl. Brady mounted quickly and settled the cat into the makeshift sling. Then he carefully released the edges of the sack.

The mother cat raked his chest with her claws. Her tiny kittens made frightened mewling noises. That distracted her and she shifted to give them room. He tried to help, which earned him another scratch on his already bleeding hand.

"Is she hurting you?" Rita asked.

"Not at all," he muttered between clenched teeth, and lightly kicked the gelding.

At the first step, the cat dug her claws into Brady's thighs. He spoke softly, but she didn't release her hold. Angry yellow eyes glared at him, as if telling him this was all his fault so it was only right that he should suffer.

With each of them holding animals on their laps, there was no way he or Rita could allow their horses to move at more than a slow, easy walk. The trip home took nearly two hours.

Everyone was waiting when they arrived. The vet took the spitting mother and her kittens into the barn to make sure they were fine. Ziggy carried Princess to the main house, and Quinn and Ralph took care of the horses.

Brady and Rita went into the house. Tex was already there, kneeling next to Princess. He had some bandages in a pile, along with disinfectant and a bowl of warm water.

"There's cube steak on the counter," the cook said. "I thought she deserved something special tonight."

"I agree," Brady told him. "I'll give her water first, though. My guess is she's been out with that cat since before dawn."

Tex pulled the dog up on his lap and supported her with one arm while he dipped her dirty paws into the water. She whimpered. Rita crouched next to her.

"It's going to be okay, sweetie. You're a brave girl. This will make you feel better so that you can get back to taking care of your cats. They missed you today. You would have been so ashamed of the way they lounged over everything. There was no order, no discipline."

Princess licked her fingers and thumped her tail against the floor.

Tex worked quickly. When her paws here bandaged and she'd had her fill of cool water and red meat, Brady carried Princess out onto the porch. She stretched out on the blanket Tex had placed on the floor and sighed her contentment.

Pokey, the pregnant tabby, jumped down from the railing and walked over to her. She sniffed the dog's face, then began grooming her. Peter appeared from under the porch, hopped up next to Princess and promptly collapsed over her back legs. Within seconds, the kitten's eyelids were sinking closed. A few of the other cats moved closer, wanting to be near their leader now that she was home.

"Good job," Tex said, and slapped Brady on the back.

"Thanks." He was too tired to smile, so he nodded instead.

"Are you still bleeding?" Rita asked.

Brady glanced down at his chest. Blood stained his shirt. "I'm not sure I want to know."

"You don't get a choice in the matter," she said. "Hit the shower. When you're done, I'll put some cream on those scratches."

"The same thing Tex used on Princess?"

"Too good for the likes of you," the older man said, then winked.

"I'm sure we can find the right preparation for your species." She brushed her hair out of her face.

She might be worried about him, but she looked as if she'd been through a war, as well. There was dirt on her face and clothing, bloodstains on her shirtfront and jeans. Her hair was loose and wild. Shadows stained the delicate skin under her eyes.

As usual, he wanted her, but this time something else joined the desire. Something more dangerous.

Faint lines of cleaner skin streaked her cheeks. Visible reminders of her tears. Rita wasn't just good at her job. She was also smart, funny and compassionate. He'd learned the truth about the latter today. In the three months he knew Alicia, he'd never seen her cry. He had a feeling it wasn't something she did, unless it was about herself. Rita was different. And while he appreciated that difference, he knew it didn't make her any safer than she'd been before.

Eight

Randi combed her damp hair and decided there wasn't time to dry it. She wanted to get downstairs before Brady. Judging from the blood on his shirt, the scratches on his chest and arms had been nasty. If he was a typical male, he would resist treatment unless she was there to force him.

She debated tying her hair back, then figured she was off duty for the night. She might as well leave it loose. At least it would dry faster than if she braided it or caught it up in a ponytail.

As she walked down the hall, she heard the water shut off in Brady's bathroom. Good. She would have time to collect first aid supplies. She vaguely recalled that the house first aid kit was kept in the kitchen, in a cupboard next to the sink.

She found the plastic box containing enough bandages, medicine and splints to service a small army. Of course, on the ranch, they weren't exactly close to a local hospital. The drive to town had been nearly an hour. So if someone was injured, emergency treatment would have to be administered on the spot.

While she was sorting through the various medicines, looking for a cream to ward off infection, Tex entered through the back door. He had a plate in one hand and a bowl in the other.

Rita stiffened when she saw him, then tried to relax.

He looked at her and gave her a slight smile. She nodded in return. Their earlier conversation hung between them, making the moment awkward. She didn't want that, but she didn't know how to change it.

"The vet's gone," he said. "Mother cat and kittens are fine. She checked on Princess, too. Her paws will heal in a few days." Tex set the plate and bowl on the counter and wiped his hands on his jeans. "I didn't think the two of you would want to come to the bunkhouse for dinner, so I brought you a couple of steaks, salad and potatoes. I took care of the men already. I can fix these up for you in a couple of minutes."

Rita stared at him unbelievingly. He was so concerned about Brady, he didn't dare leave the two of them alone? The unfairness of it all burned down to her soul. What had she done wrong? Why was she being judged?

"Don't look like that. You've got it all wrong," Tex said quickly, and shook his head. "What I said earlier...this isn't about that."

"Then, what's it about?"

"Dinner." He shifted uneasily. "This is damn hard to say, all right? Brady thinks you're special. No one cares if the two of you are just friends, or it's something else. All I'm worried about is what happens when you move on. He doesn't deserve to be used."

Randi blinked several times. It was too much information to take in. Brady thought she was special? Brady? How would Tex know that? Had they discussed it, or was it something the older man had observed?

She pushed that thought away, because there was no way to get answers to her questions. Instead, she focused on the rest of what he'd told her. That Brady didn't deserve to be used. The implication being that someone had used him before. A woman. But who?

"I'm not the kind of person who uses people," she said. "There's no reason for you to believe me, I know, but it's true. Brady's a great guy. I enjoy working for him." She enjoyed dreaming about him, too, but she wasn't going to share that particular piece of information with the ex-marine.

"You still mad at me?" Tex asked.

"I was never mad. You're just looking out for a friend. If anything, I'm envious. I want someone to care about me that way."

"You're not so bad. For a girl." He gave her a wink.

"Thank you. High praise from a man like you." She turned her attention to the steaks. "Now, about dinner. I think I can manage."

Tex winced. "I'm sure you can, missy, but—"

She cut him off with a wave of her hand, then walked to the stove and pointed. Two of the gas burners had been replaced with a grill. "Fire," she said. "Fire hot. Fire cook meat." She crossed to the microwave tucked under the counter. "Magic. Heat potato very fast." Finally, she placed her hand on her chest. "Rita smart. Rita understand fire and magic."

He rolled his eyes. "Women. Try to give them a little assistance and they get all huffy. See if I ever offer to help you out again."

She crossed to the back door and held it open. "If you hurry, you'll get back in time to watch your favorite television shows."

"Uh-huh." He crossed the floor.

When he was in front of her, she put a hand on his arm. He glanced at her. She smiled. "Thanks, Tex. For explaining what you meant. I think Brady's lucky to have a friend like you."

"Don't go all mushy on me," he grumbled, then

reached up and tugged on one of her curls. "Don't let him talk you out of putting antiseptic on those scratches. He's a baby that way."

"I'll be tough, I promise."

Tex gave her a wave and left. She closed the door behind him and returned to the kitchen. Before she could turn on the grill, there was a noise on the stairs.

"Rita?" Brady called.

"In the kitchen. Tex says I'm not to let you weasel out of first aid treatment, so let's get that over with, okay?"

He entered the kitchen from the dining room. "Don't worry. I'm not going to protest. I don't want these to get infected."

"Good. I was all prepared to—"

She glanced up and lost her ability to speak. The man had been scratched by a cat. On his chest. So that's where the injuries would be. She'd known that, but she hadn't put it all together. She hadn't actually thought about the fact that if she was going to treat them, she was going to have to see them. Which meant Brady walked into the kitchen bare-chested.

Her breath caught in her throat. Her stomach flopped over once, and heat flared on her cheeks.

Like her, he was fresh from the shower. Damp hair had been brushed back from his face. He hadn't shaved since that morning and stubble darkened his jawline. Bad enough that he was so damned handsome; worse that he was half-naked.

She'd known he was strong. Ranch work did that to a man. She'd seen the way he filled out his shirts, straining the shoulders until the fabric looked ready to rip. Now she was able to *see* the rippling muscles under tanned skin.

As he crossed the room, muscles bunched and released

in his arms and chest. Hard strength, warm, honey-colored skin, big eyes and a ready smile. This she was supposed to resist?

Then her attention focused on the scratches marring his perfect skin. From his right shoulder, across his chest to his belly, four angry red claw marks cut through flesh. Several shorter gouges dotted his right side. There were more wounds on his arms and the back of his hands.

"They look worse than I thought they would," Randi said, finally finding the power of speech. "Sit down and let's get something on them. Did you wash them thoroughly in the shower?"

"Didn't you hear me screaming?" he asked, his smile turning into a wince as he sat down. "Normally I would go all macho on you and insist on treating myself, but tonight I'm willing to admit to being a wimp. The antiseptic cream stings like a son of a bitch. Ignore my unmanly whimpers."

"No problem," she said, trying to tell herself this was about a medical problem. She was not going to think about being close to him for several minutes, let alone touching his skin. At least while he was in pain, he wouldn't notice she was hyperventilating.

She grabbed the cream and stepped in front of the chair. As she bent down, her hair spilled over her shoulder and brushed against his thighs.

"This isn't going to work," she muttered, and tossed her head back. The curls flew out of the way.

She knelt on the floor next to him. His right hand rested on the arm of the chair. She opened the tube and squeezed out a little onto her finger, then touched the cream to the scratches. He stiffened.

"Sorry," she said.

He leaned his head back and closed his eyes. "Don't

apologize. Maybe you could talk to me. That would be distracting.''

"Sure. About what?"

"Anything."

"Okay.'' She smoothed the antiseptic over the rest of the marks on the back of his hand, then moved up his arm. She tried not to notice the scent of him—something intriguingly masculine laced with the clean smell of soap. She also did her best to ignore his heat.

She was close enough to see the individual whiskers darkening his jawline, and the faint crease by his mouth, where he got a dimple when he smiled. As she moved higher, toward his shoulder, she became mesmerized by the steady rise and fall of his chest. She wanted to lay her head there and listen to his heartbeat. She wanted to touch him with her fingers, then her mouth as they—

"Rita?"

"Huh?" She blushed bright red and stared at him. Thank the Lord, his eyes were still closed.

"You're supposed to be talking."

"Oh. Right. Um, talk." She tried to think of something safe to say. "Okay, Tex brought us dinner so we don't have to go to the bunkhouse."

"That sounds nice. What did he fix?"

"There's steaks and potatoes. He offered to stay and cook, but I told him I could handle it."

"I'll cook."

She'd finished with his arm and leaned over to apply the cream to his chest. Fortunately his words were enough to distract her from her task.

"What is it about you guys? Why does everyone think I can't cook? I'm not completely useless in the kitchen."

Brady opened his eyes. "No one said you were, but my mama taught me well. I'm not going to assume that you'll be cooking dinner just because you're a woman. You put in a hard day's work, just like I did. In fact, you were up earlier. I was being polite."

"Oh." Who would have thought?

"Just, *oh*? What about a heartfelt apology?"

She smiled. "Don't you think 'heartfelt' is just a little too strong? This is a situation that calls for a casual apology."

"I'll take either one."

She touched the cream to his belly. Muscle rippled. Her mouth went dry. She had to clear her throat before she could speak. "Why don't we share kitchen duties? I'll be in charge of the potatoes and setting the table, you can take care of the meat. The salad's already made."

"Fine." He closed his eyes again. "When you're done with my chest, I've got some dandy scratches at the top of my thighs."

Randi froze.

Brady opened one eye and grinned. "Gotcha."

After dinner, Randi sipped her wine and sighed. "I am content. I worked hard this morning, helped you rescue Princess, a cat and her kittens, then finished up with a wonderful meal. Life doesn't get much better than this."

"Agreed." Brady leaned forward and rested his elbows on the table.

After she'd seen to his scratches, he'd pulled on his shirt. The logical side of her brain had been relieved. With him decently covered she was at less risk of making a fool of herself. The illogical side of her brain had murmured a protest, wanting to continue to look at his bare chest. At least she had the memories, she reminded herself. When she was alone in her room tonight, she would relive the experience of seeing and touching him.

You might be growing up, but you're still not very bright when it comes to men, she told herself. But somehow, with Brady, she didn't care. It was safe to dream about him because he wouldn't ever want her.

"I should go clean up the dishes," she said, making no move to rise.

"I'll help...in a minute." He poured more red wine into her glass, then filled his own.

She glanced around the dining room. A large hutch stood on the far wall. There was a buffet under the window. Several old samplers, obviously handed down for generations, decorated the walls. "This is such a great house," she said. "I wonder if your parents miss it."

"I'm sure they do, but they know it's waiting here for them. That makes a difference. When I got homesick, that's what I told myself."

"When were you gone?"

"I rode the rodeo circuit for nearly ten years."

"Really? I've been to a few rodeos and enjoyed them. I didn't get to as many as I would have liked. My mother didn't approve."

"Why?"

Randi stared at her glass. "Oh, it wasn't socially correct. Now, if I wanted to go to the ballet, that was fine. Or the opera. What were your events?"

"Bareback and bronc riding. I was a bull rider for a couple of years, but those guys are crazy."

She raised her gaze to meet his. "I agree. It's dangerous, but at least it's fair."

"What do you mean?"

"I don't know. I guess if a man wants to ride a bull that's his business. The bull is larger and can take care of himself. I always hated calf roping. Those poor baby calves getting caught, then hog-tied. It doesn't seem like a test of equals.''

''If they grow up to be the bull riding stock, at least they get their own back.''

She laughed. ''I like that. I'm sure most of the calves don't, but I'm going to insist on believing they do.''

They sat next to each other at right angles, at one end of the long table. The large room made Randi want to whisper, as if they could be overheard. In some way, that added to the intimacy of the moment.

''The rodeo was a good life for me,'' he said. ''I traveled, saw a lot of the country, met interesting people.''

''Women?''

He grinned. ''Some.''

''How many is some?''

''More than one, less than you would think.''

She batted her eyes. ''No details?''

''I'm not one to kiss and tell.''

''Bummer. I would love to know what it was like to be a rodeo hero.''

He shrugged. ''I was never that good. I managed to win enough to support myself, but I only made the national finals four years out of ten. Still, I wouldn't trade that experience for the world. I grew up on the road. My dad had done the same thing, so he knew a lot of people on the circuit. His friends, the older guys, kept track of me. With them around, I avoided getting into any real trouble.''

''Who keeps you out of trouble now?'' she asked, her voice teasing.

''I've outgrown the need to find trouble.''

''Oh? You talk like you're an old man yourself.''

''I am.''

She thought about his bare chest and supple muscles. "Brady, you're not much older than I."

"Nine years. It's enough."

She pushed her wineglass away. Until that moment, she'd been enjoying the conversation. "So in addition to being one of your strays, I'm also a child?" she asked, then wanted to call the words back. Even *she* had heard the hurt in her voice. But she couldn't help it. She'd wanted to be more than just someone he'd taken in—she'd wanted to be an individual. Special, as Tex had said. Obviously the cook had been wrong.

Brady frowned. "What are you talking about? What strays?"

She folded her arms over her chest. "All of us. You collect human strays the way Princess collects cats. Tex, Ziggy, Ty, even me."

His expression tightened. "I was raised to believe everyone deserves a second chance. If you have a complaint about that, you'll need to take it up with my folks." He pushed his chair back, stood up and left the room. Seconds later, the front door opened, then closed as he walked outside.

Randi stared after him. From the stiff set of his shoulders it was obvious she'd insulted him. That wasn't what she'd meant at all. Quite the opposite.

She followed him outside. Princess still lay on her blanket. Randi paused to pet her and the few cats sleeping next to her, then straightened and looked at Brady.

He stood on the edge of the porch, facing the barn. He must have heard her join him, but he didn't say anything. She wondered what she could do to make it right between them. He was the last person she wanted angry with her.

Darkness surrounded them. Overhead, stars twinkled in

the heavens. The heat had disappeared with the sun, leaving the temperature pleasant.

Slowly, she walked toward him, stopping less than a foot away. She wanted to lean against his strength, absorbing some of it for herself. Maybe that was the problem—she wasn't capable of making it on her own. Why did she always have to depend on someone else? Why wasn't her own counsel, her own company, enough?

Yet she knew this was different. In the past she'd wanted to lean on her father or her brother because she didn't want to face her problems or deal with her life. This time she wanted to lean on Brady because she had a hunch she would find something magical in his arms. His strength would become a part of her, and her strength—surely she had some—would flow into him.

She raised her hand to touch him, but instead of resting her fingers on his back, she curled them toward her palm and dropped her arm to her side. She was just one of the strays. Touching wasn't allowed.

"I didn't mean to insult you," she said.

He shrugged without turning around. "I'm not a fool," he told her. "I don't hire everyone who shows up. If I think they have what it takes, I give them a chance. In return I get loyalty and hard work."

"I've learned that firsthand. I appreciate that you gave me a chance. I didn't say it right, probably because it's hard for me to see myself as just another stray. My lifestyle has taken a turn for the worst in the past couple of months. In a way, that's sort of humbling. So I wasn't trying to make you uncomfortable. I guess the real message is that I admire you and what you've done here."

Brady grimaced. Admiration. He knew what that was like. He'd been on the giving and receiving end of it. Hero worship. Rita didn't want to be another stray, and he didn't want to be a hero.

But he couldn't tell her that, just as he couldn't tell her that he'd left the table, not because he'd been insulted, but because her description of him had hit too close to home. He did make it a habit of taking in strays, but that wasn't how he saw her.

Even though she was an employee, even though he knew better, he wanted her. In his bed and in his life. Both were dangerous, the latter very close to deadly. He knew the risks involved. He knew how bad the heartache could be. He'd been down that road before. Yet something about Rita made him want to try again. Something made him dream about her, want her, need her in the most fundamentally, soul-stirring way.

"Brady, I..." Her voice faltered.

He didn't dare turn around. He didn't want to know what she was thinking right now. Something that would remind him he was just an old cowboy with a thing for a young woman who wouldn't look at him twice on a bet.

Facing the barn, trying desperately to ignore her, he reminded himself it was for the best. When she was ready to move on, he would let her go. That's how these things happened.

Despite his intense effort not to notice, the scent of her shampoo teased him. He could feel her presence right behind him and knew she was close...close enough to touch.

"There aren't many old-fashioned gentlemen left," she said. "You're one of the good guys."

Involuntarily, he spun toward her. "I'm not a gentleman," he said through gritted teeth. "I'm not a good guy. I'm just a man, like every other man. I have flaws, and you better get your butt to your room before you witness one of mine."

Her eyebrows pulled together in confusion. "What are you talking about?"

"Dammit, Rita. Don't make me spell it out."

Her blue eyes were nearly black in the porch light. "You're going to have to. I apologized. Isn't that enough?"

"It's not about what you said, it's about what I want. Go home, little girl. Run away and play."

She raised her chin. "I'm not a child. I'm a grown woman. Stop treating me like your little sister."

"It beats the alternative."

"What does that mean?"

"You still don't get it?"

She shook her head.

She didn't have a clue. If he hadn't been so furious and frustrated, he might have laughed. As it was, something inside snapped from the pressure. He glared at her. "Then, let me explain it. I'm not a good guy at all. You drive me crazy. Every damn day you're out here in your jeans and your T-shirts, flaunting curves that—" He curled his hands into fists as words deserted him. "I know it's wrong. That's not the problem. I can't seem to resist your jokes, your laughter, your quick mind. I want you naked in my bed. I don't think that qualifies me as a gentleman, do you?"

Her mouth dropped open. "You think I'm attractive?"

"That's all you got from that? What the hell do you think I've been talking about?"

"I don't know. I'm not pretty."

He closed his eyes and groaned. "Yeah, right."

"Brady, I—"

He cut her off. He knew what she was going to say, and he didn't want to hear. He didn't want to be let down easy. "Just go inside, Rita. Go to your room and leave me alone. I won't mention this again. You don't have to worry that I'm going to embarrass you or inflict myself on you.''

"I wasn't worried about that at all."

He looked at her. Her blue eyes had widened and her cheeks looked flushed, but she wasn't angry and she wasn't leaving.

"I told you to go inside."

"And if I don't?"

Her unexpected response slammed into him like a runaway steer. He nearly staggered. "I don't have a whole lot of self-control left. I want to kiss you. I want to do a whole lot more, but I'm willing to settle for that. So if you don't run away, I won't be able to resist."

She smiled. "Gee, Brady, a clear warning like that and you say you're not a gentleman. I'd say you're the best kind." Then she raised herself up on tiptoes and pressed her mouth to his.

He was so shocked by her actions that it took him nearly two heartbeats to register what was going on. Her fingertips lay lightly on his shoulder; her body was inches from his. He could feel her heat, inhale her scent, and against his mouth was the sweetest, tenderest, most arousing touch he'd ever experienced.

Pleasure exploded. He wrapped his arms around her and hauled her hard against him. She melted into his body, her curves flowing over his hard planes, her arms embracing his neck, her thighs teasing his.

Every point of contact ignited its own fire. He raised one hand to her head and buried his fingers in her thick curls. With his other hand he followed her spine to her waist, then slipped to the side to cup the swell of her hip. She was built for a man to love—strong, round, supple.

He tilted his head and moved his mouth against hers.

Her lips parted and he licked at the open seam. A soft whimper escaped her throat. The sound bore into his chest, feeding an already out-of-control need, sending hot blood coursing through his body. He was hard and aching in seconds.

Randi clutched at Brady, wondering what on earth was happening between them. She'd been kissed before. She'd even made love a couple of times with her college boyfriend. The experience had been pleasant, but it hadn't prepared her to go up in flames. She liked Brady and admired his body, but she hadn't known he could arouse her with just a kiss.

As his tongue swept into her mouth, her legs began to tremble. The rippling in her thighs made it difficult to stay upright. She had to lean against him to maintain her balance.

He teased the tip of her tongue with his, then circled hers, igniting explosions of intense pleasure in her breasts and between her legs. She was already damp. She could feel the heat and the wanting that was as much an ache as a throb. Her breasts swelled, the nipples tightening until she had to press against his chest to try and ease the pressure.

As she clung to him, she remembered his words and the picture he'd painted of her in his bed. She wanted to be there—wanted it more than she'd ever wanted anything in her life.

He cupped her face in his hands, his fingers stroked her cheeks. The tenderness in the gesture was as perfect as his mouth against hers. He broke the kiss and gazed at her. She wondered if she looked as aroused as he did.

"Wow," he said, and smiled.

"Yeah. That's what I was thinking." She giggled softly.

"So you're not offended?"

She reached up and brushed her thumb across his mouth, then shook her head. "Hardly. Intrigued. Surprised, but not offended."

"I'm glad." He lowered his head and pressed his lips to the side of her neck. Warm, damp kisses slipped down to her T-shirt. His hands rested on her shoulders. One moved lower, drifting toward her breast. She held her breath in anticipation.

He cupped the curve gently, almost reverently. She exhaled as intense pleasure filled her. Long, strong fingers stroked her and his thumb brushed over her taut nipple. She clutched at him and sighed.

"Sweet Rita," he murmured against her neck.

It was as if he'd dumped a bucket of cold water over her. She stiffened and stared in horror.

He raised his head and looked at her. "Rita? What's wrong?"

He'd said it again. *Rita.* But that wasn't her name. Rita was a lie, just as her life was a lie. She was Randi Howell, runaway bride.

He shook her gently. "What is it?"

"I—" She swallowed as tears suddenly formed. "Nothing. I can't—"

She broke away. She couldn't do this to him. Not to Brady, who *really* was one of the good guys. He deserved something so much better.

"I'm sorry," she whispered, and did what she should have done the first time he mentioned kissing. She turned on her heel and ran to her room.

Nine

Brady paced the length of the kitchen, paused, then walked back. Once there, he glanced at the digital clock on the microwave. It was 3:58. Rita was due downstairs any minute. He'd already started the coffee for her, and he'd rehearsed what he planned to say a thousand times.

At least he hadn't had to worry about waking up on time. As it was, he'd barely slept last night. Between reliving the powerful kiss they'd shared and wrestling with guilt, there hadn't been much time for dozing off.

He heard footsteps on the stairs and turned quickly to face the doorway. A shadow moved through the darkness. There was a click and light flooded the kitchen. Rita saw him and jumped back.

She touched a hand to her chest. "Brady! You gave me a start. What are you doing up?"

She was dressed for work, dressed as he always saw her, in jeans and T-shirt. Her hair was neatly braided, her face freshly washed. As he gazed at her, something flickered in her eyes. His heart sank. She was cautious because she expected him to attack her again. How could he have done that to her?

He drew in a deep breath. "About last night," he began, and shoved his hands in his pockets. "Look. I'm sorry. I feel awful about what happened. You work for me, and as your employer, I shouldn't have put you in a position that makes you feel uncomfortable. I've never done anything like that before. I've never said those things. I don't know what got into me."

"It's okay," she said softly.

"No, it's not. As I told you from the start, I wanted you to live here in the main house so you would feel safe. And here I am, the first guy to break the rules about leaving you alone." He cleared his throat. "I want you to know that I was completely in the wrong, and that it will never happen again."

Her blue eyes crinkled at the corners as she smiled. "That was quite an apology. Thank you. I have just one question."

"What's that?"

"Were you awake all night beating yourself up about our kiss?"

Embarrassment burned hot. He averted his face and tried to look casual. "Not exactly."

"Just as I thought. One of the good guys." She crossed to the coffeepot and poured herself a cup. After taking a sip, she looked at him. "Okay, Brady, if you can bare your soul, I guess I can bare mine. Don't give this matter another moment's thought. You didn't force me to do anything against my will. I liked kissing you. I don't think it was especially smart, or something we should pursue right now. Neither of us is in a position to deal with the ramifications of taking things further, so it might be better if we just backed off for a while. Sound reasonable?"

He was too shocked to speak, so he just nodded. She flashed him another smile. "Good."

With that she walked to the back door and left. He stared after her. She wasn't angry. He'd convinced himself she would either be furious or incredibly hurt. Instead, she'd calmly admitted he hadn't forced her. She'd wanted to kiss him. She'd *liked* kissing him.

He felt himself grin and knew he would be grinning like a fool the whole day. She'd liked kissing him. Hot damn.

The barn dance fulfilled every city slicker cliché Randi had expected—and she loved it. The lodge in town was tacky and old, with dusty animal heads on the walls. The band consisted of several retired men and one woman on keyboard. They played country favorites with a rhythm that had nothing to do with what the songwriters had originally intended.

Conversation and laughter swirled around as wildly as the dancers. She watched two teenage boys spike the punch. When the preacher caught them, he actually grabbed them by their ears to pull them outside. She wasn't sure if she'd gone back in time, or had been caught up in a location shoot for a television movie-of-the-week.

This happy occasion was as different from the formal dances she was used to as filet mignon was from five-alarm chili. She'd always liked chili dogs, and now she knew why.

The people here were actually having fun. Couples smiled while they danced, children dashed around the edges of the room playing elaborate games of tag. Old ladies sat in straight-backed chairs and gossiped. New mothers showed off babies. Her mother had wanted her to be a debutante, but this was much more her style. Her dress cost less than her mother's overpriced face powder, yet she felt, if not attractive, then at least average enough to fit in.

Randi smiled. One of these days she was going to have to work on her self-confidence. Although, referring to herself as "average enough" was better than her description of "hideous"—as she'd thought in high school. She owed a little of that improvement to Brady. Three days later she still remembered every word of his declaration—his wonderful, exciting statements about wanting her. Just thinking about that night made her skin break out in goose bumps. Their kiss had been—

She shook her head. Their kiss was something she was trying not to think about, remember? It had been a wonderful experience and something best forgotten. There was no room for her in Brady's life, and wishing for the moon would only make her unhappy.

Still, she couldn't help recalling his sweet apology the next morning. Had anyone ever cared so much about her feelings? Had any other man been as concerned that she felt comfortable and safe? If she wasn't so sure she was moving on, she might be tempted to—

"Penny for your thoughts?"

She glanced up and saw Ty standing next to her. The darkly handsome cowboy raised his eyebrows expectantly. Randi flushed.

"They're not for sale. Sorry."

"Too bad. They looked interesting. Want to dance?"

"Sure."

She stepped into his arms. In the first hour she'd danced with everyone from the ranch except for Ty and Brady. Even Tex had taken her on a quick turn around the floor, all the while making her laugh with incredible tales about his life in the marines.

There wasn't a shortage of women, so she figured the guys were trying to make her feel comfortable. "Is there a conspiracy?" she asked.

"About what?"

"Everyone has danced with me. Are you guys trying to keep me from being a wallflower?"

"No conspiracy. Maybe we just like you and want to dance with you."

She wrinkled her nose. "I doubt that."

"So if I told you that you looked nice, you would dismiss the compliment?"

She glanced down at the simple blue floral print cotton dress she wore. Cap sleeves showed off her tanned arms. The garment skimmed over her waist and hips, then flared out slightly to her knees. "I think I look okay."

"Was that a thank you?"

Before she could answer, he led her through an intricate series of steps that left her stumbling and breathless. She laughed. "So you're trying to show me up?"

"I would have thought a city girl like you had taken dancing lessons."

"Really? What makes you think I'm a city girl?"

"Aren't you?" For the first time since she'd met him, Ty smiled. The faintly dangerous expression he normally wore faded slightly. He wasn't just good-looking. When he smiled he was about the most gorgeous man she'd ever seen.

She tried to remember what she knew about Ty. It was pretty close to nothing. He was good on the ranch, a natural leader. When Brady had a couple of crews working, Ty was always in charge of the second group. He was bright, capable, and she suspected he had a degree. What on earth was he doing stuck on Brady's ranch?

His hold tightened slightly, warning her of more complicated steps. She concentrated and managed to keep up as he wove them through the other dancers.

She took a shot in the dark. "What's her name?" she asked.

"Who?"

"The woman who taught you to dance?"

The smile faded as if it had never been, his mouth straightened and already dark eyes turned black with pain. "Denise."

There was something about the way he said the name. As if it had cost him plenty to form the single word.

"I'm sorry," Randi said quickly. "I shouldn't have—" She shook her head. "I'm sorry."

He shrugged. "No big deal."

But she knew it was. She'd been teasing him and had inadvertently bumped into an open wound. A thousand questions filled her mind. Who was this mysterious Denise? Why wasn't he with her? What had happened? How long had he loved her?

Randi suspected it had been for a very long time. What would it be like to be loved that much?

The song faded, then another one began. She recognized it, although she didn't recall the title. Something about an old flame burning bright. Ty winced visibly and dropped his hands to his side.

"Thanks for the dance," he mumbled, and left the floor.

Randi watched him go. She wanted to run after him and apologize, but it was too late for that. Talk about blowing it.

She moved to the edge of the dance floor and glanced at the crowd. Families and friends chatted together. For the first time since arriving, she felt out of place. Suddenly that old phrase—alone in a crowd—made sense to her.

She was a long way from home, and she had a sneaking suspicion that no one in Grand Springs was missing her tonight. Certainly not Hal. In the past couple of weeks she'd decided they hadn't even been friends, let alone in love.

"May I?"

She didn't have to look at the speaker to know he was Brady. She shivered in anticipation, then turned toward him. "Hi."

"Hi, yourself."

He took her in his arms. She tried not to notice how every nerve cell in her body instantly went on alert. It wasn't fair. She'd danced with nearly a dozen men tonight. Some of them, like Ty, had been very good-looking. Most had been charming. And not one of them had made her feel the way Brady did.

He held her gently, not pulling her too close. Which almost made her laugh, because she would enjoy being hauled up against his chest. She would even like being kissed senselessly. Was he thinking about that, too? Was he remembering their kiss, the passion flaring between them, the heat, the—

"What do you think of our country dance?" he asked.

Her fantasies popped like a balloon pricked by a needle. So much for him remembering anything about that night.

"It's fun," she said. "Everyone has been really nice. The guys have all danced with me. I tried to get Ty to admit there was a conspiracy, but he denied it."

"There isn't as far as I know." He smiled. "Dancing with you is hardly tough duty."

She looked up at the dimple in his left cheek and thought about swooning. Unfortunately, she'd never swooned in her life and didn't know how to go about doing it. She suspected Brady wouldn't appreciate the gesture. If the man had a single clue as to what he did to her he would take off for the hills.

A couple in their early sixties moved next to them. The wife asked Brady about his parents. He answered, then the older couple moved off.

"This is very different from where I grew up," she

said. "I had dance lessons for three years and I hated every one of them. The only way my mom got me to go was to promise me I could spend two hours riding my horse for every hour I went to dance class." She frowned. "All those uncomfortable silences when we were dancing. Twelve- and thirteen-year-old boys aren't exactly thrilled about the experience, either. At least we had that in common."

"So you were part of the upper crust of society?" he asked, his voice teasing.

"Not exactly. Our town wasn't big enough to have a crust, although my mother is constantly in search of one. My dad—" She stopped, remembering her father and missing him. "He was great. I was a daddy's girl, of course."

Brown eyes twinkled at her. "Of course."

The song ended and another began. Brady didn't release her and she didn't indicate she wanted to be let go. If it were up to her, she would spend the night in his arms.

"My father always believed in me, no matter how much I messed things up."

"That's what fathers do," he said.

"I know, and mine was one of the best. The only bad part was, he never made me try to fix things on my own. I learned to depend on him to always get me out of trouble. That works great when you're ten, but it's a less attractive trait at twenty."

Music and laughter surrounded them. They turned and the room spun. Randi wondered if it was safe to talk about her past like this. But it had been so long since she'd had someone to talk to. Especially someone she liked and respected. She knew she could trust Brady. Besides, she wasn't telling him anything that would allow him to locate her family.

"My mother was completely different," she went on. "She saw me as her burden in life. A daughter who was a tomboy and completely uninterested in doing the socially correct thing."

"You have a brother, right?"

"You remembered." She smiled. "Noah. He's wonderful. A doctor. Handsome, charming. Everything I'm not. I suppose I should hate him, but I don't. When Dad died, Noah was really there for me."

Brady's hand tightened on her waist, drawing her closer. She went willingly. His embrace comforted, as did his strength.

"You miss your father."

"All the time. I want to make him proud of me."

"He already is."

Randi wasn't so sure. Her father wouldn't be proud of the way she'd handled things with Hal. One of these days she was going to have to make some decisions about that situation. She couldn't hide out forever. She would have to go back and explain things. But what about the men with those guns? Were they still after her? Why had they threatened her in the first place? What—

Brady shook her gently. "Rita, come back to me."

"Huh? Oh." She'd been a thousand smiles away...or at least a few hundred. "Sorry."

"Let me guess. You were thinking about another guy, right?"

Randi stumbled a step. "Not really."

"Liar." His smile never faltered, but she thought she saw disappointment flicker in his eyes. At least, she hoped it was disappointment.

''No, it's not like that,'' she told him. ''Okay, I was thinking about someone, but it's not what you think.''

''What is it?''

They were at the far end of the room. Brady moved them away from the dancers and into the corner. Randi would have preferred to keep dancing. Not because she didn't want to talk about this, but because while they were dancing he held her in his arms. As he drew them to a stop, he released her. She twisted her hands together in front of her waist and tried not to feel rejected.

''There was this guy back home. We went out for a while. The thing is, I can't figure out why. My mother pressured me to see him. Hal's involved in politics and will probably be mayor some day. There was even talk of the state legislature.'' She shrugged. ''It's not really my thing. Anyway, we dated, and, I don't know, one day we were engaged.''

Brady withdrew. He didn't move away, but she felt him pull back all the same. ''Are you still engaged?'' Ice sharpened the edges of his tone.

''No.'' Surely Hal would consider the engagement broken when she'd run off. If he didn't, she would tell him, just as soon as she got back to town. ''The thing is, I never loved him. I'm not sure I liked him.'' She drew in a deep breath and met Brady's unreadable gaze. ''That's one of the reasons I'm here. To figure things out. You know, find out a purpose and all that.''

''You're young,'' he said easily. ''That comes with time.''

''Brady!'' She put her hands on her hips. ''Haven't we had this conversation already? I'm not a child. Why do you insist on thinking that I am?'' Hadn't their time together convinced him she was very much a woman?

Before he could answer, McGregor came up. ''Well,

lass, they're playing a two-step." The older man winked. "I suppose you could say it's our song."

She glanced at Brady, trying to figure out if she should refuse the farrier's invitation so they could finish their conversation. He nodded at the Scotsman. "Don't wear her out. She still has chores in the morning."

"Oh, I'll be testin' her a little, but I promise to return her in nearly the same condition I found her. Come, lassie. Time's a wastin'."

She was pulled into McGregor's enthusiastic embrace and swept around the room. At the end of the dance, a man she didn't know asked her to dance, then another. Thirty minutes later, when the band took a break, there was no sign of Brady. Randi excused herself and made her way over to the tables and chairs set up in a side room. A buffet line formed. She ignored it, detouring the crowd to collect a soda from the bar in the corner.

Ziggy and Quinn spotted her and called her over. She smiled and waved but kept on walking until she saw Tex sitting alone. She tapped the chair across from him. "May I?"

"Help yourself."

She sank onto the wooden seat. "I'm exhausted. All that dancing. I should have taken a longer nap today."

"You're having fun. You can sleep when you're old like me."

She rolled her eyes. "I don't want to talk about age differences right now."

"What do you want to talk about?" Tex took a sip of his beer.

Randi rubbed the sides of her soda can. "Why isn't Brady married?"

"You're going to have to discuss that with him."

"He won't tell me."

"Have you asked him?"

She shook her head. "There's no polite way to bring that up. At least not with the person involved."

"I don't think he'd mind."

She glanced at Tex. "You could hint about his past."

"Why do you want to know?"

Her gaze skittered away. "See, this is that awkward part I was talking about."

The older man chuckled. "I won't give you specific information, but I might be convinced to whisper a hint or two."

"Great. I promise to feed Princess and the cats every day for a week."

"You're doing that, anyway."

She leaned forward and rested her elbows on the table. "Then, I promise not to stop."

"Deal." He thought for a minute. "Brady's not that complicated a guy. He grew up in a secure home with great parents. Living out on the ranch, he had lots of freedom to roam around. What with ranch chores and all, he learned about responsibility early."

Randi wondered if she should hum "The Battle Hymn of the Republic" for background music. Talk about the all-American boy.

"His parents were happy together. They're still very much in love." Tex glanced around the room. "Not a lot of people can say that."

She thought about her parents' strained marriage and agreed. "It's rare."

"It's also a tough act to follow. Brady wants what his folks have. He believes in love, he's a good man. Even so, mistakes are made."

What mistakes? But she didn't ask. There was no point.

Tex wouldn't answer that kind of question. He was too loyal a friend.

"These mistakes," she said cautiously. "They can make a man not believe anymore."

"True. Sometimes it's hard to get back in the saddle...so to speak." He took another sip of beer. "There was a cowboy Brady knew on the circuit. Donny was a hell of a bull rider. Made it to the finals every year, but he never won. One day he started drinking. Turns out he had a family history of alcoholism and the liquor got a hold of him. Within a year he deteriorated to the point where he was rarely sober. He rode drunk once and nearly killed himself."

A group of teenagers walked by. The young people nodded respectfully at Tex, then at her. She smiled in return.

"What happened to Donny?"

"When he'd recovered from his injuries, Brady hired him. There was only one rule. No liquor. Donny agreed. Then one day the craving got too strong. He went out into the herd drunk and started a stampede. He lost control of his horse, fell and died." Tex frowned as if the memories crowded him. "He had no one. No family to mourn him. Just Brady. So Donny was buried in the Jones family plot, and Brady took care of his debts and his things. That's what he does for people."

"If he's busy taking care of everyone, he doesn't have time to worry about being alone," she said slowly. "Being the caretaker also allows him to keep his distance. He's always the father figure."

Tex raised his eyebrows. "Could be."

Is that what Brady was doing to her? Always talking about their age difference as a way of separating himself from her? Then, what about their kiss? Somehow that night he hadn't been able to hold the barriers in place. She'd gotten through. Yet as soon as he could, he put the relationship back on very specific terms, with him acting as mentor.

"Why this interest in Brady?" Tex asked.

"I don't know," she said. "I mean that. I just—" She shrugged. "I think he's a great guy. And I'm not going to use him," she added hastily. "Don't worry about that."

"I don't anymore."

She smiled. "Thank you. I've never met anyone like him before. Sometimes I think he's too good to be true."

"He's just a man, with faults like everyone else."

"And all of us to take care of. Who takes care of him?"

"Good question," Tex said. "Maybe you'd like to apply for the job."

Ten

For the first couple of hours of the dance Brady had managed to avoid torturing himself, but after the musicians' second break, he couldn't seem to stop himself. He stood behind the lodge, supposedly enjoying the cool evening breeze, but in reality he stared in the open windows and watched Rita dance with other men.

He told himself it didn't matter who she danced with; it wasn't his business. He ran through the "she's just an employee" lecture, followed by a stern talk on how much younger she was. He even spent a couple of minutes telling himself he didn't like dark curly hair and blue eyes. Then he stopped. He knew he had it bad if he was reduced to lying to himself about the fact that he found Rita attractive.

She was, he acknowledged, very special. And not just her looks. He liked that she wasn't afraid to work hard and that she was endlessly patient with Ziggy when his stuttering made it nearly impossible to complete a sentence. He enjoyed watching her with the cats, playing with them, talking to them, naming them when she thought he didn't know. She'd made a place for herself at the ranch. Despite being the only female, she'd managed to defuse any potential trouble by acting like everyone's sister. Even Tex had taken a shine to her.

But there was no point in letting his hormones race into overdrive. No matter how well she fit in, she wasn't staying. He'd always known that, and their conversation tonight proved it.

For the first time, she'd shared a little about her past. She'd painted a word picture of a family that while flawed, was still a force in her life. She had a mother and a brother somewhere, waiting for her. She also had an ex-boyfriend.

He grimaced, wishing he didn't know about Hal. Or the engagement.

Who was this man who had nearly claimed Rita as his wife? Why had she agreed to marry him, then changed her mind? She'd spoken of the relationship as if it had no value to her. Was that because she'd "fallen into it" as she'd claimed, or was it something else?

The music changed. He glanced up and saw the dancers swaying together as a slow song shifted the mood. Rita wasn't on the floor with anyone. He could go inside and ask her to dance himself, but he knew better. A single dance could be explained—she was his employee and it was polite to ask her. Anything else would imply interest. As if she hadn't guessed that from the kiss they'd shared.

Still, he wasn't ready to start anything with her, and he was damn well going to ignore the fact that something may already have started on its own.

"You look like you could use this," a voice said behind him.

He turned toward the sound and saw Rita standing in the shadows. She held out a plastic glass of beer.

"Thanks. Why aren't you dancing?"

"No one I wanted to dance with asked me."

He mulled that over for a second, wondering if it was an invitation. By the time he figured it might be, the song was half over and they couldn't have made it inside in time. Besides, they were both holding drinks. So instead, he led her to the bench pressed up against the lodge.

She sank down and sighed. "You're smart to be out here. This is better than dancing. My feet are sore. I'm not used to wearing high heels." She slipped off her pumps and wiggled her toes.

Brady clenched his teeth to hold back the offer to rub her feet. It wouldn't be a good idea. Aside from the fact that it would be inappropriate, he doubted he could touch any part of her without getting aroused.

She leaned back into the far corner of the bench, angling her body toward him. Light spilled out of the window, illuminating her features. Long, dark curls tumbled down her shoulders and back. Her mouth tilted up at the corners, color stained her cheeks. She was lovely and he wanted her. That and a buck would buy him a cup of coffee.

"So, Brady Jones, how come you're not married?"

He raised his eyebrows.

She laughed. "I know, I know. Talk about an unsubtle opening. However, I would like to point out that you're the one who is always bringing up the difference in our ages. So what I want to know is how an old man of thirty-three has managed to avoid the delights of matrimony? Why don't you have a passel of kids running around and making trouble? Where is Ms. Right?"

He angled toward her and rested his ankle on his opposite knee. "I want a wife and a family, but it hasn't worked out."

"I suppose it's tough to meet women on the ranch," she said. "You should train Princess to collect single ladies instead of cats. Think how convenient that would be. You could have your pick of the litter, so to speak."

He chuckled. "It's not that simple. I met a lot of women on the rodeo circuit."

"Were you wild?"

"I had my moments," he admitted. "Not that many, but a few."

"Not one of these buckle bunnies appealed?"

"Where'd you hear that term?"

She batted her eyelashes at him. "I get around. So, you didn't like any of them?"

"I don't know. I guess not. My parents are very happy together. They get mad just like any other married couple, but they also still love each other. When I was growing up, I knew their relationship was a priority to them. That was very comforting in a time when a lot of my friends' parents were getting divorced. The problem is, I don't want to settle for anything less."

She took a sip of her drink. "They sound like a tough act to follow."

"Exactly. I came close a couple of times." He set his beer on the ground. "A few years ago a woman came to town. Alicia. She drove a bright red convertible. Not exactly what we're used to around here."

"This is more truck country."

"Yeah. She'd taken the summer off to drive across the country. She wanted to learn how to ride a horse, so she came out to the ranch." Brady still remembered the first time he'd seen her, all blond hair and blue eyes, with a smile bright enough to blind a man.

"Pretty?" Rita asked.

"Beautiful, like a model."

"Figures," she muttered, then looked at him. "What happened?"

"I fell hard and fast, without bothering to look at what I was doing. She didn't fit in with the ranch at all, but I convinced myself it would work out. She hated the dirt, the dust, even the horses. She wasn't much of a rider. But I was in love for the first time in my life and I refused to face the truth.'' He thought back to that time, to his parents' worried faces. They'd tried to warn him about Alicia, but when he wouldn't listen, they'd left him alone to make his own mistakes.

"She never talked about her past," he continued. "That should have been my first clue. There were lots of secrets she kept. Once she disappeared for a couple of days and wouldn't say where she'd been, but I didn't want to pay attention to the signs. In my mind, we were meant for each other, just like my folks. I proposed and she accepted.''

"You married her?"

Something about Rita's voice didn't sound right, but when he looked at her, he couldn't see anything odd in her expression.

"Not exactly. We planned a quick wedding, nothing fancy. My parents weren't happy, but they didn't argue with me. Mom took care of all the details.''

He leaned back against the bench. Those days were so clear to him. The conversations he'd had with Alicia, the watchful concern in his parents' eyes. Everyone had guessed but him. Everyone had tried to warn him but he wouldn't have any part of it. He wanted Alicia and he refused to listen to reason.

"What happened?"

"What everyone but me expected. She never showed up for the wedding. She left me standing at the altar, waiting like a fool. Eventually some kid brought a note she'd left. She told me she'd had a great summer, that she'd enjoyed her time with me. Apparently, the whole point of her trip was to make her rich boyfriend jealous.

It had taken a while, but the trip had worked. Two days before our wedding, he'd flown out to propose and had taken her back with him. She said she hoped I understood and wished her happiness.'' He heard the bitterness in his voice. "I wished her a lot of things, but happiness wasn't one of them.''

After all this time, he couldn't let that go. He no longer hated Alicia or blamed himself. He understood what had happened. He'd been so determined to find something like his parents' relationship that he'd thought he'd found a treasure where there was only fool's gold. He didn't hate her or himself, but he was disappointed that he'd chosen so poorly. The bitterness came, not from what he'd lost, but from what he'd never had.

"What I resent the most is that she didn't have the courage to tell me to my face," he said. "She ran out on me like some kid runs away from home after breaking a lamp. The mistake was mine for thinking her an adult capable of acting responsibly.''

He glanced at Rita. She stared at him openmouthed. Her stunned expression made him feel foolish. Had he exposed too much of his past?

Before either of them could say anything, McGregor stuck his head out the window. "I thought I saw you two sittin' out here in the dark. What's wrong with you both? There's fine music playin' and dancin' to be done. Talk tomorrow when the dancin' is finished.''

When Brady didn't move, McGregor snorted. "What are you waitin' for, boy? Ask the lady to dance.''

Brady stood up and held out his hand. Even as Rita took it, he felt the tension in her body. She didn't want to dance with him. She was obviously disgusted by his story. He swallowed, feeling about as comfortable as a snake in a rocking chair store. Dammit, why hadn't he kept his sorry past to himself?

They moved into the lodge and joined the circling crowd. Rita held herself stiffly in his arms. He contrasted her posture with what had happened the last time she'd danced, when she'd melted against him.

"I know what you're thinking," he said. "That I was a fool."

She raised her head and looked at him. Pain filled her eyes, darkening blue irises nearly to black. She shook her head. "Brady, you have no idea what I'm thinking. Trust me."

Compassion and something else vibrated in her voice. Something that touched him down in his heart.

"Rita?"

She pressed her lips together. "If you knew how I hated that name."

"What name?"

"Never mind. Brady, I think you're very wonderful. Alicia was obviously stupid and self-centered and greedy. She had no idea what she'd found in you. If she'd known, she would never have gone back to her boyfriend, no matter how rich he is. I'm sure she hates herself every day, and deeply regrets what happened."

"I doubt that."

"Then, you're wrong." She tugged on his hand until they moved out of the path of the other dancers and were standing to the side. "You're a very special person. I admire you so much. You're a good man and you deserve a unique woman. I know you'll find h-her."

Her voice broke on the last word. She shrugged helplessly, then turned and ran outside.

Randi stumbled into the darkness and pressed her palm

to her stomach. Taking deep breaths wasn't helping enough. She was going to throw up.

What had happened? How could this be true? Dear God, please let him be lying. Brady couldn't have been left at the altar. It was too unbelievable. It was too ironic.

She sucked in air and tried to calm herself. Her heart thundered in her chest, her legs were shaking, her throat tightened as she fought tears.

It wasn't fair. It just wasn't fair at all.

She turned around, trying to figure out where she was, needing to find out how to get away. She saw someone walking toward the parked cars. She peered, trying to place the familiar stride.

"Ty?"

The man paused.

She rushed toward him. "Ty, are you going back to the ranch? Can I have a ride?"

He blended with the darkness. There was something forbidding about his size and strength, but right now she would have accepted a ride from the devil himself.

"What's wrong?" he asked. "You sound upset."

"Nothing's wrong. Okay, I am upset, but it's not important. It's just—" She broke off and realized tears blurred her vision. She swore under her breath. "I'm fine. Can you please take me home with you?"

"Sure. The truck's this way."

She followed him to the pickup, then climbed into the passenger seat. Ty didn't speak and she was grateful. In a matter of minutes, they were on the main highway, heading back to the ranch.

Thoughts swirled through her head. Of all the crimes for Alicia to commit. Why couldn't she have been unfaithful, or been married, or secretly a man? Why did she have to run out on her own wedding? No wonder Tex had been concerned about Brady being used. That's exactly what Alicia had done.

The pain made it hard to breathe. As Randi attempted to draw air into her lungs, she found herself slamming directly into the truth. There was only one reason why Alicia's duplicity bothered her so much—only one reason why she raged against the unfairness of the situation. Because it made it impossible for her to explain about *her* past.

She hadn't realized how much she'd come to care about Brady, how much she'd wanted to be with him, until that chance was ripped away.

There would be no understanding, no miracle. When Brady found out the truth, he would despise her. He would see her exactly like the woman who had betrayed him.

She leaned her head against the cool window and fought the tears. This wasn't a situation she could bargain her way out of. She couldn't call Noah and have him make it right. She'd created a problem all by herself, and she had no one but herself to blame.

Oh, sure, she could say those men with guns were the reason she had abandoned Hal, but it wasn't true. She'd decided to run *before* she'd seen the men. Once again, she'd chosen the easiest way out. Instead of facing the consequences of her actions, she'd acted irresponsibly. This time, she was going to get stuck paying the price for the rest of her life. She'd met a man she respected and liked and admired—maybe even loved. A man she'd found herself dreaming about. A man she'd just lost as surely as if she'd betrayed him with his best friend.

It wasn't until the silence surrounded her that she realized they'd returned to the ranch and were parked behind the bunkhouse. She glanced around at the familiar structure, the outline of the trees against the star-filled sky, and knew she would miss this place.

"Wanna talk about it?" Ty asked.

"Thanks for asking, but it won't help."

"I bet Brady could fix it."

Randi made a sound that was half a burst of laughter, half a sob, then covered her mouth. "He's a major part of the problem," she mumbled, then dropped her arm to her side. "I wish—" She shook her head. What was there to wish for?

Ty leaned back in his seat. "The nights get real long out here. If we were a different sort of people, we could use each other to forget."

Despite the pain in her heart and the tears on her cheeks, she smiled. "That's the nicest invitation I've had in a long time. Thank you."

He gave her a wry smile. "I wasn't kidding."

"Me, either. I wish I could take you up on it. Life would be a whole lot less complicated. But if I were the kind of woman who could forget my troubles in your bed, I wouldn't be suffering right now. And if you were the kind of man to help me do that, you wouldn't still be missing Denise."

He flinched. "Well said. So here we are. A sorry collection of misfits with nowhere else to go. What does that say about us?"

"We all need lots of time in expensive psychological therapy."

He chuckled. "Probably." He turned toward her. "I'm willing to listen if you want to talk about it."

His offer touched her. Mostly because she knew how he avoided getting involved. "Thank you. Talking won't help and I'll start to cry, then you'll be uncomfortable."

"I could handle it."

"I don't think I could. But you're not the crying type, so if you want to talk about her—"

"No," he said quickly, cutting her off.

"I didn't think so."

They sat in silence. Randi told herself she should go inside, but she wasn't ready to be alone. What had started out as the perfect evening had turned into a nightmare.

"Do you love him?" Ty asked.

She knew the "him" in the question was Brady. "Has it been that obvious?"

"No. I've noticed a couple of things, but I wouldn't have put them together if you hadn't said he was your problem. Don't worry—no one's talking about you. At least not that way."

"I'm not sure I want to know how I'm being talked about."

"You're avoiding the question."

"I know." She bit her lower lip. "I'm not sure I know what love is. I haven't ever really loved anyone. At least not romantically. I care about him. I like him and respect him." She wanted him, but she didn't tell the cowboy that. He'd probably guessed it on his own. "Did you love her?"

Ty reached forward and clasped the steering wheel. His grip tightened until the tendons in his hands stood out in stark relief. "I lost her."

"How?"

"I was a fool."

His pain filled the cab, making her tremble. Compassion joined her own suffering. As he'd said, they were a sorry collection of misfits, belonging nowhere.

She leaned over and kissed him on the cheek. "'Night, Ty. Thanks for the ride."

Before she could straighten, he cupped her face and

stared into her eyes. For the first time, the shutters were down and she saw into the blackness of his soul. The open wounds there startled her. Who was the woman he'd lost? How had he survived this long without her? Is that what love did to a person? She wasn't sure she could handle that.

Ty stroked her skin with his thumb. "I hope you aren't offended, but you have no idea how much I wish you were someone else."

She blinked quickly, but couldn't hold back the tears. One slipped down her face. "I know what you mean." She stepped out of the cab and headed for the house.

Once there, she walked from dark room to dark room. Moonlight caused the furniture to cast faint shadows. She imagined she could hear voices from the past, laughter and happy conversations. This family loved so well, the emotion lingered long after the people were gone.

His presence surrounded her, nearly as tangible as his touch had been. She was wishing for the moon, yet wishes and dreams were all she had left. Fantasies about a future that could never be.

Why was she surprised? She'd never planned to make this her permanent home. She'd always known she was moving on. But that had been *her* choice. Now it wasn't anymore. Now she had to leave before Brady found out the truth. She would rather he thought she simply didn't care or that she wanted to move on, than for him to suspect her feelings, or to later learn what she'd done and despise her.

Eleven

The bald man stared at the ringing phone, wishing he didn't have to answer it. There was no news to report.

"Yes," he said, placing the receiver to his ear.

"Have you learned anything?"

"Yes. We've been checking small towns all along the interstate. She went to Albuquerque after Phoenix."

"Very good," the voice on the other end of the phone said, sounding faintly surprised. "You're making progress."

The bald man didn't respond. Eventually he and his associate were going to have to come clean and admit that Randi Howell's trail went stone-cold after Albuquerque. They'd been searching for nearly a week without a single break.

"I have some information that may help you," the caller said, as if he could read their minds. "There's a large horse and livestock show in northern New Mexico this coming weekend. Someone from town, Travis Stockwell, will be there. She might try to set up a meeting."

The bald man wrote down the pertinent information. "We'll keep looking around here," he said, "then get to the show in plenty of time. If she's there, we'll find her."

"Just remember what I told you before. You must silence her *before* she speaks to the police. If she makes it back to Grand Springs—"

"We understand. She won't be around long enough to return to Grand Springs."

There was a click and the caller hung up. The bald man replaced the receiver. His associate continued to toss his cigarette pack into the air. "What's the word?" he asked.

"We've got a break. Someone from Grand Springs is going to be at a livestock show a couple hundred miles north of here. We'll stake it out and watch to see if she shows up. If she does, we've got her." He pulled the nine millimeter pistol from its holster and pointed it at an imaginary target.

"Boom!" he said, and smiled. "Just like that."

Brady tied Captain in a shady spot near the barn, then walked into the tack room to collect the brushes and combs he would need to groom the gelding. It was a mindless chore at best, one he should leave to Rita or one of the kids he hired. But the past couple of days since the dance had played hell with his ability to concentrate, and he needed to do something to clear his head.

He grabbed currycombs, a dandy brush, hoof pick and a couple of cloths, then headed back to his horse. Starting at the animal's head, he worked smoothly and efficiently, seeing to Captain's gleaming coat.

Maybe he shouldn't have told Rita the truth, he thought for the thousandth time that day. Yesterday he'd spent as much time mulling over the matter. Had he made a mistake? Had he been wrong to share that kind of personal information with her? It wasn't that he didn't trust her, it was more that he wasn't sure she'd wanted to know the sordid details of his past.

Looking back, he realized the problem wasn't anything she'd said or done, it was the silence. He'd expected more of a reaction from her. Some sign that the information had meaning. But she hadn't said much of anything. She'd looked shocked then, at the first opportunity, had run off. Why?

Did she think he was a fool? If so, she had to get in line to accuse him of that. He knew he'd been a fool, and so did his family. He'd acted without thinking, because he thought he'd been in love with Alicia.

With the hindsight of time, he now understood the truth about that summer. He'd been desperate to find what his parents had. He hadn't wanted to face the fact that he might spend the rest of his life alone. So when a pretty woman had interested him, he'd been ready to jump in with both feet, ignoring the advice of people he respected, turning his back on obvious clues about her character. He'd been blind to all but what he wanted to see, and in the end, he'd paid the price.

He tried to convince himself it didn't matter what Rita thought about him. But it wasn't true. For some reason, her opinion counted. And her silence had unnerved him. What had she been thinking? Did she understand that he was sharing his past with her in the hopes—

Of what? he asked himself. Why, after years of not talking about Alicia, had he finally spilled his guts? Had he been hoping for a reaction that would give him a hint as to her feelings? He grabbed the dandy brush and squatted down by the gelding's front legs. That was it, he told himself. He'd wanted some clue as to what she thought about him. By sharing his past, by being the first to open up, he'd hoped to convince her to do the same. He'd wanted to test the waters with her.

She was such a mass of contradictions. All soft and giving with Princess and her cats. She'd responded to his kisses with enough heat to leave him burning and hard for days. Then, when he'd apologized, she'd brushed his words aside, saying she'd enjoyed the kissing as much as he had. Did she want him? Did she think about being with him?

He brushed the mud from the gelding's legs and hooves, then straightened. Did it matter what Rita wanted from him? Her past stood between them. How could he care about or trust someone so obviously on the run from something? He'd shared some of his secrets, but she hadn't responded in kind. She'd run off, and maybe that was why. She wasn't prepared to expose herself to him.

He leaned against his horse and exhaled slowly. He was in way deeper than he'd first thought. Based on his previous experience with women who dropped into his life, he might very well be headed for another heartache.

"You hiding out here?"

Brady turned toward the sharp voice and saw Tex walking toward him. "I'm grooming Captain. That's not hiding."

"You think I haven't noticed you moping around, but I have. You wanna talk about it?"

"There's nothing to say."

"Uh-huh." Tex reached into his jeans pocket and pulled out a slice of apple for the gelding. "This wouldn't have anything to do with Rita, would it?"

Brady had bent over to brush the gelding's rear legs. He was glad the ex-marine couldn't see his face and know he was lying. "No, why?"

"I thought you might be thinking about her as something more than just the groom. The way you two have been talking and such."

Brady knew Tex was hinting around, trying to find out if there was any "and such" to discuss.

"Your point is?"

"You're not involved, are you?" the cook asked.

That Brady could answer honestly. "No."

"Good." Tex sucked in a breath. "I guess it's none of my business, but I'm going to tell you, anyway. I thought you were the one she was interested in. I'll admit I was more than a little worried. She's not as coldhearted as Alicia, but she could be just as dangerous, even more. Anyway, I was all set to warn you off, but that's not necessary."

Tex had Brady's full attention now. He straightened and stared at the older man. "What are you talking about?"

"I had it wrong," the ex-marine said. "It's not you she's interested in. It's Ty."

Brady gripped the brush he held. "Ty?"

Tex nodded. "I left the dance a little early. When I came back to the bunkhouse, I saw them in his truck, and they weren't just talking." Tex's gaze narrowed. "That bother you?"

About as much as getting a leg cut off, but Brady wasn't about to admit that. Nor would he acknowledge the sudden coldness in his body or the hollow ache in his chest. "No. Should it? If their relationship starts to cause trouble around the ranch, then I'll speak to them. But until then, it's their business."

Tex studied him for a moment, then nodded. "That's what I figured, but I wanted to make sure. I thought you might have had some feelings for the girl."

"Sorry, no." He even managed a smile.

Tex continued to talk for a few minutes, but if tortured, Brady couldn't have said what the conversation was about. His mind was occupied elsewhere. Rita and Ty? Was it possible? Was it true? What about the kisses he and Rita had shared? What about their dance, when her body had melted into his? What about their conversations, the things they'd shared? Hadn't that meant anything to her?

Disappointment, hurt, anger and confusion ripped through him. He wanted to track Rita down and demand to know what the hell she was doing with the cowboy. He wanted to beat Ty until his employee's handsome face was reduced to a bloody mass. He wanted—

"Where's Rita?" he asked, trying to act casual, hoping he hadn't cut Tex off in midsentence.

"She went to town. With Ty."

"Okay, thanks."

Tex said a couple more things and strolled off. Brady finished grooming the gelding, put the animal in its stall, then headed for the house.

But there was no escape in the place that had always been his sanctuary. Rita's presence filled the old house until there was barely room left for him. He paced, alternatively listening for the sound of a truck and telling himself he didn't care if she never came back.

She wasn't his business. He had no right to her. He didn't care about her, and even if he did, what did it matter? He couldn't trust her, not with so many secrets between them. So there was an attraction—it happened all the time. It didn't mean anything. Wanting and love weren't the same thing at all. Wanting was about sex, and loving was about forever. He'd given up on forever the day Alicia had left him standing alone in the church.

So Rita was interested in Ty. Fine. Good. He wished them well. He would put any thoughts of her from his mind and get on with his life.

As he said the words, he meant them. Really. Which didn't explain why he crossed to the window every few minutes, listening for the sound of a pickup truck returning to the ranch.

* * *

"Are any of them calicos?" Felicia, the owner of a hair salon, asked. "I adore calicos."

"There are a pair of sisters," Rita told her, meeting her gaze in the mirror. Felicia worked at the next station, teasing an older woman's blue hair into a sizable coiffure. "They're very sweet. About a year old. They're not big cats, maybe ten pounds a piece."

Felicia, close to forty and with a figure that would make Dolly Parton blink, sighed. "Two little calico girls. You know what? I'll take them. You give me a call next time you're coming into town so I can have time to buy the supplies they'll need. They should have plenty of room. I've got the whole upstairs." She pointed to the ceiling of the shop. "They can play down here during the day." She smiled. "Calico cats, just like I've always wanted."

"They've already been fixed," Randi said.

Felicia laughed. "Good thing. There are a couple of tomcats running around town, acting as wild as any cowboy I've ever met."

Mary Alice, the young woman working on Randi's hair, gave her a shy smile in the mirror. "You just want the ends trimmed, right?" she asked as she combed Randi's freshly shampooed hair.

Randi nodded. "My hair is impossible, so that's about the best you can do. At least long enough so I can tie it back. I cut it short several years ago and it was a disaster."

Felicia winced. "Don't cut it, honey. Your hair is beautiful. If you knew the ladies who come in here begging for a perm that will make their hair look like yours. You can't even imagine. I can try, but the best stylist and the best products don't even come close to that natural curl. You be grateful. Besides," she added with a sly smile, "some men really like hair like yours."

Everyone joined in the laughter except for Randi, who got a sinking feeling in the pit of her stomach. "You have beautiful hair, Felicia," she said, desperately hoping to change the subject.

Felicia touched her blond waves. "I work at it, honey. Two hours every morning. But then a girl in my position has a certain reputation to uphold."

Mary Alice picked up a pair of scissors from the table in front of Randi's adjustable chair and began trimming. Conversation drifted from Felicia's reputation for beauty, to who was currently pregnant, and to a debate over whether or not there would be any fall weddings. Randi closed her eyes and let the words flow over her.

She was pleased Ty had come by the stable and offered to let her join him on his way to town. Another day on the ranch and she would have gone crazy. There was only so much tension she could survive without exploding. Not that she had anyone to blame but herself. She was torn. Part of the time she wanted to be with Brady so badly she could taste it. She thought about him, dreamed about him, went out of her way to see him and talk with him. When she wasn't dying to be with him, she was anxiously planning how to get away from the ranch. Twice she'd packed up her duffel, only to unpack it. Fortunately she didn't have a lot of things, and all the packing and unpacking didn't take much time.

Her feelings fluctuated like a pendulum, falling out of the rational zone at each end. She was acting like a crazy person, and there was nothing she could do to stop it.

The facts were very easy to understand. She really cared about Brady. There were some feelings she wasn't ready to explore, at least not yet, but for now she felt comfortable admitting to caring. But—and here was the bad news—whatever he might think about her now, as soon as he found out the truth about her past, he was going to despise her. There was nothing she could do about changing what she'd done, and there was no way to justify her actions. So they had no future. The best thing for both of them was for her to leave.

The problem was, she didn't want to go. She wanted to stay and pretend it was all going to work out. At least for now. Eventually she would have to do the right thing and move on. Maybe she would even head back home. It was almost time.

"Speaking of weddings," Felicia said, then winked at Randi. "I saw you dancing with Brady Jones last Saturday. You looked very involved with each other."

"Gee, Felicia, you saw me dancing with everyone last Saturday night," Randi said calmly, hoping her cheeks didn't blush and betray her discomfort. "If I had to pick the person most interested in me at the dance, I'd say McGregor, although he's a little old."

"I don't know." Felicia finished smoothing her client's blue-white hair, then reached for a can of hair spray. "I've known Brady all his life and I think he was showing some interest in you."

Randi was torn between wishing the other woman was right and knowing that their attraction would only cause heartache. "Brady's a gentleman," she said lightly. "He doesn't date the help."

Felicia scoffed. "Most of his help are guys, honey. Don't sell yourself short. I'd bet my last can of mousse that you've got his attention in a big way."

Maybe, Randi thought. For now.

An impulsive act had brought her to the only place she thought she might be able to call home. That same act made it impossible to stay.

Mary Alice put down her scissors. "That should do it. Nice and even." She fluffed the drying curls.

"Hey, gorgeous."

She glanced up and saw Ty standing in the entrance to the shop. All conversation ceased as every woman's attention focused on the tall, dark cowboy.

Ty didn't seem to notice. He strolled in, tipped his hat to the ladies and stopped behind Randi's chair. "You about ready?"

Randi glanced at Mary Alice. "How much do I owe you?"

The young woman blushed bright red. "F-fifteen dollars," she stammered, gazing at Ty as if she'd never seen a man before. Maybe she hadn't, at least not one that good-looking.

Randi paid the woman and left a large tip. On her way out, she promised to give Felicia a couple days' notice before bringing the calico cats to her.

"What's it like to do that?" she asked when they were on the sidewalk.

"Do what?" Ty asked, falling into step with her.

"Stop traffic, reduce intelligent women to incoherence, that sort of thing. You know, be gorgeous."

He shrugged uncomfortably. "Sometimes it's a pain in the butt."

"I notice you're not denying the statement."

He grimaced. "I've had it happen enough times to figure out that for some reason, many women find me physically appealing. When I was younger, I used that to my advantage. One day I grew up."

She wanted to ask more questions about the lessons he'd learned along the way. Were his looks the reason he had lost Denise? But she didn't ask. For one thing, it wasn't her business. For another, she understood all about wanting to keep secrets.

"I finished what I needed to do in town," he said. "You want to head back?"

"Sure."

They walked to Ty's truck, then drove back in companionable silence. But the closer they got to the ranch, the more her mood changed for the worse. Tension filled her. If only there was a simple solution for her problem.

As they turned off the main highway, Ty glanced at her. "You've fallen for him, haven't you?"

She didn't have to ask who the "him" was. "Looks that way."

"I think he's hot for you, too. Is there a reason it can't work out?"

Brady hot for her? She glanced at Ty, torn between wanting to ask him why he thought that and wanting to act unconcerned. "I, um, have a few other things going on in my life," she finally said, settling for the truth and avoiding the dangerous ground of Brady's feelings.

Ty turned into the driveway in front of the main house and stopped the truck. When she went to leave, he put a restraining hand on her forearm. "For what it's worth," he said, staring out the front window, "My advice is to give it a try. There are few things worse than regrets. They kill you slowly, eating you alive from the inside out." He stared at her. "I know."

For once she could read his emotions in his dark eyes. Raw pain flared out. She caught her breath, wishing there was something she could say or do to ease his discomfort.

"I'm sorry," she murmured.

"Don't be sorry, just don't do what I did. Love is worth it, Rita. Take a chance. If you don't, you have to live with

the memory of what could have been. Regret is forever.
Trust me, it's no way to spend a life.''

He leaned close and kissed her cheek. She closed her
eyes briefly and wished there was some hope for him. But
who was she to offer advice?

"Thanks," she said. "For everything."

"You bet, kid."

She slid out of the truck and slammed the door shut
behind her. Poor Ty. Was that her destiny, too? Was she
going to be caught up in a past she couldn't change and
couldn't forget? That's not what she wanted, but did she
get a choice?

When she walked in the house, she was surprised to
see Brady standing at the foot of the stairs. At the sight
of his familiar face, the warm brown eyes and the dimple
hovering on his left cheek, her heart picked up its cadence.
She had the strongest urge to throw herself in his arms
and beg him to make love to her. Fortunately, she managed to bite back the words.

"Hi," she said, and smiled.

He didn't smile back. It took her a couple of seconds
to register the tension in his body. "Rita." He nodded.

"What's wrong?" she asked.

"Nothing. I would like to have a moment of your time,
if that's not too much trouble."

She swallowed. Had she done something wrong? Had
he guessed her secret? "Go ahead."

He shifted his weight, then stared at a point just beyond
her right shoulder. "You're relatively new to the ranch,"
he said. "As your employer, I feel a certain responsibility
toward you that goes beyond your job performance.
Therefore I feel obligated to say something I wouldn't
normally mention."

She'd never been very good at double-speak. "I don't understand."

"Then let me be more plain. Ty is a good man and an excellent leader. But he's a loner by nature. What you do with him on your own time is your business. However, as a—" He hesitated. "As a friend, I feel obligated to warn you he's not the kind of man you can count on to be there."

She half wanted to turn around to see if there was someone else he was talking to. "None of this makes sense," she said. "Ty and I aren't involved. He gave me a ride into town, but we weren't spending time together. I went shopping and got my hair trimmed." She frowned, thinking. "I don't know what he did."

Brady brushed off her comments with a wave of his hand. "I don't want to know the details of your relationship. I just wanted you to know what you were getting into."

"There's no relationship. I'm not getting into anything."

He took a step toward her. "I saw him kiss you."

"On the cheek."

"Tex saw you kissing after the dance."

She felt as if she were fifteen and had been caught necking with a boy her parents had forbidden her to see. "Also on the cheek. He was talking about his past. If you must know, we were sympathizing with each other and the rotten luck we've had in the game of love. He's just a friend."

"I don't want to hear this, Rita. You don't have to explain."

"I know that. I *want* to." She shifted her packages to her left arm and planted her right hand on her hip. The sensible action would be to thank him for his concern and go up to her room. However, she couldn't bear to have him think she was interested in someone else. "I appreciate that you're concerned about me, but you have it all wrong."

"Why won't you admit you're seeing the guy?"

His obvious annoyance made her temper flare. "Because I'm not. We're friends. Nothing more. Yes, he's good-looking and he's been very nice to me. So what? I'm not the least bit attracted to him. If you're worried about me making a fool out of myself over a man, then you're way off base with Ty. If I was going to act on my feelings with anyone it would be with y—"

She clamped her hand over her mouth, as if the physical action would draw the sound back into her throat. It didn't. The half word hung there between them, echoing until the confusion in Brady's eyes faded and comprehension dawned.

Heat flared on Randi's cheeks. The sensation was so strong, she didn't need a mirror to tell her she was bright red. She dropped her hand to her side and raced for the stairs.

"Rita?"

She didn't respond to his call. She kept running until she reached her bedroom and slammed the door shut behind her. Once safely alone, she sank to the floor and buried her face in her hands. No matter what, she was never, ever going to be able to face Brady Jones again.

Twelve

As soon as Randi finished the last bite of her dessert, she murmured a quick excuse, pushed back her chair and fled the table. No one else seemed to notice, but Brady stared after her and wondered how long she was going to avoid him. Since the previous day, when she'd admitted she was attracted to him, not Ty, she'd been ducking in and out of buildings, turning up late for meals, then leaving early, all in an effort to stay out of his way.

Brady got up and followed her. They had to get this situation straightened out. There was no way she would be able to relax while she was worried about what she'd said—or almost said. Besides, the whole thing was his fault. If he hadn't confronted her about Ty, she wouldn't be feeling badly now. And if Tex hadn't come to him and said that he'd seen Ty and Rita together, Brady wouldn't have thought twice about her friendship with the cowboy.

As his long legs ate up the distance to the house, he grimaced. It all came back to Tex. Had the older man really thought there was something going on or had he pulled a fast one? Tex wouldn't mind twisting a tale to suit his purpose, especially if he thought it might make Brady admit his feelings for a woman. Tex was forever on his case, reminding him Alicia wasn't the only female on the planet.

When Brady opened the front door, he heard footsteps on the stairs. "Rita?" he called.

The footsteps slowed.

"Could you come down here, please?" he asked.

The steps sounded again, this time advancing instead of retreating. She came into view, feet first, then long, shapely legs, round hips, full breasts and finally her face. She wasn't smiling. Tension tugged at the corners of her mouth. Her dark blue eyes were wide with trepidation and her joined hands twisted together.

He held open the front door. "Why don't we talk out here," he said, motioning to the porch and thinking a more public place would ease her discomfort.

She perched on the far side of the top stair. He settled next to her. They both stared at the barn. Sunset wasn't for another hour or so, but the heat of the day had already started to ease.

"I'm sorry about what happened yesterday," he said. "I shouldn't have jumped to conclusions."

She cleared her throat but didn't say anything. So she wasn't going to make it easy.

"Tex went on about you and Ty being together," he continued. "Thinking about that made me a little crazy. I guess what I'm trying to say is that I like you, too."

He glanced at her. Color stained her face. She gave him a darting glance, then faced front again. "Okay."

There were several heartbeats of silence. Now he was the one clearing his throat. He was tense and felt about as awkward as a newborn foal. "I guess we're equally uncomfortable," he said.

"You're not blushing," she pointed out.

"Would that help the situation?"

"I'm not sure if it would help, but I'd feel better."

He chuckled and she joined in the laughter.

"Friends?" he asked, glancing at her.

She nodded. "Sure. Friends. I guess if you can forgive this, you can forgive anything."

"Oh, I haven't forgiven you."

Her eyes widened. "What?"

"Lady, you kept me up most of the night. I couldn't get your words out of my head."

The blush returned to her face. "I can't explain what happened. I just sort of blurted it out. If I could take it back—"

"I wouldn't let you," he said, interrupting. "You're not allowed to retract that statement. Ever."

Her mouth tilted up at the corners. "If you feel that strongly about it."

"I do."

What he didn't bother telling her was that it was more than her words that had robbed him of sleep. All night he'd imagined her in his bed, next to him, under him. He'd wanted her in ways he hadn't wanted a woman in years. He'd wanted to touch and taste her, to bring her pleasure over and over again until she was exhausted and glowing.

But he didn't share his fantasies, just as he hadn't walked down the length of hall between their rooms. Because as long as she had her secrets, as long as he wasn't sure he could trust her, he wouldn't risk it all again. He'd done that once, and he'd learned the price involved. No one had to teach him that particular lesson twice.

Princess strolled by the porch with her herd of cats in attendance. The pregnant tabby hung back, her swollen belly barely clearing the ground.

"That one's going to pop soon," he muttered. "I wonder how many kittens she'll have."

"At least a couple dozen."

He stared at Rita. She laughed and held up her hands.

"Sorry. Just kidding. I'm sure no more than five. If it makes you feel any better, I found homes for the two calicos while I was in town yesterday. Felicia, the lady who owns the hair salon, is going to take them."

"Great. We get rid of two and add five. I want to call the vet and find out how soon I can get the tabby and that new mother cat Princess found fixed. I don't want any more litters. Between them, we're going to add another ten cats at least."

"I know."

He grimaced. "You don't seem to understand the gravity of the situation. It's getting out of hand. We can't have this many cats around."

"Don't worry, Brady. Princess takes care of them, and I'll find more homes. Have a little faith. Or take a vacation. You need to get away."

"I was thinking of doing just that." At her look of surprise, he added, "There's a horse and livestock show next weekend. It's in New Mexico, and not all that far from here. I'm thinking of buying a couple of bulls."

"Good idea. You'll come back refreshed and calm."

"I'm perfectly calm."

"Not about the cats."

He shrugged. "I'll admit the cats make me crazy." He looked at her, at the dark curls tumbling down her back, at her profile, with her perfect nose and tempting mouth. "You want to come with me?" he asked without thinking.

He didn't want to call the words back—at least, not if she accepted. Rita turned to look at him. Questions filled her eyes, questions he couldn't answer. He didn't know why he'd asked her. It had been an impulse. Maybe time alone together and away from the ranch would allow them to— He didn't know what. He just wanted her company.

"Where is it going to be?" she asked.

He named the town.

She thought for a moment, then nodded slowly. "I'd like that."

He read the hesitation for what it was. "Are you afraid of your past catching up with you?"

He hadn't realized how much he wanted her to deny it until she agreed. "That's a risk," she said.

Secrets. Always secrets. "Why are you on the run?"

She faced front again and didn't answer. He told himself to let it go, it wasn't any of his business. Yet it was. If he was getting involved with her, if he was starting to feel things for her, he had a right to know.

He swore silently. What happened to the lesson he was supposed to have learned the first time he'd been burned? Hadn't Alicia taught him anything?

Apparently not. Here he was, thinking about a woman with a mysterious past. What the hell was wrong with him?

"You don't trust me," he said flatly.

She shivered. "It's not that."

"Then, what is it?"

"I can't explain."

"Why not? What is so horrible?"

She pulled her legs to her chest and dropped her head to her knees. "Nothing. I mean, I have done a few things, but it's not too awful. I'm not a murderer or anything. I just can't tell you."

"You don't want to tell me. There's a difference."

"Yes," she whispered.

"Dammit, Rita!"

She raised her head and stared at him. "Why does it matter?"

Instead of answering with words, he slid toward her. One part of his brain reminded him this was not a good way to prove he'd learned his lesson. His rational side pointed out it was still daylight and they were in plain view of anyone who happened to be looking. But the rest of him, the part of him that wanted her and needed her, didn't care. He placed his hands on her arms, turning her to him.

She could have protested, but didn't. She could have run away, or stopped him with a word. Instead, as he lowered his head, bringing his mouth to hers, she parted her lips in anticipation of his kiss.

He lost himself in her heat. The willing warmth of her mouth drew him in, and he settled against her as if coming home. Her arms wrapped around his neck while her fingers buried themselves in his hair. She shifted, straightening her legs so they could lean closer to each other. He cupped her face, holding her still as he traced the sweetness of her lips before dipping inside.

As their tongues touched, passion exploded. His body tensed in arousal. A soft cry escaped her throat, and she shuddered. He rubbed his hand against her back, moving up and down, feeling her muscles contract as she strained toward him.

He wanted to lie her on the porch and make love to her. His body cried out for that release. He could stand up and pull her into the house where they would have privacy. Would she accompany him? Would she share his bed? He thought about asking. Instead, he eased back slightly, pressing soft, tender kisses on her cheeks, her jaw, then down her neck.

"You do know it's still daylight," he murmured against her skin.

"Uh-huh." She arched her head when he nibbled on her earlobe.

"Anyone could be watching."

"Let them get their own girl."

He chuckled. "I like that attitude."

Randi gazed at the man who held her so tenderly, the man whose kisses made her forget herself both physically and emotionally.

"I want to make love to you," he said.

His brown eyes flared with a passion that thrilled her. No one had ever wanted her the way Brady did. She leaned forward and pressed her mouth to the base of his throat. He sucked in a breath. Her lips clung to him as she tasted the forbidden essence that was his alone.

Every part of her vibrated with need. Between her legs, her feminine place dampened in readiness. She wanted to be with him, under him, accepting him into her, joining with him in an age-old dance of love. While the fantasy was nice, reality made it impossible.

He reached behind her head and untied the ribbon holding her hair in place. As the curls sprang free, he captured a few in his hands. "Why do I sense you just refused my invitation?" he asked.

She dropped her gaze to her lap. "Because I did."

"Why?"

A simple question. Gathering strength from deep inside, Randi forced herself to meet his gaze. "Because you're a decent guy and you deserve better. I like you, Brady Jones. I respect you and admire you. If circumstances were different…" She sighed. "But they're not. I can't make you any promises while I'm living a lie. We both know making love can be the biggest promise of all."

His face tightened with frustration. "What lie?" he asked, his tone sharp with annoyance. "What are you talking about? What's so important that it forced you to run away?"

She took his hand in hers. "All my life my father or

my brother have rescued me from harm. If there was any kind of problem, I ran home and Daddy fixed it. When Daddy was gone, Noah took over. That's not how it's going to be anymore. I refuse to be that little girl. This time I need to fix my problems myself.''

When he would have spoken, she pressed her fingers to his mouth. "No, don't say anything. The truth is, if I let you make this all better, I haven't learned a thing. Worse, I won't be anyone you'd be interested in. Face it, Brady, you're a strong man with a sense of right and wrong. I guess the word I'm looking for is *moral*. Do you want someone who isn't like that? Do you really want to get involved with someone who isn't your equal?''

He stared at her. In a way she felt as exposed and bare as if they *had* just made love. Emotionally, she'd never been this naked before. She'd confessed her darkest secrets, laying out her vulnerabilities for him to accept or reject.

"And then what?'' he asked. "Say I leave you alone to sort out whatever this is, when you've fixed it, will you stay?''

Would she stay? She shuddered, knowing that he'd asked the one question she would have sold her soul not to hear. The one question she couldn't answer.

"I don't know.'' She squeezed her eyes shut. "I'm not saying that to be cruel, but because it's true. I don't know anything.'' She clutched his hand and forced herself to look at him.

"You are the best man I've ever met,'' she said earnestly, trying to convince him with her words and her heart. "You are so very special, and I believe I could care about you in ways that terrify me. But there are things you don't know, things I can't tell you right now. And when I can tell you, you may not look at me like you are now, with affection and desire. You may despise me and want me to go. But if you've already asked me to stay and I've said yes, you'll be too much of a gentleman to retract your invitation. I would never put you in that position, so I won't agree to stay. Later, when you know everything, ask me again.''

"Tell me. What is this deep dark secret you're keeping between us?"

"I can't," Randi said. "Not now."

Brady surged to his feet. "I hope you enjoy playing with other people's lives," he said, his voice thick with anger. "It's a nice speech. You get to sound noble, all the while you're refusing to risk any part of yourself by trusting me."

She'd meant every word she'd said. His rejection of her honesty fueled her own temper. "Don't talk to me about being noble. You're the expert. You play at being perfect and showing the rest of us up, when in reality, you're terrified to get involved. You surround yourself with strays because you always get to be the rescuer and the one in charge. You never have to be vulnerable to anyone. You never have to reveal yourself. You show up and you're the good guy, a real knight in shining armor. The trick is, you hold yourself back. While you're spending all that time rescuing the world, you don't have much left to get really involved. You don't risk your heart. If I leave, I reaffirm your view of the world. If I stay, you'll always be the guy who rescued me. Either way, you come out looking great. I don't believe you let yourself care enough to allow any of this to hurt you, so no matter what, you're going to win."

Brady glared at her. "If that's what you think, you don't know me at all." He turned on his heel and stalked off.

She stared after him, watching him disappear into the barn. He was wrong, she did know him. She understood him, his good points and his flaws, and neither mattered. She'd still fallen in love with him.

Two days later, Brady still couldn't forget what Rita had said. No matter how many times he told himself they weren't true, her words continued to haunt him.

So what if he surrounded himself with strays? That was hardly a crime. In some circles, giving people a second chance was a *good* thing. He was only continuing a tradition his father had taught him.

But that wasn't her complaint, a voice in his head whispered. It was that he used the act of rescuing to hold himself emotionally distant.

That wasn't true, he thought as he leaned back in his chair. He stared at the walls of his office. He wasn't emotionally distant from anyone. He had friends. Tex, some of the cowboys, a few men in town, kids he'd grown up with.

"I'm not a snob," he said aloud. He wasn't holding himself out as a moral example to the rest of the world. She'd made him sound like some East Coast prig.

But no matter how many times he tried to discredit her words, a voice inside whispered she had spoken the truth. At least some of it had been dead-on. He *did* occasionally demand a certain emotional distance in his relationships. He *wasn't* always as open with people as he could be. Even her accusation that he feared getting too involved was true. He swore. Where did that leave him? Was he a jerk? Too horribly flawed to inspire affection in others?

She'd held up a mirror, and he'd been forced to take a good look at himself. Was it her fault he didn't like what he saw?

Brady slammed his hands on his desk. He was willing to admit she might have had a point. About a few things. Maybe he could be more emotionally accessible. He remembered several times when he'd acted as mentor to young cowboys he'd hired. At least he'd thought of them as young when he hadn't been more than a year or two older. By becoming their mentor, he made sure they weren't ever close friends.

"Dammit, Rita," he muttered, and knew his annoyance was with himself. What was he supposed to say to her? Why would he assume she even wanted to talk to him?

Then he remembered the rest of her words—when she'd said he was the best man she'd ever met. That she could care about him. He'd ignored all that because she'd pricked his pride. Because she hadn't said she would stay.

What right did he have to dictate her life? Until he knew her secrets, he couldn't make judgments about her decisions. He wanted it to be different. He wanted her to be free to be with him so they could explore what each of them felt.

He rose to his feet and headed for the front of the barn. Rita was where he'd expected her to be, grooming the horses. Despite their words and his ignoring her for two days, she continued to do a great job.

She looked up when she saw him approaching. His chest tightened as he took in the dark shadows under her eyes and the faint slump in her shoulders. She watched him, but didn't speak.

He paused in front of her. "I'm sorry," he said.

She shook her head. "No, I am. I crossed the line. No matter what else, I still work for you. I shouldn't have—"

"Yeah, you should have. A couple of cuffs to my ears wouldn't have been wrong, either."

She smiled at that. "I didn't know you liked the rough stuff."

He grinned, then sobered quickly. "Rita, I'm confused by all of this. You, how I feel, your secrets, and most of all, what's going to happen."

"Me, too," she whispered. "I never meant..." Her voice trailed off.

"Tell me about it." He absently patted the gelding. "Maybe we should start over. Try being friends for a while longer."

"I'd like that."

"Good. You still want to go to the livestock show with me?"

She nodded.

"We leave in the morning." He started to turn away. She touched his arm and he paused.

"Thanks, Brady. For everything."

Affection shone in her eyes. Affection and something that made his heart beat a little faster. He returned to his office, walking with the confidence of a man whose world has been restored.

When had he handed Rita that kind of power? And what was going to happen to him when she finally had to leave?

Thirteen

The crowd surged around them like water in a river. Randi tried to remain calm.

"You okay?" Brady asked.

She nodded. "I think I've been isolated too long. I've forgotten what it's like to be out among people."

"I get that feeling myself." Brady slipped his hand through hers. "I won't let them steal you away," he promised.

"Thank you." As his fingers entwined with hers and he tugged her close to his side, she was able to smile. With Brady around, she might actually start to relax.

The livestock and horse show drew buyers and exhibitors from all the western states. In addition to the animals, booths displayed everything necessary for a well-run ranch as well as plenty of items for the home. There were western clothing manufacturers and leather companies, people selling odd jars of spices for making everything from beef to rattler more tasty. Various universities sold sweatshirts, while conservationists preached about the value of recycling.

Then there was the food. Beef on a stick, churros, ice cream, hot dogs, pretzels, Mexican entrées, and more exotic fare including venison and snake.

Randi wanted to get lost in the crowd, but for now, she was too nervous. Part of what she'd told Brady was true—she *did* find it uncomfortable to be around so many people. When she'd first gone on the road, she'd stayed away from busy places because it was safer...or so she'd thought. But over the past couple of months, she found she liked a more solitary existence. On the ranch, there were plenty of people around if she wanted to have a conversation, but Brady and the cowboys were different from a crowd full of strangers.

The other reason she was nervous was that she kept expecting to see someone she knew. The idea was ridiculous. What were the odds of a friend from Grand Springs showing up here? Still, she couldn't shake the feeling of impending disaster. If not a friend, what about those men with guns?

She clutched Brady's hand tighter, enjoying both the physical connection and the feeling of safety. With him around, she knew she was going to be all right, no matter what happened.

But as the mass of people increased, she found her nerves drawn tight. Telling herself she was unlikely to be recognized didn't help. While the crowd protected her, it also made it impossible for her to stare at every face. She shouldn't have come with him.

Yet she hadn't had a choice. In the past week, she'd had a sense of time running out. Soon, she would have to move on to another temporary place, or back to Grand Springs. Either way, she was going to have to leave Brady behind. And she didn't want to. Not yet. Not ever.

"You hungry?" Brady asked.

Randi touched her free hand to her stomach and tried to sense anything but faint fear. "I could probably eat."

"Rattler tacos?"

She glanced up at his smiling face and wondered how she would survive without him. She grinned in return. "Sure, but I want to watch you eat one first."

"I've had rattler before."

"Let me guess, it tastes like chicken."

He raised his eyebrows. "How'd you know?"

"Everything weird tastes like chicken. At least that's what people try to convince us unsuspecting types. I've yet to taste anything other than chicken that really tastes like chicken. I'm convinced it's all a ploy so that we have to eat the nasty thing you guys just tried."

He bent down and kissed the tip of her nose. "That made no sense at all."

"My point is that I think I want beef on a stick."

"Sounds good to me." He headed them in that general direction.

"When does the bull auction start?" she asked.

"Tomorrow. I want to buy at least two, maybe three. I've been tracking bloodlines on the computer. I'm going for the leaner stock. If I could come up with a low-fat filet mignon, I'd be rich."

Two young boys darted toward them. Brady released her hand and stepped aside. When the kids had zoomed past, he moved close again and put his arm around her shoulder.

"Any horses?" she asked.

"I think we have enough for now. What do you think?"

"I agree. They get worked steadily, but they all have a couple of days off to rest."

"Agreed. So I'll concentrate on the bulls."

She leaned against him, absorbing his heat. The sun was bright, the afternoon warm. Smells from the livestock blended with barbecue and meat smokers. Conversation and laughter surrounded them in a pleasing cacophony.

She would remember this, she told herself. Whatever happened, they would have had this time together.

"Brady? Brady Jones?"

Brady stopped when he heard his name and turned toward the sound. Instinctively, Randi stepped free of his embrace, prepared for flight. But she didn't recognize the man approaching.

"Travis!" Brady grinned and held out his hand. "What are you doing here? Why aren't you heading for a rodeo?"

Travis shrugged. He was good-looking, in a rugged sort of way, with sun-streaked brown hair and brown eyes. He winked at Randi. "Ma'am," he said, pulling off his cowboy hat.

Brady turned to her and touched her arm. "Rita, this is an old friend of mine, Travis Stockwell. We were on the rodeo circuit together. Travis, this is Rita Howard. She works for me."

"Hi," Randi managed to say past the tightness in her throat.

"Nice to meet you." Travis plopped his hat back on his head. "I got hitched," he said.

Brady raised his eyebrows. "You're married? What happened? You get struck by lightning?"

"Just about. I got hurt pretty bad at the last one and took some time off to heal." Travis smiled proudly. "While I was getting better, I met a woman. Her name is Peggy and we're married."

Up until that point, Randi had only been half listening to the conversation. While the two men chatted, she'd been scanning the crowd, trying to find the source of a sudden prickling at the back of her neck.

Peggy? She blinked. She knew a Peggy. Peggy Saxon who worked in City Hall back in Grand Springs. Her chest tightened.

Stop it! she ordered herself. They couldn't be the same

woman. There were thousands, probably millions, of Peggys in the country.

Brady slapped Travis on the back. "I don't believe it. Congratulations."

"Thanks." Travis grinned. "I sure didn't expect something like this to happen to me." He glanced at Randi and winked. "I was one of those guys who liked the rodeo circuit and thought I'd be single till I died. But Peggy and the babies have changed me."

Babies? Her heart froze. Randi felt as if she couldn't move. Peggy Saxon had been pregnant...very pregnant the last time she, Randi, had seen her.

"Babies?" Brady asked.

"It's a long story."

Randi forced herself to speak. "Where did you find this wonderful new family?"

"My hometown, Grand Springs. It's a nice town in Colorado." He looked at Brady. "You'd like it there. Now, stay right here. I want to introduce you to my bride. If I can find her."

She had to get out of there, Randi ordered herself. She had to! Now! But it was impossible to think, impossible to move or breathe. Oh, Lord, what if Travis recognized her? What if Peggy walked up and saw her? Who else could it be but Peggy Saxon from Grand Springs? The same woman who spoke to Randi every time she'd gone to visit Hal.

Images began to spin in front of her eyes. Run! a voice in her head screamed. She decided she'd better listen.

She touched Brady's arm. "I don't want to be rude," she said through stiff lips, "but I'm not feeling well. I need to find a rest room."

His eyes darkened with concern. "You look a little pale. Go on. I'll catch up with you by that tent," he said, pointing to a green-and-white striped tent at the entrance to the food area. "Are you going to be all right?"

She nodded, then turned away. She walked toward the rest rooms, then ducked behind a vendor stall selling earrings. From here she could see Brady talking to his friend. A couple of minutes later a woman joined them. Randi bit back a groan. It was Peggy. The three of them chatted for a bit, then they split up. Travis and Peggy headed in one direction while Brady made his way to the tent.

Randi closed her eyes and tried to think. She'd never seen Travis Stockwell before, so it was unlikely he knew her, either. Even if her running away from her wedding had made the paper, it would have been in the back pages, and wasn't something likely to interest a rodeo cowboy.

Peggy was another matter. She would know Randi on sight and would be very intrigued at the events surrounding the wedding. But she hadn't acted as if she'd seen anything unusual. Surely if Peggy had spotted her, she would have said something and Brady would have reacted. Yet nothing about his body language indicated anything unusual.

After taking a couple of deep breaths to clear her head, she walked to the tent. Brady waited for her. He frowned when he saw her. "You still look pale. What's wrong?"

"Nothing," she said, touching his arm. "I think it's just a reaction to the crowd. Really. I'm fine. What happened to your friend?"

"Travis and I are going to have a drink later. But only if you're sure you're going to be all right. I don't want to leave you alone otherwise."

She searched his brown eyes, reading the caring there. Caring and affection, and nothing else. Peggy hadn't seen her. Randi's secret was safe.

As she stared at Brady, she was filled with a strong

desire to make love to him. She'd done nothing to deserve this wonderful man in her life. If things had been different, she would have wanted to be with him forever. But they weren't. Sharing his bed would imply a commitment she wasn't ready to make. No, she was ready to make it, but he wouldn't want it, once he knew about her. Maybe she should just come clean, she thought. And she would, she promised herself, suddenly realizing it was time to stop running from him, as well. As soon as they got back to the ranch, she would tell the truth about her past. She just wanted these few days together, first. Sort of a last chance for them.

She wrapped her arms around his waist and held him tightly. "I'm going to be just fine," she said. "Enjoy your drink with Travis. But first, I'm suddenly starving."

"Rattler taco?"

She laughed. "You're an amazing man, Brady Jones."

He tugged on her braid, forcing her to look up at him. "That's what all the girls say."

"Guess what?" she teased. "In this case, all the girls are right."

The smoky bar reminded Brady of countless others he'd frequented when he'd been on the rodeo circuit. Places with scarred floors and cold beer on draft. Whenever he found himself in bars like this, or meeting with friends from the "good old days," he waited for a yearning to go back to his youth. When a good ride meant the difference between money in his pocket or not, and the women had been pretty, starry-eyed and willing. Not that he'd been all that eager to take them up on what they offered, he thought with a grin.

But no matter how many old friends he met up with, or how many bars he stopped in, the yearning for those

days never came. They'd been lots of fun, a hell of a way
to see the country and grow up, but that time was over.
Now his life was where it should be. If he occasionally
fought the demon of loneliness, he'd learned to win that
battle. One day he would find someone to love. Maybe
he already had.

He searched the crowd, then spotted Travis already
seated at a back booth. The cowboy motioned him over,
then pointed to the frosty glass waiting.

"I thought you'd be thirsty," Travis said, and took a
drink of his beer.

Brady grinned his thanks. "You always were a thoughtful fellow." He took a sip of his beer and leaned back in
the seat. "Tell me what's been happening with you."

Travis talked about his injury and the temporary job
he'd had driving a cab. When he explained how he'd met
his wife, Brady sat up straight.

"You delivered her babies?"

"Yup." Travis beamed with obvious pride. "Twins. It
was easy."

"You go to hell for lying same as stealing, Travis. It
might have been a lot of things, but I'll bet it wasn't
easy."

Travis's humor faded. "That moment changed my life
forever. I've got Peggy, and the babies. Me!" He pointed
at his chest. "Who would have thought it?"

"Not anyone who knew you."

"Yeah, well, I'm not the only one with surprises. What
about you? What are you doing hiding Grand Springs'
famous runaway bride?"

Brady had raised the glass to his lips. Now he set it
down, untasted. His stomach constricted tightly as a cold
foreboding swept through his body. "You know Rita?"

Travis leaned forward and shook his head. "Not me.

Peggy. And I know her name's not Rita, Brady. You don't have to pretend with me.'' He lowered his voice. ''Peggy used to work at City Hall in town. She saw Randi visiting from time to time. Her fiancé's a member of the city council. His mother was the mayor, but now that she's dead, he's been acting in her place.''

Brady couldn't believe what he was hearing. Rita wasn't Rita? She was from Grand Springs and she was a runaway bride?

''Whose fiancé is acting as mayor? Rita's, ah, Randi's?''

Travis nodded. ''Sure. Peggy says Hal is a jerk, so I don't blame the girl for running out. She left him standing at the altar in front of God and everyone. Just disappeared. It was the day we had that big blackout. I remember. Peggy had the twins right then. What a mess.''

He continued to talk about the thirty-six-hour blackout, but Brady wasn't listening. He was barely breathing. Dear God, it couldn't be true. Not his Rita. She couldn't have betrayed him that way.

But she had. She'd run out on her wedding, leaving some poor bastard to be humiliated. Just like Alicia had done to him.

''What's wrong?'' Travis asked. ''You don't look right.'' His mouth dropped open. ''You didn't know, did you.''

Brady slowly shook his head. ''I knew she was in trouble, but I didn't know what kind. She's been working at the ranch for over a month.''

''I'm sorry.''

''It's not your fault,'' Brady said grimly. It was Rita's—make that Randi's—fault.

He felt like a fool, or worse. When he thought about how he'd told her everything about Alicia. Jeez, she must have had a hell of a laugh at his expense, thinking she and his ex-fiancée had a lot in common. Did she get a kick out of destroying men's lives? Was his next?

Fury rose in him, fueled by embarrassment and the loss of expectation. He'd had plans for them. Dreams. He'd thought when things settled down for her maybe they could—

He rose to his feet and tossed a couple of bills on the table. "Sorry, Travis, but I'm not good company right now. Can we do this another time?"

Travis nodded grimly. "I didn't mean to mess things up," he said.

"You didn't. You made things more clear for me. Thanks, buddy. I'll be in touch."

Brady left the bar and drove back to the hotel. Thoughts tumbled through his mind. He tried to figure out what he was going to say to her, but he couldn't focus on anything but his rage. No wonder she hadn't wanted to tell him her secrets. There was no way for her to come off as anything but a lying, cheating bitch.

He crossed the parking lot and walked quickly to the four-story building. Their rooms were on the first floor, in the back. Rooms, he thought with a grimace. He'd given her a room of her own. Ever the gentleman. Ever the sucker.

When he reached her door, he raised his hand, made a fist and pounded loud enough to wake the dead. There would be no excuses this time. No matter what, he was going to get the truth out of her.

The loud pounding brought Randi off the bed like a shot. She dropped the book she'd been trying to read. "Who is it?" she called.

"Brady."

"Oh, you're back earlier than I thought."

She rushed to the door and unlocked it. Before she could turn the handle, Brady did it for her and pushed into the room.

"How was your drink?" she asked.

He slammed the door shut and stared at her. Instinctively, she backed up a step. The anger on his face made her nervous, but what really got her heart rate up was the pain and disappointment lurking in his eyes.

"Brady?"

"That's me. Brady Jones. It's been my name my whole life. But you can't say that, can you? *Randi.*"

She pressed a hand to her throat. Dear God. "You know." It wasn't a question.

He nodded, then walked to the window. "Yup. Me and Travis had quite a little chat. Turns out you're something of a celebrity back home. That would be Grand Springs, right? Seems the whole town is talking about the runaway bride. After all, it's not every day a young woman runs off and leaves her intended standing at the altar. But it does happen. I've had some personal experience with that. But then, you're already familiar with my story, aren't you."

She retreated to the bed and sank down onto the mattress. "I'm sorry," she whispered, covering her face with her hands. "I was always afraid it would come to this. I never meant—" She paused, not sure what to say. It was so hard to think. Her entire body ached with pain and cold. She'd seen the look in his eyes. He loathed her. The worst of it was, she couldn't blame him.

"You never meant to what? Lie? But you did. You lied from the moment you showed up at the ranch. Leaving out facts about your past is the same as lying. Did you have a good laugh when I told you about Alicia? Did you think I was a fool, just like your fiancé? What was his name?''

"Hal," she said automatically. "And no, I never thought you were a fool. Alicia is the stupid one. She should never have left you."

"How kind of you. I wonder if Hal has someone offering him comfort right now."

"He doesn't need comforting," she said. "He never really cared about me."

"That's a convenient way to justify your actions. Unfortunately, there's no way to prove it's true. His actions suggest otherwise. After all, he was willing to marry you."

His tone indicated Brady wasn't sure why any man would want to have anything to do with her. She fought tears, knowing that giving into them would only leave her more vulnerable. She had to pull herself together, to find a way to convince Brady that she—

She bit her lower lip. Convince him of what? Her crime was there for everyone to see. She'd done exactly what he accused her of—she'd run out on her wedding, exactly the way Alicia had run out on him. At least she hadn't been running off to be with another man, but she doubted he would consider that much in her favor.

"It's not what you think," she said dully, and straightened. He still stood at the large window. The sliding glass door was open to let in the afternoon breeze. He placed one hand against the screen.

"Why don't you tell me what it was like?" he asked.

The silky smoothness of his voice didn't deceive her. She knew he was still furious, yet maybe he was willing to listen. Did that mean he would give her a chance, or was he going to try to trip her up? Either way, she had to risk it. She couldn't let him walk away hating her.

"Everything I told you about my past is true," she began. "My mother is very interested in the Grand Springs social scene. I've always been a disappointment to her."

"Gee, I know what that feels like," he said.

She winced, then continued. "I never had serious boy-friends. There were a couple of guys in high school, but nothing I wanted to pursue, and a relationship or two at college. When I came home after graduation, my mother started inviting Hal over. I knew what she was doing, and I even knew why. Hal has a political future. If her daughter was related to the mayor, or the wife of a future state legislator, my mother's social position would be guaranteed."

"None of which excuses what you did."

"I know." She pulled one leg to her chest and rested her forehead against her knee, then closed her eyes. It was easier to confess her weakness in the dark. "I just sort of went along for the ride. I suppose I kept thinking something would happen to stop things, or that I would find out I really liked Hal. But it didn't stop. We were dating, then engaged, and one day I woke up and we were getting married."

She sucked in a breath. "I never loved him. I didn't know what love was." Until now. Until a strong, noble man had entered her life. But she didn't say that. Brady wouldn't believe her. Besides, it was a cheap trick and she was determined not to resort to that.

"There I was, alone in the bride's room, listening to the music. As I stared at myself in the mirror, I knew I couldn't do it."

"So you ran."

"Yes. Yes, I ran and it was wrong. I was young and stupid and I've grown up." She raised her head and stared at his stiff back. "I made a mistake. A huge one. I was afraid that if I tried to get out of it my mother would convince me to go through with the ceremony."

He turned to face her. The fury remained, as did the contempt. Her heart sank.

"That's it?" he asked.

She nodded. "I've changed, Brady. I've learned my lesson. I'm not that young woman anymore. I'm responsible. Look at the job I'm doing for you. You don't have any complaints, you've said so yourself. Please try to understand."

His gaze narrowed. "If you're so grown up, why didn't you go back?"

It was the one question she couldn't answer. What was there to say? The truth?

"Forget it," she said. "There's no point."

"Yes, there is. Rita—" He grimaced. "Randi, why didn't you go back?"

"I couldn't." She lowered her foot to the floor and stood up. "All right, if you want to know the reason, I'll tell you. You're not going to believe me, but it's the truth. I swear it is." She drew in a breath and squared her shoulders.

"When I was running out of the Squaw Creek Lodge, where we were holding the ceremony, I heard some people talking in the corridor. I didn't want them to see me so I ducked into one of the meeting rooms. I was on my way back out when I realized I wasn't alone. There were a couple of men in the room. When they realized I'd interrupted them, they pulled guns on me. They were going to kill me. I haven't gone back because I don't know what to do about those men. I don't know who they are or what they want with me."

She felt the tears forming. As Brady's expression hardened into disbelief, the first one trickled onto her cheek. She brushed it away impatiently.

"I knew it," she said softly. "You don't believe me. Do you really think I would make up something that stupid?"

Before he could answer, someone knocked on the door. "Who is it?" he called impatiently.

"Room service."

He glanced at her. She shook her head. "I didn't order anything."

"You have the wrong room," Brady said loudly.

"It's this room. An order for Randi Howell, in 104. That's you, right miss?"

Randi felt as if she were in a plane and they'd suddenly descended ten thousand feet. Her ears absorbed the sentences, but as if through a thick cloud of pressure. The world reduced itself to two words. *Randi Howell.*

"How do they know my name?" she asked, too stunned to do anything but stare at Brady.

His eyebrows drew together. "They shouldn't. The room is registered under my name. They shouldn't even know about Rita Howard."

There was another knock. "Miss, your order."

"Come on!"

Brady grabbed her hand and pulled her toward the sliding glass door. Before she'd caught her breath, he'd tugged her outside and onto the small patio. A low, thigh-high block wall separated the small space from the parking lot.

"Climb," he ordered. Seconds later, the front door slammed open.

Randi swung one leg over the wall and glanced back. Her eyes widened. "They're not the same men," she said, unable to believe what she saw. But the guns they were holding looked identical...and just as deadly.

"Get down!" Brady roared, pulling her off the wall and onto the ground as a loud popping explosion filled the air.

Fourteen

When Randi hit the ground, Brady threw himself on top of her. The echo of the gunshot faded.

"You get her?" one of the men asked.

"I don't think so."

Brady glanced around frantically. They were in a two-foot-wide planter that was more parched earth than plants. From there, asphalt stretched out to form the parking lot.

"Let's go," he whispered urgently.

Randi nodded, scrambling up as soon as he did. Brady grabbed her hand and pulled her to the left, following the line of the patios instead of making a break for the parked cars. He thought they would have more cover here. Besides, his truck was in this direction. If they could make it past two more rooms, they could duck behind the large rented moving van up ahead, then plan a strategy for getting to safety.

Behind them, the men spilled out onto the small patio. "Where the hell are they? Check those cars out there. They can't have gotten— There!"

Brady didn't waste time glancing back. "Duck!" he yelled, and jerked Randi hard to the right.

She hunched down and half stumbled after him. The rental truck was only a few feet away. Pulling her along with him, he sprinted for cover. Something slammed into the ground at their feet. Randi screamed.

"Aim higher. Don't worry about hitting the guy. We can figure out how to deal with that later."

Brady sucked in a breath and dove for the truck. As they rounded the corner, he felt the *whiz* of a bullet by his left ear.

"Too close," he said as they paused for a second. "We've got to get out of here."

Randi nodded. Color drained from her face. He gave her hand a reassuring squeeze. "Don't worry. We're going to head for my truck. It's over there." He pointed to the black pickup.

She nodded. "Okay," she managed to say between pants.

"Keep low. We'll weave between cars. Don't waste time looking back."

He took off at a run. Randi kept up, her footsteps blending with his. He could hear the men behind them, the rapid pounding on the asphalt. Then there were other sounds. People screaming there were men with guns in the parking lot. Shouts to call the police.

He looked up and saw his truck. Digging in his pocket, he found his keys. When they reached the vehicle, he unlocked the driver's door, then pushed Randi in first.

"Keep down," he commanded.

She scrambled in. He followed on her heels, closing the door while inserting the key. The engine roared to life. He hit the gas and aimed for the exit. To his right he saw the two men staring at him. There was no sign of the handguns, although both of them looked furious enough to kill with their bare hands.

The hotel parking lot dumped out onto the feeder road for the interstate. Brady was already going sixty-five when the truck burst onto the smooth blacktop. Five miles later two smaller highways intersected their path. He took the second, heading west for about twenty miles, then going north for another forty. By nightfall, the hotel was nearly two hundred miles behind them.

"I don't expect anything to happen," Brady said into the phone. "But tell the men to be on the lookout. Those two goons got a good look at my license plate, and I'm sure they can trace it. Lying low is the logical next step, so while I'm sure someone will be watching the ranch, I doubt they'll come in with guns blazing."

He listened while Tex reminded him that twenty years with the marines had left him an expert at combat.

"Consider yourself in charge of defending the place," Brady said, only half kidding.

"How's Rita?" Tex asked.

Brady glanced at the woman sitting on the edge of the double bed closest to the bathroom. "Okay for now. We'll spend the night here and make some plans in the morning. I'll keep you informed."

"Tell her—" The older man paused, then sighed. "Tell her to take care of herself. You take care of her, too."

"I will."

"And yourself. You're no good to anyone if you get your ass shot off."

Despite his tension, Brady smiled. "I'll remember that. I'll be in touch." He hung up the phone.

Silence filled the room. He returned his attention to Rita—Randi. She sat stiffly, her back straight, her eyes fixed on the motel room's only door. She'd folded her arms, clutching them tightly to her chest, but he didn't know if that was to ward off danger or to hold herself together. She hadn't said much of anything since they'd made their escape. He'd been too busy trying to get them to safety to bother with questions, but now he had several.

Yet he wasn't sure he could ask them. Rita—damn, Randi. When was he going to get used to her new name?

Randi was close to collapse. He would have to tread carefully.

Giving himself time to come up with the right thing to say, he glanced around at the motel room. It was barely big enough to hold the two double beds and a narrow dresser. The fixtures in the bathroom were about thirty years old. The entire place needed paint, but it was clean and in a tiny town he'd never heard of. Chances are the bad guys hadn't heard of it, either.

He moved to her bed and sat down next to her. Her only acknowledgment of his presence was her words. "They'll find us."

"Not likely. I'm not sure where we are, so how could they know?"

"They found me once."

True enough, and he wasn't sure how. "I took the license plates off the truck the last time we stopped for gas. We've been off the interstate for a hundred and sixty of the last two hundred miles. You're safe."

"For now."

She turned to him, and he saw the fear darkening her blue eyes. Her skin was ash-colored, her mouth trembling. He reached up and tucked a strand of curls behind her ears.

"If it makes you feel any better, I believe you now," he said.

A faint smile tugged at the corner of her lips. "Good." She shook her head. "I'm sorry, Brady. Sorry for lying to you, sorry for getting you involved in all this. I'd apologize for coming to the ranch in the first place, but I can't. Whatever happens, I'm not sorry I met you."

He wanted to read something special into her words, but he knew she was still functioning on raw nerves. She didn't know what she was saying.

"No apologies necessary," he told her.

"I think one or two are probably required." She relaxed and let her hands slip down to her lap. "I know what you're going to ask me. You want to know why they're after me. I don't know." Her eyes filled with tears. "I swear, I don't know. They saw me and pulled guns and I have no idea why."

"Hush," he murmured, and pulled her close.

She came willingly to him, leaning her head against his shoulder and wrapping her arms around his waist. With one hand, he stroked her hair, with the other he traced a line down her spine.

"Start at the beginning," he said. "Tell me exactly what happened that day."

She gave a strangled sob. Hot tears dampened his shirt. He rocked her gently, whispering soft words of concern.

She clung to him for several minutes. He felt her heartbeat slow slightly and her cries quieted. While he thought about what had happened and wondered how the hell they were going to get out of this mess, a part of him acknowledged the pleasure of holding her. Supple feminine curves flowed against the hard planes of his body. Heat enveloped him, stirring blood and need. He forced away any thoughts of desire, knowing that wasn't what she needed from him, but it was too late. The ache in his groin grew, as did his arousal.

"I was in the bride's room," she said, her voice muffled as she pressed her face into the crook of his neck. "My mother had rented the local ski lodge for the wedding. I was pacing because I was scared. They were about to start the wedding march and I'd just figured out I didn't want to marry Hal."

She raised her head and looked at him. Tears filled her eyes and streaked her cheeks. "I swear I didn't plan to run, Brady. I didn't know what else to do."

''I know, honey. It's all right. Don't worry about that. Just tell me what happened.''

She sniffed. ''I took off my shoes because I didn't want to make any noise. I grabbed my purse and I ran to the exit. Only I didn't get all the way out the first time. As I told you before, I heard voices so I ducked into one of the meeting rooms. While I was waiting for the people in the hall to pass, I realized I wasn't alone. There were men in there with me.''

''They saw you?''

She shook her head. ''Not then. I was shocked and embarrassed. I thought they were doctors. My brother's a doctor, and I was terrified they might know me. I didn't want to be seen running away.'' She wiped her face with the back of her hand, then leaned her head against his shoulder.

''Then what?''

''Then I tried to leave. The room was sort of L-shaped, with a screen. I could hear them talking. They were drinking coffee, I think. Yes, they were, because I remember the smell of it and the sound of clinking, like the coffeepot had hit the edge of a mug. Anyway, I opened the door and was prepared to sneak out, only I stepped on a carpet tack and screamed. Not loud, but loud enough.''

He felt her tense. ''Okay. Relax. Don't worry about it.'' He kissed the top of her head. ''I'm here and you're fine. So you cried out. Then what?''

''They came after me. I turned around, and this guy had a gun pointed directly at me. I remember thinking I could see that he was going to kill me. It was in his eyes. I couldn't do anything but stand there and wait to die. Then the lights went out.''

''What?''

She nodded. ''I know it sounds insane, but that's what happened. The lights went out. Like a power outage or something. I ran. When I got outside, a guy in a semi picked me up and took me to Phoenix.''

"That's it?"

"Yes. I know it sounds crazy. I've been over it a bunch of times. If they'd been selling drugs or doing anything illegal, I would have understood. But they weren't. They were just talking.''

Men who "just talked" didn't go around killing people, Brady thought grimly. There was something else going on. "Did you ever contact the police?"

She sighed. He felt warm breath fan his throat and tried to ignore the erotic sensation. "No. At first I was too scared to think clearly. After a while, I doubted what I'd seen. But I was nervous enough not to risk going back.''

"If they weren't doing anything obviously illegal then they must be worried about what you overheard. What did they say?"

"I can't remember. Something about Jo."

"One of the guys there?"

"No, a woman. They said 'she.'" She paused. "Jo will take care of the old broad. That's her—'' She stiffened. "Her, what? Something like…oh, damn. Wait! Specialty. That's it. I thought they were talking about a woman taking a nursing job. Obviously I was wrong.''

Those two sentences didn't seem enough to kill over. "That's it?" he asked.

"I didn't hear anything else."

"You said the men who shot at us today weren't the same ones you saw then, right?"

"Right. I remember a guy with a beard. At least he wasn't there today. I'm not sure about the other one. I can't remember what he looked like.''

"If different men are chasing you, someone is serious about this."

"I know. What am I going to do?"

He cupped her shoulders and eased her back a little. "*You* don't have to worry about this tonight because *we're* staying right here. In the morning we'll come up with a plan together. I'm going to help you through this, Randi."

His gaze locked with hers. Some of the fear faded from her eyes. "Always the gentleman," she said. "Do you still despise me?"

"I never did."

Randi studied Brady's familiar face. While she was worried someone was trying to kill her, if she had to be in danger, there was no one else she would rather have on her side. Brady was a rock. Smart, steady, solid. When he said they would get through this together, she found it easy to believe in him.

"Don't think about it anymore tonight," he said, pressing lightly on her head until she rested it on his shoulder. "You're safe here. Are you hungry?"

"No." She couldn't imagine eating. She couldn't imagine sleeping, either, but that was a problem for later.

She shifted. Brady stiffened, as if uncomfortable. Awareness dawned. She'd wrapped her arms around him as if she was an octopus and she showed no signs of letting go. He must think she was trying to make a pass at him. Her face flooded with heat.

"I'm sorry," she said, moving back quickly and clearing her throat. "I forgot myself. I didn't mean to—" Words failed her, and she was reduced to making a meaningless gesture with her hands, trying to indicate she hadn't meant to throw herself at him.

"It's okay."

She dropped her gaze to the worn blue pattern of flowers on the bedspread. "No, it's not, but it's kind of you to pretend that it is."

"Randi?"

"Yes." She continued to stare at the spread, wishing there were a casual way to apologize. It was nerves, or the tension of the moment. How could she have been so unaware? Why hadn't she noticed the way she was pressing against his body, flattening her breasts against his broad chest. He must think she was a wanton of some kind or—

"Randi, look at me."

Slowly, she raised her gaze to his. Instead of looking disgusted, he had a faintly amused expression. Lurking laughter made his eyes crinkle.

"I liked it," he said.

She shivered. "You're just being kind."

"No, I'm being honest. I wasn't pulling back, I was trying to keep you from knowing how much I liked it."

She blinked. At first his statement didn't make sense. How could she know how much he liked being close to her? Then she got it. "Oh." She blinked again and made her gaze stay firmly on his face. If she didn't concentrate, it would automatically drop lower, so she could visually confirm what he'd already admitted. "Oh."

"Yeah, 'oh,'" he said wryly. "Don't worry. I'm not about to make a pass at you."

Well, why the hell not?

For a moment she didn't breathe. Dear Lord, had she said that or merely thought it? By the look on Brady's face, the calm, if slightly self-deprecating expression, she'd only thought the words.

"Stop looking at me like that," he said.

"Like what?"

"As if you want me to do something we're both going to regret."

Hunger descended with the speed and power of a tornado springing unexpectedly from the heavens. Need and desire caught her up in a vortex she could neither explain nor control. She could only hang on and endure.

She told herself it was just the danger and the circumstances. She would be attracted to anyone who happened to be with her right now. Yet, even as she thought the words, she knew they weren't true. She'd admired Brady from the first moment she'd met him. Time had turned admiration into liking and then into love. Love, true heartdeep affection. That was the reason she wanted to be with him. Even if they couldn't ever share a life together, she wanted to know what it was like to join fully with the man of her dreams.

"You have no idea what you're asking," he said, inching away from her.

"Don't I?"

"Randi, I can't play this game."

Tears filled her eyes. "If you knew how much it wasn't a game. If you knew how much I care about you."

"Don't cry." He slid forward, gathering her against him. "Please. I'll do anything."

"Really?"

He chuckled. "Brat."

She brushed the tears away and looked at him. "I'm not a child. I'm a woman."

His expression tightened as if he were in pain. "Believe me, I know."

"Good. Just so we understand each other."

Their gazes locked. It was like their very first hug, on the stairs in front of his house. She wasn't sure who moved forward first. She didn't know if she reached for him, or if he gathered her closer still. She only knew that suddenly he was holding on to her as if he would never let her go. His mouth dropped to hers as she surged toward him.

The kiss was like coming home. Familiar, welcoming,

yet lighting a fire that burned so hot, every cell in her
body glowed. She wrapped her arms around his neck and
buried her fingers in his thick, short hair. His head tilted.
She parted her lips, anticipating the moment he would
brand her with his tongue.

But he didn't plunge inside right away. Instead, he circled her mouth, carefully seducing every inch of sensitive
skin, dipping in slightly, then withdrawing in a dance designed to leave her trembling uncontrollably.

He supported her back with one hand and moved the
other down her side to her hip, then lower to the curve of
her derriere. He squeezed gently, making her arch against
him. Long fingers kneaded sensitive flesh. Through the
layers of her jeans and panties, she felt his touch, the
sweep of his thumb across the back of her thigh.

His tongue dipped into her mouth, distracting her momentarily. He tasted of masculine temptation and incited
the kind of passion that made lovers willing to risk everything.

The kiss was endless as he discovered her, then withdrew, inviting her to explore him, to learn the secrets of
what made him moan or stiffen or retaliate with a moist,
sweeping caress.

His hand moved up to her belly, then higher toward her
breasts. She stilled, anticipating those strong, skilled fingers touching sensitive skin.

He did not disappoint. First he stroked the underside of
her curve, then he circled, as if encroaching on sacred
ground. Her breasts swelled with his touch, her nipples
tightened into twin points of aching sensation. When his
thumb brushed against one peak, she whimpered.

He broke the kiss. "If you knew how long I've wanted
to do that."

"If you knew how long I've been waiting for you to
do that."

His gaze met hers. Bright fire danced in his dilated pupils. "You could have said something."

She laughed softly, the sound turning into a moan as he rotated the tight bud between his thumb and forefinger. "Right. The horses are healthy and exercised. By the way, would you please touch my breasts?"

"I would have said yes."

He lowered her back onto the mattress, then leaned over her. Instead of reaching for the hem of her T-shirt, he bent down and pressed his mouth to her covered breast. Through the layers of T-shirt and bra, she felt his hot breath, then the tantalizing pressure of his teeth.

Fire burned a path from her nipple to the swelling heat between her thighs. Her toes curled, her hips arched and she had to bite back a cry.

She clutched his head, holding him in place, urging him to do more and then more. He fulfilled her request, shifting his attention from one breast to the other, teasing them both until she couldn't catch her breath. Then he placed a hand on her belly and began to move it lower.

Long fingers reached for and found the tiny point of her pleasure. He rubbed the spot, pressing so she could feel him through the thick fabric of her jeans. Her head tossed from side to side. It wasn't enough.

As if reading her mind, he undid the button, then lowered the zipper. Still nibbling on her taut breasts, he inched under her panties, searching for, then finding, the waiting heat between her legs.

When bare fingers met damp desire, she jumped and clutched at the bedspread. He raised his head and looked at her. "You want me," he said, his voice thick with equal parts passion and wonder.

"What did you think?" she asked.

He smiled. "I'm not sure." He rubbed her, then dipped lower. "Wet," he murmured. "I never thought—"

She didn't get to hear what he thought. He leaned down and kissed her, plunging inside her mouth at the same time he began rubbing over and around the place designed for her pleasure.

He moved back and forth, exploring slick flesh, learning her secrets, all the while kissing her into mindlessness. She writhed on the bed, finally pushing her jeans and panties off her hips and kicking them to the floor.

"Better," he murmured against her mouth. "Spread your legs."

She did as he requested. He moved his hand lower and traced the entrance to her feminine place. A shudder rippled through her.

"Yeah," he said softly. "Want it. Want me."

"I do, Brady. I want you."

Now it was his turn to shudder. He brought his fingers back to the pleasure place and stroked it. Her breath caught and she found herself moving faster and higher. In some distant part of her brain she was aware that he was watching her, watching the feelings drifting across her face, noting the flush she could feel spreading up her neck to her cheeks.

Then she didn't care. Everything in the universe focused on that tiny place on her body, on the steady cadence of his fingers, on the way he urged her higher, to give it all to him. Her blood raced faster, her head tilted back. She clutched at the bedspread and dug her heels into the mattress.

"Now," he whispered, and in that last moment of coherence, she wondered how he knew.

She disappeared for a heartbeat, suspended in another dimension. His fingers continued to circle around, then the feeling exploded and she returned to a symphony of pleasure-filled release. She called his name in a hoarse voice she didn't recognize and clutched at him when he finally held her close.

He stroked her hair until her breathing and her heart rate returned to normal, then smiled when she asked why he had all his clothes on.

"You're still dressed," he said, fingering the hem of her T-shirt.

"Only part of me."

"That's true. The interesting bits have been exposed." He raised his eyebrows suggestively.

"Are you going to cooperate, or do I have to force you?" she asked, wondering when in the past lovemaking had ever been this much fun. Those two young men in college had both been so intense and she'd been so nervous, there hadn't been room for laughter.

"Force me?" He seemed to consider that option. "I think I like it."

"I thought you might."

She pushed at his shoulder until he stretched out on his back. While his hands stroked her legs and bare buttocks, she busied herself with his shirt. When it was unbuttoned, she pushed the edges back and exposed the well-muscled expanse of his chest.

Years of working outdoors had left him tanned and fit. Various scars showed that his life had occasionally flirted with danger. She traced the random patterns of the scars first with her fingers, and then with her tongue.

He tasted salty, yet faintly sweet. The combined flavor was addictive, and she suspected she could feast on it for the rest of her life and never have enough.

A narrow ribbon of dark hair began at his waist. She touched the exposed inch or so, then reached for his belt buckle. As she worked the metal clasp, he half sat up and pulled off his shirt. Before she reached for his button fly, he tugged at her T-shirt.

"I want to see you," he said.

She pulled the shirt off in one movement, then sat back on her knees while he unfastened her bra. The undergarment fell away, exposing her breasts. He stared reverently, then cupped them. Fire flickered in her belly, banked ashes flaring once again to life.

This time he was the one to quickly unfasten, then kick off his jeans and briefs. He urged her to stretch out on top of him, long legs tangling, bodies rubbing, heat flaring at all points of contact.

When he rolled her onto her back and knelt between her thighs, she smiled at him. Whatever their past or their future, they would have this moment of belonging. This was where they were destined to be—joined as one.

He entered her slowly, easing into her tight, waiting heat. The cords in his neck bulged and his muscles tensed in both pleasure and restraint. He cupped her breasts, teasing her nipples until she found herself beginning the journey again.

He withdrew only to enter her, deeper, harder, faster, pushing her higher. She surged with him, gripping his hips to express what her lack of breath wouldn't let her say. How much she wanted him. How much she needed him.

And when his body paused on the brink of completion and she found herself soaring with him, she managed to find her voice long enough to whisper how very much she loved him.

Fifteen

Brady lay in the warm bed and listened to the sounds from the shower. A quick glance toward the window showed him it was barely dawn. After last night he supposed he should be tired. He and Randi hadn't slept much. They'd turned to each other again and again, making love, exploring, touching, holding as if this was to be the best time they would ever have.

Or the last.

He pulled her pillow over and slid it behind his back as he sat up. Was it their last time? He didn't have an answer. In the magical moments of her release, she'd whispered that she loved him. He wanted to believe she told the truth. He wanted to say the words himself. But he wasn't sure. Was it him, or the danger of the moment? Had they joined together because their hearts and bodies could no longer deny intense feelings, or were they reacting?

She'd turned the shower off. He stared expectantly at the door, picturing her all damp and pink, wondering how he could want her again so quickly. He wouldn't have thought his body capable of so much passion. Certainly Alicia had never inspired him to such a level of performance.

She hadn't inspired him to love, either. Looking back, comparing what he'd felt for his former fiancée to what he felt for Randi, he realized if this was love, the emotion was new to his life. With Alicia, he'd obsessed. With

Randi, he wanted to belong. With Alicia, he'd experienced passion and pleasure, even some fun times. With Randi, he felt the connection down to his soul, as if by being together, they'd bonded on a cellular level. Whatever happened in the future, he would not be able to move on easily. She would always be a part of him.

The bathroom door opened and she stepped out into the bedroom. As he'd pictured, she was damp and glowing. She'd wrapped her long hair in a towel piled on her head. Another barely covered her torso. Long pale legs tempted him, and it was all he could do not to throw back the sheets and invite her into bed. But the worry in her eyes made him ignore the throbbing desire between his thighs.

"Good morning," he said, holding out a hand.

She crossed to him and sank next to him on the bed, then squeezed his fingers. "You're smiling," she said. "Good. I was terrified you would have second thoughts."

"About being with you?"

She nodded.

"Never." He touched her face, then her shoulder. "Never," he repeated. "And you?"

She closed her eyes. "Last night was the most perfect experience of my life." She looked at him and blushed. "I hope you don't think I usually behave like that."

He leaned forward and kissed the tip of her nose. "Only with me, lover. Only with me."

She pulled the towel from her hair and began to finger-comb the wet, tangled strands. "The shower isn't very modern, but it works and there seems to be plenty of hot water."

He waited, knowing she didn't really want to talk about the shower.

She sucked in a breath. "Okay, the thing is, I've been thinking. It's time for me to go back to Grand Springs."

As the knife that was her words sliced through him, he

hung on to the fact she'd said Grand Springs instead of "home."

"Today?" he asked, hoping she couldn't see how she'd hurt him. He knew what would happen when she returned to that place. She had a life waiting there, a family. It might not be home right now, but it had been and it soon would be again. He would lose her forever. But hadn't he always known that was a possibility?

She nodded. "The sooner I go back, the better. I want to talk to the police and tell them what happened. They might not believe me, but I have to try. Plus, I've got a bunch of family stuff to deal with. My brother, my mom." She wrinkled her nose. "Hal."

He dropped his hands to the bed and curled his fingers toward his palms. By squeezing his fists very tight, he forced himself to ignore the sensation of his life's blood seeping away. How was he supposed to survive without her? Why hadn't he known losing her would hurt this much?

She gave him a faint smile. "You'll probably be glad to get rid of me."

"I wouldn't say that."

"Really?" She bit her lower lip. "I'm glad, because I was wondering..." Her voice trailed off.

He watched her, memorizing the features of her face, wondering when she'd become so important to him. Being with her was all he wanted. He didn't care about who she was or what she'd done in the past. Yet he couldn't tell her that. Not now. Not when she was ready to return to the place she belonged.

"Would you come with me?" she asked in a rush. "I know it's tacky to ask you, and I wouldn't except I'm a complete wimp and I don't want to be alone. It would just be for a couple of days. You know, getting to Grand

Springs, then seeing me through everything. It would be boring and awful and I have no right to expect—"

"Yes," he said, cutting her off. "I'll come with you and stay as long as you want."

Her bright smile eased a little of his pain. "Are you sure?"

"I'm happy to do it, Randi." He would do anything to stay with her a few more days. Anything to put off the inevitable.

She flung herself at him and he hauled her close. As his mouth descended to hers and she parted her lips to accept him, he wondered how many more times they would be together. In the silence of the morning he heard a faint ticking sound, as if the best part of his life was slowly slipping away.

"You've caused more than a little trouble, young lady."

Randi squirmed on her seat and resisted the urge to duck her head. She felt as if she'd been brought before the principal for speaking out of turn in class. But the middle-aged man in front of her wasn't the principal. Frank Sanderson was Grand Springs' chief of police. He stared at her with piercing brown eyes.

Brady dropped his arm around her shoulders and gave her a reassuring squeeze. "Randi had no way of knowing about the mayor's murder when she left town three-and-a-half months ago."

The chief of police's expression didn't soften. "You could have called."

He sounded like a scorned suitor. If she hadn't been so nervous, she would have laughed. "I didn't think anyone would listen."

"I'm listening now." Sanderson leaned forward in his

chair. "Start at the beginning. Don't leave anything out. It's important."

Randi sucked in a deep breath and recounted the events of her almost-wedding day. When she mentioned the two men talking, Sanderson started taking notes.

"What did they say? Be as exact as you can."

She closed her eyes and tried to put herself back in the meeting room. She'd been anxious to get away before anyone realized she was missing. She inhaled, trying to recall the smell of coffee.

There was the clink of the carafe against a mug, muffled voices, then, "Jo will take care of the old broad. That's her specialty."

"Dammit!"

Randi jumped and opened her eyes. Sanderson grimaced. "Jo's a woman. So that confirms it. Olivia Stuart's killer *was* a woman."

Randi glanced at Brady. He shrugged, obviously as confused as she was. Sanderson caught the look. "It's a long story. All we know for certain was that someone gave Olivia a shot of a drug whose effects simulated a heart attack. We had suspected that the killer might be a woman. Son of a bitch." He picked up the phone and punched in a few numbers, then quickly recounted what he'd just been told. When he hung up, he took Randi through the rest of the events of that day.

A half hour later Sanderson was satisfied that he'd gotten everything he needed. "You're free to go," he said.

Randi stared at him. "What about the men after me?"

"I'll arrange to leak this information to the media. Once word is out that you've told us everything you know, you should be safe. But you might want to stay out of sight for a couple of days. Your family will take you in?"

She nodded, a little stunned by the course of events. "My mother and my brother."

"Either would be fine. I wouldn't worry, Ms. Howell."

They said their goodbyes and were shown out of his office.

Once in the hallway, Randi stared at Brady. "I'm in shock."

"Me, too. I figured what you'd heard had to be important, but I never thought it was part of a murder investigation."

"Do you think he's right? About the men not having a reason to kill me now?"

Brady took her hand in his. "Yeah, I do. You'll need to be careful for a few days, but I think the danger is past. You've told the police what you know. You're of no use to them now."

She shook her head, trying to shake off the surreal feeling. "I could have solved all my problems by talking to them that first day," she murmured. Then she realized that wasn't completely true. She wouldn't have learned all she did on the road. She wouldn't have met Brady. She wouldn't have fallen in love. Even knowing about the terror she would have to live through, she wouldn't go back and change anything.

"Now what?" Brady asked.

"I have to figure out what's next." Several uniformed officers walked past them and entered the chief's office.

"Let's get out of here," Brady said. "We can talk in the truck."

He kept her hand in his as he led the way through the maze of desks and cubicles. Before they reached the door, someone called her name.

"Miss Howell?"

She turned and saw a tall, lean blond man staring at

her. His intense gaze was unnerving. She instinctively inched closer to Brady. "Yes?"

"I'm sorry to bother you, but one of the officers mentioned you'd shown up at last." The man gave her a wry smile. "I was hoping you'd recognize me."

She frowned. "I'm sorry, I don't know you."

"I wasn't invited to your wedding?"

Randi blushed. She had a bad feeling she was going to be talking about the wedding for the next several weeks. Despite the passage of time, it seemed still to be fresh in everyone's mind.

"I'm not sure, Mr...?"

"Smith," he said. "Martin Smith. I've lost my memory. A few people suggested I might have been a wedding guest. Hal doesn't know me and I was hoping you would."

Randi shook her head. "Sorry, no."

"Thanks." He turned away. "Oh, welcome home."

Home. This wasn't home anymore, she thought as she and Brady stepped out of the police station and onto the street. She glanced around at buildings she'd seen countless times, and not one of them made her feel welcome.

She could picture individual streets in her mind, she knew the exact locations of stores and restaurants. Grand Springs was familiar to her. And completely foreign. There was nothing for her here. Not anymore. The town hadn't changed—she had.

"How are you holding up?" Brady asked.

"I've been better." When he stepped close, she allowed herself to lean on him. "My head is spinning. The mayor was murdered, and I had one of the puzzle pieces in my memory. That poor guy—Martin Smith. I was shot at, but until he can remember his past, he's lost his whole life. I can't believe everything that's happened while I've been gone."

"Sort of like missing a month of your favorite soap opera."

She laughed. "Exactly."

"What now?" he asked.

She wanted to find somewhere private and make love with him. She wanted to be in his arms, joining with him the way they had so many times last night. She wanted to tell him again that she loved him and hear him say the words back. She wanted to know that she always had a place at his side.

But he hadn't responded to her heartfelt confession, nor had he talked about the future. She had a feeling that if she hadn't asked him to spend some time with her, he would have dropped her off and returned to the ranch without once looking back.

She'd worried that he would despise her once he knew the truth. Well, he knew it now and he didn't despise her. Unfortunately, he didn't seem to love her, either.

She squared her shoulders. Before she worried about her future—or lack of future—with Brady, she had a few pieces of her past to deal with.

"You're going to hate this," she said. "But I have to talk to Hal."

His dark eyes never wavered from her face. "No problem. If I don't like the look of him, am I allowed to beat him up?"

She laughed. "Yes. Please."

Both men stared at the phone. On the fourth ring, the bald man picked it up. "Yes?"

"Randi Howell spoke to the police today. She told them everything. Perhaps you and your associate didn't understand that this was important?"

The bald man swallowed as his back began to prickle.

The cold sweat crept down his neck and around to his chest. "We nearly had her."

"Nearly isn't good enough. We're very disappointed."

Panic flared low in his belly. Dear God, they were going to die.

"Please take the next flight back," the voice continued. "We'll be waiting." The line went dead.

He slowly replaced the receiver.

"What?" the other man asked.

"As you'd expect. They want us to take the next flight back."

"Forget that. I'm not going to let them put a bullet in my head just because the girl got away. A friend of mine has an import company in Singapore. He wants me to come work for him. Same sort of job, less trouble if you screw up. Interested?"

The bald man thought about the alternative. There was no way to fix this problem. If the woman had spoken to the police, killing her now would accomplish nothing. He could return as he'd been ordered, or he could make a run for it.

"I'm interested," he said, picking up his small overnight case and wondering how many movies they showed on a plane trip to the Far East.

Brady stirred his black coffee, then put the spoon down when he realized the action betrayed his nervousness. He told himself to relax, that the outcome of Randi's meeting wasn't his business. Yet he couldn't convince himself of the lie. Of course it was his business. Randi was meeting with Hal Stuart, her former fiancé.

He leaned back in his seat. There was no point in straining to hear the conversation. While he'd settled in at the back of the diner so he could watch what was going on, Randi and Hal had a booth up toward the front. Even if they spoke loudly, the conversation from other patrons and the clink of dishes muffled their words. He was at right angles to them. All the better to torture himself with, he thought grimly. He could see them looking at each other, catch every nuance of body language, and watch them either reconcile or break up.

Maybe he should have waited in the car. It would have been easier not to watch. Yet it was like staring at the scene of an accident. Even though he didn't want to look, he didn't have the strength to turn away.

At least Hal Stuart wasn't the paragon he'd feared. While the man was fairly tall and in some circles might be considered handsome, Brady found his perfect blond hair, tanned skin and practiced smile too polished for his taste. Hal reminded him of an old-fashioned snake oil salesman. What had Randi ever seen in him?

Watching her now, it was obvious she was battling with the same questions. When they'd first met, Hal had been cautiously friendly. He'd held out his arms for a hug. Randi had offered a tight smile instead. Brady had breathed a sigh of relief. The last thing he wanted was to watch the woman he loved give herself to another man.

Hal leaned forward in the booth and spoke earnestly. His manicured hands cut through the air, emphasizing what he said. Randi nodded a couple of times, then shrugged. She still wore the same clothes she'd had on yesterday. Worn jeans and a faded T-shirt. He'd offered to take her by her mother's house so she could collect some clothes, but she'd refused. Her long hair hung loose around her shoulders. She looked like a pagan goddess.

Suddenly Randi and Hal stood up. They shook hands across the table. Hal left without giving Brady a single glance while Randi headed toward the rear booth.

"Hey, good-looking," she said, sliding in across from

him. "What'd you think about Hal? I noticed you didn't beat him up."

"If he'd tried anything, I would have. So, what happened?"

She smiled. "We talked about the wedding. I told him my concerns. He agreed that under the circumstances it would be best not to resume the relationship. End of story." She wrinkled her nose. "I can't believe everything is turning out so well. Why on earth did I resist coming home? The police believed me, Hal accepted the broken engagement without a whimper. All that's left is talking to my brother."

"And your mother."

"Oh, Brady, why'd you have to go and spoil my mood? I was doing fine until you mentioned her."

"You know you have to talk to her."

"Yeah, but she's going to get on my case about Hal, and she's going to want me to move back with her."

Thoughts of either made his blood run cold. In his head he knew Randi wasn't coming back to the ranch with him, but in his heart, that was all he wanted. Nothing was easy.

Randi took a deep breath and let it out slowly. "I guess it's time for me to finish growing up. If you can handle a little more trauma, I'd like you to come meet my brother, Noah. He got married while I was gone. One Howell runs out on her wedding, another gets married with almost no warning at all. What a family. You gotta love us, right?"

He smiled. "Absolutely."

"I see you finally decided to use some of the money they pay you," Randi said, linking arms with her brother and glancing around at his beautifully furnished living room. "I thought you were going to be trapped in that bachelor apartment forever."

Amanda, Noah's pretty wife, laughed. "I think we would have been perfectly happy there, but Noah insisted. As soon as we were married." She met her husband's gaze and they shared a moment of silent communication.

"I'm glad Noah and Amanda have this house," Melissa Howell said from her seat by the fireplace. "It's important for someone in Noah's position to have the right kind of residence."

Brady leaned against the window frame and watched Randi roll her eyes at her mother's comment. They'd finished dinner a few minutes before and had moved into the living room for more conversation.

He'd caught Randi's worried gaze a few times during the meal. She was obviously concerned because he was so quiet. When they were alone, he would reassure her that he was fine. This was her family, and she needed time to catch up with them. While he appreciated her bringing him along, he couldn't help feeling like the odd man out.

Melissa Howell smoothed her silk skirt and turned toward him. "Mr. Jones, you own a ranch? Is that what my daughter told me?"

"No, you don't, Mother," Randi said, leaving her brother's side and approaching Brady. "You're not going to grill him. Brady Jones hired me when I had no references and no way to prove myself. He's been a terrific friend to me, and I refuse to let you ask about his family name and net worth."

Melissa, all sleek hair, perfect makeup and expensive jewelry, made a slight expression of distaste. "Randi, I'm sure I don't know what you're talking about."

"I'm sure I do."

"Brady doesn't look like he needs defending," Noah said.

"Your brother's right," Brady told her as she reached him and took his hand. "I can take care of myself."

Randi's blue eyes crinkled at the corners as she smiled. "Maybe, but you've been taking care of me for the past couple of months, so it's only fair that I return the favor." She leaned forward and whispered, "Besides, my mother can be very determined. After all, she talked me into marrying Hal."

"What are you telling him?" Melissa asked. "Stories, I'm sure. My youngest has always had the most peculiar notions."

Amanda broke in with a statement about ordering a bedspread. There were so many fabric swatches to choose from. Momentarily distracted, Melissa gave her daughter-in-law her full attention as they discussed the merits of the various offerings.

Randi gave her brother a thumbs-up signal. "He made a great choice," she murmured to Brady, leading him to a settee as far from her mother as possible. "Amanda handles Mom like a pro. With her around, the situation might be bearable."

Brady settled next to her on the small sofa. In the soft light her skin was luminous. She wore her hair pulled back from her face and twisted into order at the base of her neck. Protesting the entire time, she'd finally agreed to visit her mother's house long enough to collect some clothes. He'd stopped at a local store for some supplies of his own. In their run from the bad guys, they'd been forced to leave their luggage behind.

"Why are you staring at me?" she asked. "You hate this, don't you? You hate being here." She sighed. "I don't blame you. Family stuff. I'm sure your parents are a blast, but the Howells are not known for rollicking good times. I'm really sorry this is so boring. We'll leave soon, okay?"

He touched her cheek, noting how mysterious her eyes appeared. He'd never seen her in makeup. The cosmetics emphasized her strong features, adding to her allure.

"Actually, I was thinking about how great you look."

"Really?" She shook her head. "You're just saying that. I know I'm not hideous, but I'm not really—"

He touched a finger to her lips. "Yes, you are really pretty. I've always thought so."

Her gaze locked with his. The moment reduced itself to the two of them, and he wished they were alone together so he could show her how much he loved her.

"Hey, brat," Noah said, coming up to join them. "I'm glad you're back."

"Me, too." Randi angled toward her brother but didn't let go of Brady's hand. "I'm sorry about running off."

Noah's gaze narrowed. "Time away seems to have done you some good. You've grown up."

"Finally."

Noah turned to Brady. "I don't think any of us have thanked you for taking care of Randi. She's annoying as hell, but we would have missed her if we'd lost her permanently."

"My pleasure," Brady said.

Conversation continued. Brady found himself resisting being drawn into the family's inner circle. Not because he didn't enjoy their company, but because he knew he didn't belong here. While he liked visiting the city, his life was back on the ranch. Money wasn't the issue—his family's fortune easily fit into the category of what Melissa Howell would consider acceptable. The problem went deeper than logistics or finance.

He watched Randi laugh at something her brother said. She fit in here, in this room, with these people. He had no right to ask her to leave.

She deserved better than he could offer. She'd been

right about him, about the way he picked up strays in his life so he could emotionally hold back. He'd grown up in the bright reflection of his parents' love and had wanted the same for himself. Instead, he'd found Alicia.

Then Randi had entered his world and shown him light and love he could claim as his own. But it was too late for him. For them. She belonged here—he had nothing to offer her but a life of isolation in a desolate corner of the country.

Doing the right thing was going to hurt like hell, but do it he would. Because that was all he knew. He would love her, and loving her, he would let her go.

Later, when they'd made their excuses and left, Randi leaned against him as he unlocked the truck. "Do you have any thoughts on where you want to stay tonight?"

"Gee, I was sort of hoping we'd stay at your mom's."

She slapped his arm. "Don't even joke about it. At her place, there's no way we could share a bed. Even if I got up the courage to sneak down the hall to join you, I wouldn't be able to relax. It would—" She broke off and bit her lower lip. "You didn't want us to sleep together, did you. That was the whole point. Oh, I should have seen—"

This time she stopped talking because his mouth covered hers. He kissed her deeply, tasting all of her, holding her tight, rubbing his arousal against her belly until she couldn't doubt what he was thinking.

"A hotel would be nice," he said, raising his head slightly and raining kisses on her face.

"Hmm, or we could just do it in your truck."

"Not too comfortable."

"How would you know?"

"I researched the concept thoroughly in high school."

"Maybe you need more practice."

He glanced at her and smiled. "I would prefer a real

bed where I can make love to you slowly. I want to take your clothes off one by one, touching and tasting every part of you, bringing you close again and again until you're powerless and panting.''

Her mouth opened, then closed. She blinked. Finally she said, ''Okay, that works. A hotel it is.''

Sixteen

Randi stood at the bedroom window and stared at the beautiful grounds that, in a few short months, would soon be covered with snow. The irony of her situation would have been amusing if it hadn't hurt so much. Just three months ago she'd been in the Squaw Creek Lodge ready to be married. Last night she'd stayed in one of the rental condos. Once again being in Squaw Creek Lodge was about to turn her life upside down. Only this time she wasn't the one leaving. This time she was the one being left.

She sipped coffee from a mug and listened to the silence. He hadn't said a word...yet. He didn't have to. She knew him now, understood his moods, his thoughts. She'd seen the world through his eyes. There were disadvantages to loving a noble man.

They'd spent last night as they'd spent the night before. Making love. He'd taken her in his arms and together they'd experienced perfect joy. If he'd been anyone else, she would have assumed that was enough. But he wasn't anyone else, he was Brady Jones. The kind of man who always did the right thing.

"Why do you leave me?" she asked, her voice soft and shaking slightly.

She heard muffled footsteps on the thick carpet, then felt the pressure of his hands on her shoulders. They both wore the luxurious robes provided by the lodge. Even through the thick, expensive terry cloth, his touch warmed her. Once he was gone she would never be warm again.

"I don't want to," he said.

"Then, don't. Stay with me, or ask me to stay with you."

There! She'd said it. Put it out on the table, so to speak.

"It's not that simple."

"Why not?"

He tried to turn her toward him, but she resisted. Her eyes burned and she didn't want him to watch her cry. Not when they might be seeing each other for the last time. She stared out at the view, trying not to notice when the trees blurred and blended with the sloping grounds.

"I was wrong to judge you," he said. "You made the best of a bad situation and I admire that. You're a hell of a woman, Randi. Tough, gutsy, beautiful."

She sniffed. He was lying about the beautiful part, but right now she didn't care. She set her coffee mug on the window sill. "Then, don't go."

Or ask me to come back with you. But she'd already offered a broad hint that she would accompany him if requested. She wasn't going to beat that point to death. If he wanted her there, he would tell her. Obviously he didn't.

"You have a life here," he continued. "Family, friends. Grand Springs is a pretty nice little place."

"Paradise," she murmured, blinking away the rest of the tears.

He sighed, then moved closer and rested his chin on her head. "You were right about me. I've been holding back part of myself from my friends. I've been making it easier for myself because I didn't want to get burned. Selfishly, I'm glad, because now I can let you go. We both know it's for the best. I can't give you what you have here."

She spun toward him. "Brady, no. Don't do this. Don't leave me." She clutched his hands in hers. "I love you."

His dark gaze met hers. He smiled faintly. "I love you, too, Randi. I have for a while. Even before I knew anything about you. I think you're very special. We'll always have this time we've spent together."

She hadn't thought it could hurt more, but it did. Hearing that he loved her and that he was still willing to let her go was the worst trick of all. "Just like Bogie and Bergman," she said. "We'll always have these few weeks. Great. Forgive me for wanting to have more—a real relationship." She pulled away and turned back to the window.

She stared unseeingly at the scenery. "Someday you're going to have to risk it, Brady. You're going to have to find the courage to put yourself on the line and ask for what you want. You can't hide behind doing the right thing forever."

"That's not what I'm doing." He sounded annoyed. Good. At least anger was an emotional response. Better he hated her than just tolerated her.

"You're still afraid to risk it all," she said. "The words are meaningless without the actions to back them up. I love you. I'm willing to leave everything behind to be with you. I'm willing to put my heart and soul out there to see if we can keep the magic alive for the rest of our lives. What are you willing to risk?"

He didn't answer. She heard movement in the room, but didn't dare turn around. A few minutes later, he said, "This isn't how I wanted it to end."

Her whole body ached. "That's the difference between us," she said. "I never wanted it to end at all."

Pain tightened her throat. She wondered if she was going to die from the hurt, or if she would simply learn to live with the awful emptiness inside. Did it matter? Without him did anything matter?

"Goodbye, Randi," he said. The front door opened, then closed, and he was gone.

She continued to stand at the window until her legs trembled from fatigue. Then she dressed and collected her few possessions. At the front desk the clerk told her the bill had already been paid. Brady had been a gentleman right up to the last. She thanked the clerk and arranged for a cab to take her to her mother's. She needed to retreat and lick her wounds for a few days. Eventually she would have to figure out what to do with her life, but not now.

During the cab ride home, she leaned back in the bench seat and closed her eyes. Now what? She had to make something of her life. She would have to figure out how she wanted to spend her days, then get a job and make plans. Whether she liked it or not, there was the future to think of.

But instead of considering travel or moving to another city, all she could see was the ranch. Princess and her cats, Tex, the cowboys. And Brady. Always Brady. What would he say when he got home? What would he tell everyone? Would they forget her right away or would they remember? Would Brady hire another groom, and would that new person erase all traces of a woman named Rita Howard? Would Ty ever try to return to Denise? Would the cats find homes? Would—

"You all right, miss?" the cab driver asked.

Randi glanced at him. "I'm fine."

His obvious discomfort made her realize she was crying. She brushed her fingers against her cheek and was surprised to feel moisture.

Would Brady suffer as she suffered, or would he simply go on with his life?

When the cab dropped her off, Randi stood staring at

her mother's large home. She didn't want to go inside. There was nothing for her there, nothing but a lifestyle she'd never understood. Should she start out fresh and immediately look for an apartment? Should she—

"Noah will know," she said, and started toward the front door. She would call him and he could tell her what—

She paused in midstride and shook her head. No. There would be no phone calls to Noah or anyone else. This was her life and therefore her decision. She was supposed to have grown up. If she wanted advice, fine, but she was through abdicating responsibility. She would give herself a couple of days to get over the worst of the pain, then she would make a plan. Despite losing Brady, she would have to go on. Somehow, she would find—if not happiness—then at least contentment. Eventually.

Three days later Randi hadn't come to any decisions. At least none that made sense. She'd considered becoming a nun or maybe going to teach English in a foreign country. Both options required a commitment she wasn't ready to make.

The only fact of which she was certain was that she still loved Brady. She was going to love him for the rest of her life. Three sleepless nights had convinced her of that fact. She'd also become aware of a faint but persistent voice mumbling some rather unpleasant truths. Brady wasn't the only one guilty of not trying hard. He'd been noble and had not asked her to leave her life behind. But *she'd* let him walk away without insisting they deserved more.

Given his past, how Alicia had treated him, it was understandable that he was reluctant to pressure a woman to be with him. So perhaps he'd been waiting for her to demand his attention. Unfortunately, she was also suffering from a case of the "maybe I'm not enough" syndrome and had been more than willing to act as the martyr.

After driving her small two-seater aimlessly around Grand Springs for the better part of the afternoon, she decided to head back toward her mother's house. If she and Brady were both letting fear ruin something as magnificent as love, then they were obviously too cowardly and stupid to deserve happiness. But if they didn't love each other, who would?

She smiled at that twisted logic, her first smile since he'd left her. Her mind cleared and she finally figured out what she wanted to do with her life.

She was going to live on Brady's ranch. If he didn't want her in his bed, then she would work in his stables. At least she'd been a great groom. She would stick around for as long as it took to convince him she wasn't running off and she wasn't pining for life in Grand Springs. Despite being as relationship-impaired as herself, Brady had moments of brilliance. He would figure it out in time. If necessary, she would enlist the cowboys' aid in her campaign.

As she pulled in the driveway, she spotted an unfamiliar car parked by the back door. Randi stopped behind it and got out. Her mother hadn't said anything about company.

Not wanting to get involved in yet another discussion about why she'd run off from her own wedding and where she'd been all this time, she snuck in through the kitchen.

An unfamiliar sound stopped her. She paused, one foot on the backstairs and listened. Was that laughter? Was *her* mother laughing? A low chuckling sound mingled with the higher pitched amusement.

Her mother was entertaining a man?

Unable to resist taking a peek, Randi walked quietly through the kitchen and peered around at the living room.

Sure enough, her mother sat on the stark white sofa. Her dark hair was sleek, her dress more appropriate for a fancy night on the town than a regular afternoon. Perfectly manicured hands moved through the air, punctuating her conversation. Then Melissa Howell laughed again.

"Mom?" Randi said, involuntarily.

Her mother glanced up. Instead of scolding her for showing up in jeans and a T-shirt or offering some other criticism, her mother did something Randi had never seen before. She blushed.

"Oh, Randi. You're back."

If Randi hadn't known better, she would have sworn her mother was disappointed.

"I didn't mean to interrupt. I'll just head upstairs."

"You're not interrupting. I've been entertaining your company while you've been gone."

"My company?"

Her heart began to pound in her chest. She hurried into the living room. But the man rising to his feet wasn't Brady. It was Tex. The ex-marine, dressed in a work shirt and jeans, looked as out of place in her mother's perfect living room as Randi had always felt. She hoped the heavy weight of disappointment sinking in her stomach didn't show on her face.

"Tex. What are you doing here?"

The older man shrugged. "You left a few things behind. I thought I'd drop them off." He pointed to a small pile of clothing on the love seat opposite the sofa.

She forced herself to smile. "That's nice. You didn't have to come all this way. You could have boxed it up and sent it."

"Not all of it."

He glanced at her mother's lap. There, curled up on a fluffy cushion of formal silk, was a small black kitten.

Randi's eyes filled. She swore she wasn't going to cry, but her voice cracked as she said, "P-Peter?"

The kitten stirred, yawned, then mewed sleepily. His eyelids fluttered as he sank back to sleep.

Her mother touched the kitten's head. "Tex was telling me that Peter didn't care for the long trip. He looked tired and hungry. I gave him some tuna and water, then he went to sleep. I hope you don't mind."

Randi wasn't sure which part she was supposed to mind. "That's great. Thanks." She looked at Tex. "Are you heading back tonight?"

"No."

Melissa Howell cleared her throat. "Well, I thought it was so kind of your friend to return your belongings and bring this precious kitten. Tex and I have been talking and, well, I've invited him to stay for a couple of days. You know, to recover from the trip. It's the least we can do."

"Sure," Randi said, wondering when the aliens had first taken over her mother's body. "No problem. Are you two doing okay entertaining yourselves or do you want me to hang around?"

"Oh, we're fine," her mother said brightly. "We're going out shortly to get a litter box and supplies for Peter. I thought I might set up a bed somewhere upstairs."

"Great." Randi backed out of the room. "I'll be in my room."

As she climbed the stairs, she didn't know whether to laugh or call for the men in white coats. Her mother had actually let a pet into her house. This from the same woman who had often complained about her children simply playing with neighbors' animals. But the kitten was the least of it.

Her mother and Tex? *Her* mother?

Randi shook her head. It's not that Melissa wasn't attractive. If anything, she could easily pass for a woman much younger. She dressed well, was socially correct and had many qualities that Randi kept trying to appreciate. But her mother and *Tex*.

She sat on the edge of her bed, trying to take in what was happening. Good thing she was already planning to leave. Things were just too weird around here.

She'd barely finished packing a suitcase when there was a knock on the door. "Come in," she called.

Tex stepped into the room. He glanced around, taking in the designer bed covering and matching drapes, the pale bleached-oak furniture, the numbered lithographs on the wall. "I don't care much for your decorator," he said at last.

"Me, neither."

He nodded. "I've asked your mother to dinner and she's accepted. Seeing as I had an opinion about you and Brady it only seems fair to let you voice yours about your mother and me."

She studied the tall, proud man. He was about ten years younger than Melissa, but that wasn't likely to bother either of them. "Does she know what you do for a living?"

"I told her right off. She knows I was in the marines, too."

Randi laughed. "Let me guess. She wants to see your tattoos."

He grinned. "We're negotiating that."

Tex and her mother. "I wouldn't have put the two of you together, but if you think you really like her, then have a good time. Don't worry about me being here to cramp your style. I'm leaving."

He looked at the packed suitcase. "Going anywhere special?"

"Back to the ranch. I'm going to make Brady see sense, whether he likes it or not." She clenched her hands into fists. "Am I making a mistake? Has he forgotten all about me?"

Tex moved next to her and gathered her into a bear hug. "That boy's moping around like a she-cat without her cubs. He won't eat, can't sleep. Generally, he's suffering."

Some of the pain around her heart eased. "Good. He deserves it. I'm determined to convince him that we belong together."

"I don't think he'll need much convincing."

"I hope you're right."

"I generally am."

She stepped away and glared at him. "Then, why'd you go and tell Brady that Ty and I were involved? We weren't."

The ex-marine grinned. "Hell, I knew that, but I thought it might give Brady something to think about."

"You lied!"

"Uh-huh."

"I should warn my mother about you."

"I think the lady can take care of herself."

At noon the next morning Randi pulled off the side of the highway. To her left was the beginning of Brady's ranch. She gazed at the familiar, desolate landscape and wondered how Brady had ever thought she would want to live anywhere else.

While her sense of homecoming gave her courage, she wasn't sure how to approach him. She needed the exact words to tell him that she loved him and that they belonged together.

The sun warmed the car and she unrolled the window. A flicker of movement caught her eye. She squinted, then laughed as she recognized a familiar canine making her

morning rounds. She stepped outside and called the dog.
"Princess! Over here."

The shepherd yipped joyfully and trotted toward Randi.
She squatted down and hugged the dog, then scratched
her ears.

"How you doing, girl? You look much better." She
checked the animal's paws and found they'd healed. Princess licked her face, trotted a couple of steps toward the
ranch, then paused expectantly.

Randi slowly rose to her feet. Princess barked encour-
agingly, as if telling her to come on. As ideas went, it
wasn't a bad one. Maybe she wouldn't have to say anything at all to Brady. Maybe she could just show up.

After making sure her car was out of the flow of traffic,
she locked the doors and started after the dog. They were
only about a mile from the main house. While she got her
morning workout, she could think of what she wanted to
say to Brady.

Brady stared at the bowl of stew in front of him. Although the food was excellent, he wasn't hungry. He
hadn't been hungry in days. He couldn't survive much
longer if he didn't start eating, but nothing tasted right.
And it wasn't because Tex had decided to deliver Randi's
belongings. The temporary cook prepared fine meals, at
least that's what the men told him.

He dipped his fork into the rich mixture, then grimaced.
He wasn't himself. Nothing was going wrong, but it
wasn't right, either. The ranch, usually his refuge, had
become a prison. The joy was gone and he knew why.

But knowing why and fixing it were two different
things. So he missed Randi. He hadn't expected any different. He loved her and she wasn't with him; life was
hardly going to be happy. Before, with Alicia, he'd been
able to bury himself in work. Now that wasn't an option.

He couldn't escape the memories, the wanting, the needing.

Ty slammed down his fork and glared across the table. "I quit," he said.

The already silent room became charged. Everyone stopped eating and stared.

Brady looked at his second-in-command. "That's your right."

"Damn straight." Ty stood up. "Wanna know why?"

Brady had a bad feeling he knew what was coming. "Not really."

"That's what I thought. You want to get off easy. You want to take the coward's way out."

Brady deliberately set his napkin on the table and rose to his feet. "Maybe you and I should take this outside."

"Fine."

Ty stood up and stalked to the doorway. Once there he glared over his shoulder. "You've had this coming for a long time."

Brady followed silently.

They stopped in the yard, under the shade of the trees planted by his great-grandfather nearly eighty years ago. Ty tossed his cowboy hat aside and raised his hands to chest level.

"Come on, boss man. You go first. Hit me. Hit me hard, because maybe then you can forget you were stupid and cowardly enough to let her go."

"Is that what this is about?" Brady asked, furious the other man dared to bring up Randi. "You wanted her for yourself and you lost her. Is that it?" He assumed a fighting stance.

Ty shook his head. "I never loved her, but if I had I would have kept her here instead of abandoning her in a place that never once made her happy. So hit me, dammit, because I'm looking forward to beating some sense into you."

Brady circled the cowboy. "I didn't abandon her. She belongs there."

"Then, why was she crying over you?"

"Over me?" He made the fatal error of dropping his hands. The blow came sharp and fast, clipping his chin and sending him staggering across the yard. The pain was unexpected and sharp. He'd forgotten that fighting hurt like a son of a bitch.

The other men spilled out of the bunkhouse. "W-what are you d-doing?" Ziggy demanded.

"Getting his attention," Ty said grimly. He glared at Brady. "You ready to listen now?"

Brady touched his split lower lip and felt blood. His chin throbbed, and he was going to have a bad case of whiplash.

"There's nothing to listen to. You're not making any sense, Ty. I did the right thing." He realized all the men were staring at him, their expressions accusing. "I did," he said defensively. "You should have seen her mother's big house. The family has money."

"And you don't?" Quinn asked.

"That wouldn't m-matter to her," Ziggy said.

"She loves you," Ty yelled.

"I love her, too," Brady yelled back.

"Then, why the hell were you stupid enough to leave her behind?"

Brady stared at his men. Their concern touched him. All they wanted was for him to be happy. They thought Randi was the woman to make that happen. They were right.

"Damned if I know," he said, and knew it was true. Because he was afraid, maybe? Because he hadn't wanted to take another chance? He'd played it safe and now he was paying the price. He was going to have to learn to live without her.

Impossible, he thought, knowing he would rather risk rejection than spend the rest of his life wondering what could have been.

He looked at the men in the yard, at Ty willing to quit to make him see reason. They were his friends. He'd started out rescuing them, but somehow it had changed. Now he was the one in need of rescuing.

"So I just go ask her to come back?" He didn't wait for an answer. "What if she says no?"

Ty exhaled impatiently. "She won't."

"You don't know that."

"Yeah, I do."

"She loves you," Ziggy said. "Don't blow it."

Brady touched his still-bleeding lip. "Fine. I'll drive to Grand Springs and tell her I want her to come back. We all want her to come back. But I'm the one who's going to marry her. Got that?"

A cheer erupted from the men. Ty stepped forward and slapped him on the back. Brady faked a glare. "Didn't you just quit?"

"Nope."

"I didn't think so. I'm going to leave right away. While I'm gone—" A familiar barking cut through his conversation. Brady groaned. "Not another cat. I refuse to accept even one more." He turned toward the sound. "Princess, you take whatever you found and—"

But the figure following his dog wasn't a stray cat. Brady thought his brain might be playing a trick on him, punishing him for acting so stupidly. But she wasn't an illusion brought on by no sleep or food. She was heartbreakingly real. He wanted to say or do something, but he found he couldn't move.

Randi paused by the barn and smiled tentatively. "Hi."

The men mumbled greetings. There was an awkward pause. Ty gave Brady a shove in her general direction, then said, "Good to see you back. We've got work to do. We'll see you later."

She nodded, but her gaze settled on Brady, not the other men.

As the cowboys drifted off, he moved toward her. He took in the casual shirt she wore, the worn jeans and boots, her hair pulling loose from its braid. "You're beautiful," he said.

She flushed. "Thanks. Ask me why I'm here."

"Why are you here?"

"Because I have the answer to your question."

She waited expectantly. He frowned, trying to recall what questions they would have in common. Then he remembered. "I asked you if you would stay here when all your other problems were solved."

She nodded.

He stared at her face, at the emotions flickering in her eyes. How could he ever have considered living a life without her at his side? "You didn't have to come back to me," he said. "I'm glad you did, but I would have come to you."

She touched his lower lip and winced. "I can see you had a little help making that decision."

"No. Ty helped me figure it out, but I already knew the truth." He touched his chest. "In here. Where it counts." He took her hand in his and brought it to his mouth, then kissed her tender skin. "I love you, Randi. I know you have a family and a life in Grand Springs, and I have no right to ask you to give that up, but I'm asking, anyway. All I have to offer you is this ranch, this crazy existence out here in the middle of nowhere. I want to marry you. I want us to have a bunch of kids and grow old together."

Her smile was radiant. "Are we going to drive to the tip of South America when we're old and gray and explore the continent?"

"Maybe."

"I wouldn't have it any other way." She flung herself at him. "I love you, too," she said, her voice muffled against his chest. "I have for a long time. Grand Springs isn't home to me anymore. This is where I belong. With you and the land. With the cowboys and Princess and all the cats."

He pressed his lips to hers, ignoring the faint throb from his cut. The tender kiss ignited a contentment deep in his heart. He felt something blossom inside, a happiness so steady and so bright he knew it would last a lifetime...maybe beyond.

She pulled back and frowned. "I have to warn you, Tex might not be coming back. He's at my mother's house right now. Doing Lord knows what. I know it sounds strange, but I think they might really be right for each other."

"Tex and your mother?" Brady tried to imagine the couple and couldn't.

"I'm not kidding. He brought Peter and my things." She flashed him a smile. "Mom didn't only take a shine to Tex, but also to the kitten, so although I brought my stuff back, I didn't bring Peter."

"Good. We have too many cats now."

She laughed. "I swear one of these days I'm going to get you to admit you actually like the cats."

"Maybe."

He wrapped his arm around her shoulders and led her to the house. They had a lot of catching up to do. First, though, he was going to take her upstairs and make love to her. Then they would discuss the details of their wedding. Finally, they would get on with the business of being happy together.

She paused at the base of the stairs and wrapped her arms around his waist. "Did you formally propose?"

"Yes."

"Did I formally accept?"

"I don't think so."

She kissed him. "Brady Jones, I'm proud to marry you." She started up the stairs and paused. "Maybe my mom and Tex will come and live here."

He groaned. "Don't even think about it."

She laughed and he joined in. They linked hands and continued climbing the stairs, taking the first steps of a journey that promised a lifetime of laughter, joy and love.

* * * * *

continues with

MARRIAGE BY CONTRACT

by Sandra Steffen
available in February 1998

Here's an exciting preview....

One

"Somebody help me. It hurts. Make it stop. Please, make it stop."

It had been almost three hours since a mud slide took out the power in Grand Springs, Colorado, and the rain had yet to let up. Nurse Bethany Kent slid her arm around the teenaged girl who was doubled over in pain near the door to the emergency room, and placed her hand on the girl's abdomen, which was taut with another contraction. "Dave," she called, "Find Dr. Petrocelli. Stat. We have another mother in labor."

"What's your name?" Beth asked as Dr. Amanda Jennings joined her and the two women helped the young mother to an examining room.

Blue eyes rose to hers. "Annie. Annie Moore. Will you help me?"

Nothing in all Beth's thirty-five years had ever touched her more deeply than the entreaty and the unusual flicker of bravery in Annie Moore's eyes. Blinking back the tears that always seemed close to the surface these days, Beth nodded. "I'll help you."

She was in the process of helping Annie into bed when Dr. Tony Petrocelli pushed into the room.

"Hello," he said matter-of-factly. "I'm Dr. Tony Petrocelli."

The line creasing his lean cheek and his notorious half smile didn't seem to faze the girl. Squaring her jaw and straightening her shoulders, she said, "I'm not having the baby tonight. It's ten weeks early. So just make it stop."

Beth spared another glance at Dr. Petrocelli. She'd never understood how a man with his Don Juan image could also have the reputation for being one of the best obstetricians in Colorado. But he did. And while Beth held the girl's hand and showed her how to breathe, Tony conducted a quick examination.

Going around to the other side of the bed, he looked directly into Annie's eyes and said, "Your labor is too far advanced to stop. This baby wants to be born...now."

The girl cried out with the next pain, and there was no time to reassure her. She breathed when she could, pushed when she had to, and wept, her face contorting in pain. And then, after a momentary stillness, a baby's weak cry wavered through the room.

"It's a boy!" Dr. Petrocelli called.

"A boy?" Annie cried. "Is he all right?"

"He's tiny, but he has all ten fingers and toes."

"Can I hold him?" Annie asked. "My sister's name was Christie, so I'm going to name him Christopher."

Beth placed the baby in his mother's arms for but a moment while the doctor cut the cord, then whisked the newborn away toward the neonatal unit upstairs. Annie's voice stopped her at the door. "Promise you'll take care of him for me?"

Holding the baby close, Beth turned. The young girl looked weak and exhausted and so alone Beth would have promised anything. "I'll take care of him, Annie. You have my word."

For some reason, her gaze trailed to where Dr. Petrocelli was standing. He was tall and dark, and, even tired, his features were striking and strong. But it was his eyes that held her spellbound. His look warmed her in ways she hadn't expected, and didn't want to examine.

The baby moved in her arms, and the moment broke. With one last glance at Annie, Beth turned and left.

August 15

Bethany walked through the automatic door of Vanderbilt Memorial and headed toward the stairs to the third floor, the social worker's words still echoing through her head.

"I know you love Christopher, Bethany. And I think you'd be a wonderful mother. But the court system prefers two-parent homes, especially in infant adoptions. I'm sorry, but I'm afraid your only hope is to get married."

Beth was no stranger to marriage. She'd been married for seven long years. Forcing her worries to the back of her mind, she strode down the hall to the nursery, scrubbed her hands and donned a sterile gown. The sadness and despair she felt faded the instant she took Christopher in her arms.

She kissed his cheek, his chin, and the tiny fold of skin at his neck. "Hello, sweet pea," she whispered. "How's my big boy today?"

He was two-and-a-half months old, and nobody had seen Annie Moore since she'd left the hospital shortly after he was born. She'd given him a name and filled out his birth certificate. And then she'd left. The fact that she'd signed the birth certificate was complicating the adoption process.

"Forever" was what Beth wanted with this child. As she stared into Christopher's eyes, a yearning so deep and so strong wrapped around her heart. "Christopher," she whispered, "you really are a miracle baby, do you know that?"

She fed the baby his bottle, burped him and changed him, then stood next to his isolette and watched him sleep.

"Your only hope is to get married." If only wishes made things so, she thought to herself, finally turning to leave, her footsteps quiet and slow.

A man's voice drew her from her thoughts. "The hospital board wants to promote you to head of obstetrics, Tony, but they think it would look a lot better if you were married."

Everybody in the hospital knew Dr. Noah Howell's voice. And there was only one Tony on staff at Vanderbilt Memorial.

Suddenly, an idea too absurd to contemplate froze her feet to the floor.... *It seemed that the gorgeous Dr. Petrocelli suddenly needed a wife, and she needed a husband! Perhaps there was hope, after all.*

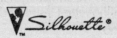

WAYS TO *UNEXPECTEDLY* MEET MR. RIGHT:

♡ Go out with the sexy-sounding stranger your daughter secretly set you up with through a personal ad.

♡ RSVP yes to a wedding invitation—soon it might be your turn to say "I do!"

♡ Receive a marriage proposal by mail— from a man you've never met....

These are just a few of the unexpected ways that written communication leads to love in Silhouette Yours Truly.

Each month, look for two fast-paced, fun and flirtatious Yours Truly novels (with entertaining treats and sneak previews in the back pages) by some of your favorite authors—and some who are sure to become favorites.

YOURS TRULY™:
Love—when you least expect it!

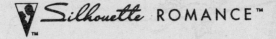
▼ *Silhouette* ROMANCE™

What's a single dad to do when he needs a wife by next Thursday?

Who's a confirmed bachelor to call when he finds a baby on his doorstep?

How does a plain Jane in love with her gorgeous boss get him to notice her?

From classic love stories to romantic comedies to emotional heart tuggers, **Silhouette Romance** offers six irresistible novels every month by some of your favorite authors! Such as...beloved bestsellers **Diana Palmer, Annette Broadrick, Suzanne Carey, Elizabeth August** and **Marie Ferrarella,** to name just a few—and some sure to become favorites!

Fabulous Fathers...Bundles of Joy...Miniseries... Months of blushing brides and convenient weddings... Holiday celebrations... You'll find all this and much more in **Silhouette Romance**—always emotional, always enjoyable, always about love!

SR-GEN

Silhouette

SPECIAL EDITION

SPECIAL EDITION

Stories of love and life, these powerful
novels are tales that you can identify with—
romances with "something special" added
in!

Fall in love with the stories of authors such
as **Nora Roberts, Diana Palmer, Ginna Gray**
and many more of your special favorites—as
well as wonderful new voices!

Special Edition brings you
entertainment for the heart!

FIVE UNIQUE SERIES
FOR EVERY WOMAN YOU ARE...

▼ *Silhouette* ROMANCE™

From classic love stories to romantic comedies to emotional heart tuggers, Silhouette Romance is sometimes sweet, sometimes sassy—and always enjoyable! Romance—the way you always knew it could be.

SILHOUETTE® *Desire*®

Red-hot is what we've got! Sparkling, scintillating, *sensuous* love stories. Once you pick up one you won't be able to put it down...only in Silhouette Desire.

Silhouette®SPECIAL EDITION®

Stories of love and life, these powerful novels are tales that you can identify with—romances with "something special" added in! Silhouette Special Edition is entertainment for the heart.

SILHOUETTE·INTIMATE·MOMENTS®

Enter a world where passions run hot and excitement is always high. Dramatic, larger than life and always compelling—Silhouette Intimate Moments provides captivating romance to cherish forever.

▼ SILHOUETTE YOURS TRULY™

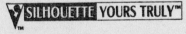

A personal ad, a "Dear John" letter, a wedding invitation... Just a few of the ways that written communication unexpectedly leads Miss Unmarried to Mr. "I Do" in Yours Truly novels...in the most fun, fast-paced and flirtatious style!

SGENERIC-R1